PRAISE *Dreaming Anastasia*

"Joy Preble has given readers an intriguing tale of magic, tragedy, love, and betrayal…Be prepared to fall into this story."

—*YA Books Central*

"*Dreaming Anastasia* is a story of love and loss on many different levels. It was a wild, fun, and sweetly romantic ride."

—*Galleysmith*

"Preble's blend of fiction, history, and folklore is spellbinding… I am smitten."

—*The Never Ending Shelf*

"A very entertaining and original story."

—*The Book Lush*

"I really enjoyed this book. It made me want to research the Romanov family and the fairy tale character of Baba Yaga… *Dreaming Anastasia* is easy to read and an enjoyable story. Thank you, Ms. Preble, for a great read."

—*Teens Read Too*

"Once it gets going, it's impossible to put it down! The adventure is so irresistible that almost all teen readers will enjoy this book."

—*Mrs. Magoo Reads*

PRAISE FOR
Haunted

"Equal parts spooky, sassy, sinister, and sexy, Joy Preble's *Haunted* lingers beyond the last page."
—Cynthia Leitich Smith, *New York Times* bestselling author of *Tantalize, Eternal,* and *Blessed*

"The will and desires of seventeen-year-old Chicago high school student Anne, a mysterious, wild-haired Russian rusalka (mermaid demon), and the infamous Baba Yaga collide in a complex story of love, betrayal, and revenge."
—*Booklist*

"The interweaving of the story with Russian folklore and history is seamless and clever. Despite the complexity of the plot, it's easy to follow, and the twists and turns will keep you flipping pages at breakneck speed."
—*Dale's Place*

"Lovely, lyrical writing…a riveting and interesting sequel to a lovely series!"
—*Zoe's Book Reviews*

"*Haunted* is a wonderful and imaginative story for both older teens and adults alike. Entertaining and magical to the very last page."
—*Long and Short Reviews*

ANASTASIA
FOREVER

JOY PREBLE

sourcebooks
fire

For Rose, Lily, Sylvia, and Lena—who struggled
to get the journeys they deserved.

Published by Sourcebooks Fire, an imprint of Sourcebooks, Inc.
P.O. Box 4410, Naperville, Illinois 60567-4410
(630) 961-3900
Fax: (630) 961-2168
teenfire.sourcebooks.com

Library of Congress Cataloging-in-Publication data is on file with the publisher.

Printed and bound in the United States of America.
VP 10 9 8 7 6 5 4 3 2 1

"Again and again the two of us walk out together
Under the ancient trees, lie down again and again
Among the flowers, face to face with the sky."

—*Rainer Maria Rilke*

VIKTOR

After a certain number of lifetimes, one becomes capable of much if only out of sheer repetition. Like a magician's sleight of hand, I learned to trick the world into seeing things the way I wanted.

Only later did I come to realize that there was more to my story than what showed on the surface. Magic has a price. Anything of value always does. It was one I was willing to pay. But even I did not understand the true cost.

When I was a boy, my mother told me the tale of Koschei the Deathless. My mother's eyes grew bright and her skin went pink as though the telling was of great importance. Later I would know why, but even then I understood I needed this story. Marina—for she let me call her by her name; it was only just the two of us after all—always knew.

I was Tsar Nicholas's son—not that my father ever acknowledged me. But Marina made sure I understood that it was both my truth and my destiny. It forced us all to places we might not otherwise have gone: my mother to Baba Yaga's forest, my father to a blind refusal to see what needed to be seen, and me…well, that is quite another tale.

"Stories within stories," Baba Yaga loves to say. "Secrets

within secrets." How clever she thinks she is, this witch who has toyed with me since my mother first went to the forest to seek her. But she was not clever enough to stop me. Not clever enough to know the power of her words.

Koschei was a man who couldn't die. Or rather, who couldn't be killed. He had hidden his soul—as the tales go—inside the eye of a needle, tucked inside an egg that sat inside a duck, inside of a hare, locked in a solid iron box, and buried under a tree on some island that blinked and vanished as it saw fit.

As I grew older, I heard other versions. Sometimes the chest was made of gold. Sometimes the island was in a different ocean. Sometimes Koschei could be weakened. But always, always he lived. As long as his soul was hidden away, as long as he had made it impossible to find, he lived.

This was the seed my mother's story planted in me. That if I could not be my father's son, could not have the legacy of a tsar, immortality would have to suffice. I would cheat death and gain the knowledge and the power that came with living over and over.

I only knew this: I was willing to sacrifice my half sister for what I desired. My sweet Anastasia, who believed in me so deeply that, like our father, she blinded herself to what I really was. This is, I think, my only regret. That even as I found delight in the ease with which I was able to manipulate her to my cause, a piece of me ached at the destruction of this beautiful girl. Was I a monster? I prefer to see myself as a pragmatist. Still it pains me—the look on her face that day we came back from the forest. The day I lost my immortality and Anastasia chose to return to the fate that I believe would have been hers anyway. Although by then truth was a fluid thing for me; when I told her I was sorry, I was not lying.

I asked Baba Yaga to take me because there was no other way to survive. No other way to gain access to all that I was about to lose: the magic, the spells, the secrets that reside underneath. I could not be other than what I have become.

Still, even the witch was unsure of my motives. I took pleasure in that for it proved my strength. I had found a way to compel the mighty Baba Yaga. The Bone Mother. The Death Crone. She was mad with it, unable to do anything but snap up a Romanov.

For a long time now—at least as time goes in Baba Yaga's hut—I have belonged to the witch. She has owned my body and often my spirit, but not always my mind. And in those moments when she grew distracted or bored or mournful for her Anastasia and curious about Anne, I watched and learned and plotted. Always I knew there was a way. One day I understood what it was.

The witch had transformed my physical self by then— honed me down to bone in her own image. But as long as I breathed, as long as I could think and had strength enough to crawl, it was enough.

Koschei, I thought, as I brought the witch her sweet tea. Koschei, I repeated over and over in my mind as I huddled in the bed that was once Anastasia's. As I pulled the ragged comforter over the sticks that were my legs. Koschei, I said as the witch's black cat, her *koshka*, flicked its tongue at my fingers, harsh like sandpaper against skin as transparent as tissue. I bled onto the floor, deep red drops much thicker than anything else about me.

Here is what I hoped for that also came true: my great-great-granddaughter's heart betrayed her. Anne opened the door just enough. She let me free. She made her promises. And watched in shock as I rose from the dead.

Resurrected.

Oh, the sweetness of the horror on their faces as Baba Yaga's horseman galloped off with me. I surprised them all: my captor, my descendant, my protégé. Even sweet Lily who falsely believed she would have her revenge. She swims still, cursed as a *rusalka*. I am free.

The story goes like this: no one leaves Baba Yaga's forest the same as he entered. And that is true for me. I have left much behind. But transformation is good for the soul. If I cannot be what I hoped, then I will be something else. Better to prevail than to bemoan my losses. My will is intact, my life eternal once more. This time I will be more vigilant.

Secrets within secrets. But I won't tell. They'll have to kill me. Except that's the point. They can't.

ETHAN

JUST BEFORE MORNING I DREAM OF RUSSIA. I'M A BOY AGAIN, walking to town with my father, our boots making prints in the snow. The sun is shining and it's deeply cold outside, so cold that our breath puffs in tiny clouds of mist. I like walking with my father. Our house is small and cramped, but here I can move and stretch and talk man to man.

In my dream, things go wrong very quickly. It begins with a scream. We both turn as we hear the sound and run through the snow-covered grass toward its source, the river. Our footsteps crunch on the ground as we go, a harsh squeak each time our boots hit the frozen snow. I reach the riverbank first.

A girl is struggling in the water, her heavy coat dragging her down. She stares up at me, another scream gurgling from her lips as she slips under, then flounders to the surface, hands slapping the water wildly.

"Leave her." The command comes from my father. Only when I turn to look at him, he wears Viktor's face. "You can't help her. You'll never help her. You're not strong enough."

I ignore him, kneel at the water, and reach for the drowning girl. "Grab my hand," I tell her. "I'll pull you up." It makes no sense that the water is deep so close to the shore. But this is a dream.

"Fool." My father's face is still Viktor's. "You think you know. You think you understand."

"I can't let her die." And in my dream I know this is Lena, the girl from our village who drowned but didn't drown. Who smiled at me with sharp teeth after she arose from the water, dead but not dead. Changed into a rusalka who beckoned me with a bony finger to join her in the depths. As a boy, I had run in terror, knowing that the boundaries had been broken, that there was another world which existed parallel to my own. A world where humans could transform into evil things. Where grieving mermaids waited to drag me under.

"She's not dead. She's chosen what she wants."

I reach for her anyway. The water's almost frozen over, and the cold stings sharply as my arm plunges in. But in my dream, I'm still a boy and I can't stretch far enough. The rusalka treads water just out of reach.

"Help me," she says. Her face is contorted with fear, but her eyes glimmer with something much darker. "You and the girl. Your Anne. Tell her, Ethan."

With the mention of her name, Anne appears next to me, standing where Viktor had been. Or where my father had been. In my dream, my mind muddles with the shifts of people and moments. My arm is still thrust in the river, up to my elbow in the icy water.

"You haven't told me everything," Anne says. "You know that's not fair, Ethan. Keeping stuff from me. I thought we were partners."

"She's drowning," I tell her. "We need to help her."

"She can wait. You and I need to talk. Something's changed, E. I can feel it. You said you didn't have power any more. That you gave the last of it to me. But that's not exactly true, is it?"

Her words startle me. How could she know? Then again, how could she not? We're connected in more ways than either of us understand. The conduit between us has continued to grow stronger.

"Don't leave me," the rusalka calls to us. "Don't let them take me. I'll tell you a secret. You just have to come closer."

Around me, the air shimmers with cold in the sunlight. The rusalka shrugs out of her heavy wool coat. I watch as it sinks out of sight. She reaches one thin, bare arm toward me.

"You need to let the witch take her," she whispers. "It's the only way. She has to know what to see. She has to know where he's been. Where you've been. Inside the insides, Ethan. Once she's heard the story enough times, she'll know what to do. She'll know how to stop him."

Anne squats down next to me in the snow. She peers at the mermaid. "No one's taking me anywhere until I'm ready to go. Promise or no promise."

The creature in the water bares her pointy teeth and makes a sound like a hiss. The air shimmers again. Above us, Baba Yaga's giant mortar flies into view, her pestle stirring the frigid air. It dips lower and lower until it hovers hugely above us, close enough that I can feel the heat of the witch's breath as she speaks from inside.

"Your girl has much to learn, Ethan."

"I'm not his girl," Anne says. "I don't belong to him. Or you."

"Child." Baba Yaga leans over her mortar and sends both her hands hurtling to the ground where they scuttle along the shore, flicking their fingers in the icy water. "So sure that you know. This is what I love about you."

The hands on the ground move in the blink of an eye. Skitter behind us before I can react and push at our backs. We fall together into the water, Anne and I, as the rusalka screams and Baba Yaga howls and somewhere out of view, Viktor laughs.

The cold is unbearable. I reach for Anne, but I can't even see her anymore in the darkness of the water.

"You just have to let go," the mermaid says from somewhere near me. "Anne is right. You've been holding things back. So many things, Ethan. Let go. Let yourself remember. And see what happens."

I hold my breath for as long as I can as I sink deeper and deeper. And just as I think that I'm dying, I wake up.

ANNE

A S NIGHT TURNS TO MORNING, I DREAM OF MY BROTHER, David. I'm in the hospital with him. It's not the night he died, but it's close. That last week before he finally let go, we were there with him almost all the time. My parents were terrified to leave, convinced that if they moved outside his room, he'd die while they were gone.

I sit on the side of his bed holding his hand. His skin feels waxy and unfamiliar—like his hand belongs to someone else. We're all pretending that things are going to be okay, even though the doctors have made it clear that this relapse is probably his last. They don't say that stuff lightly in the cancer wing; they're more about treatment and clinical trials and okay, let's do another round of chemo. But nothing is working and David is tired. Today is the first day he hasn't asked what else the doctors are going to try. The first day that I know in my gut that he really is going to die.

The thought of that numbs me and terrifies me. He's drifting away and I can't stop it. I hate this about death—that in the end we really have no control. It's like the dark cousin of the *Lion King* song I liked so much when I was a kid, that one about the circle of life. But when someone you love is dying, it feels more like a straight line.

Or as David said before he was so exhausted that he began slipping quietly from us, "I guess I'm not going out the same way I came in, am I?" We both laughed over this because let's face it, there's a visual attached and it is kind of funny. Not that funny, I guess.

In my dream, David asks me for water. "Thirsty," he says.

I fill his mug from the pitcher on the table next to the bed and help him hold it while he drinks through the straw. Each swallow sounds impossibly loud, like he's already emptied out inside and the water is tumbling into nothingness. I watch a blue vein pulse on the side of his bald head.

When he's done, I set the mug on the table and lie down next to him, my head on his pillow, my cheek next to his.

"You're going to be okay, you know," he whispers. My pulse starts to race because I know he's talking about dying; only suddenly that's not what he's talking about at all.

"I've always known. Even when you were just a kid. Not that I'd let you know. I mean you're my little sister. I'm supposed to give you a hard time and all."

We're lying so close that I can feel his breath as he speaks— short little puffs that smell like medicine. "Known what?" I ask him.

He hesitates, and I study his eye that's looking at mine. We both have this strange little golden zigzag pattern around the iris. *Cat's eye*, my mother calls it. *You both have cat's eyes.* At least that's what I think she says. I'm dreaming still and things aren't always what they seem.

"What?" I ask David again. "What is it that you know about me?" I'm genuinely curious now. I place my hand on his shoulder, careful not to press too hard. Even in my dream, I know how just the lightest of touches pains him.

"You're a witch." He grins—the old David under there still, the one who used to tease me about my braces and swore me to secrecy when he realized I'd overheard him telling one of his buddies that yes, he and Abby Uslander had slept together. Abby Uslander who we didn't talk about much anymore. After she kept crying every time she visited the hospital, he'd finally told her to stop coming, and then cried his own secret tears when she'd done what he'd asked.

My heart skips a beat. I sit up. "What?"

"No, really. She told me while I was sleeping. It was like a dream, but I don't think it was. Anyway, it made sense. It felt like I'd always known it. You understand?"

"Who told you?" I ask gently because I figure he's hallucinating or something. The meds are strong. This is what I'm thinking in my dream.

"Lily. She's so pretty, isn't she? I wish Mom knew how pretty Lily is. But Mom can't see her, can she?"

Another skipped heartbeat. My breath catches in my throat. Does David know about Lily? Does he understand what she is? The part of me that knows I'm dreaming says that this is impossible. David died before I even met Ethan.

"It's okay, little sis. I know. That's the thing about dying. You get to know stuff. Secret woo-woo stuff." He grins again like it's funny.

I try to wake up. If I know I'm dreaming, then I can wake myself up, right?

"You need to listen," David says. He presses his hand against my arm—his palm very cold. "She told me. Really. But you're going to have to figure it out for yourself. What's inside you—it's everything. Like Baba Yaga told you. It's about what's been, what is, and what will be. It's the small stuff, Anne. If you stand too close, you just don't see it. You have to look at it the right way. And then you'll see. Understand?"

"No. David, I—"

David grips my arm tighter. Our foreheads touch and his palm warms against my skin. "Anne. Really. It's important. You could change things, you know. Lily. Mom. Me. And that guy Ethan. She told me about him too. How you saved him. She says you're not sure about him. But I told her that my Anne is always sure. You learned that from me, right, sis?"

It's a dream, I tell myself again. Just a dream.

I look at my brother. Watch as he morphs into Anastasia, lying on the bed next to me, her brown hair tangled, her face pale as death, hands fisted at her sides. She morphs again and David's back, same as he was. But only for a moment. He changes once more, and even in my dream my stomach lurches.

This time it's Viktor I see lying there, face skeletal, eyes dark as ink. He smiles at me, his teeth white as bone. "You could have the secret, Anne," he says. "Just as I do. But you're not brave enough, are you? Just a weak little girl."

Somehow I force myself awake. *Breathe, Anne. Breathe.* I slip out of bed and shuffle down to the kitchen to brew some coffee. It's not even morning, just barely four, but I know I won't sleep anymore so I might as well mainline caffeine into my system.

Halfway down the stairs, the aroma hits me. Someone's beat me to the coffeemaker.

"Hey," my mother says as I walk into the kitchen, half convinced that I should hightail it back upstairs and avoid what's coming next. "Couldn't sleep. You either, huh?"

I shake my head. No.

The coffee drips into the pot, the sharp scent drifting up my nose, a dark, thick smell.

"I dreamed about David," Mom says. In the soft glow of the night-light, I can see tears glistening in her eyes. She sighs. "I wish he was here, Anne. I wish I could have done something. Anything."

I shift my gaze to the coffeepot. Underneath my skin, the witch's power stretches and grows. I force it down. Nothing surprises me these days—not the magic tapping at my insides, or that Mom and I have both dreamed about David.

I want him back too, I think, but I don't say it. Does she want me to? I don't know.

Viktor, I think, is right. I'm weak. If I wasn't, it wouldn't hurt so much that this is all Mom says. Her gaze slides down to my fingertips, flickering with that stupid power.

But she doesn't say anything else, just rises to her feet and pours herself a cup of coffee. Holds up the pot. "You want?"

"You know what?" I say. "I think I'm going to shower first."

Upstairs, under the water, I let myself cry.

Chicago,
The Present

Wrigley Field, Tuesday, 12:22 PM

Anne

It's the middle of the afternoon, and the David dream is still with me. So is my awkward moment with Mom in the kitchen. As for the dream, does it mean something? Of course it does. Everything means something these days. Which, let me say, totally sucks.

As do the Cubs, but if you're a fan, you're a fan. That's the way it works in Chicago. Every year, we hope for the best. Every year, we're monumentally disappointed. Sometimes I think we'd be more disappointed if they actually won. It would throw off the "we lose but we can handle it" mentality. Possibly this gets us through our ridiculous winters.

This is what I explain to Ethan as we park ourselves in our seats. They're great ones—main level, first-base side—because my dad shares season tickets with his law firm. I've shoved a huge bag of peanuts in my backpack because that's what we always do in our family. Over the years, David and I have eaten our way through thousands of peanuts. We used to buy them at Wrigley, but we'd go through so many bags that my mother started buying a jumbo pack at the grocery store and bringing them in her purse. Lots of things have changed in my world, but baseball traditions have stuck.

"If my dad had his way," I say, unpacking the peanuts and plopping the plastic sack on Ethan's lap, "they'd remove the lights from Wrigley. He's totally old school about this. Do you know that Wrigley didn't have lights until like the eighties? Day games only."

Ethan digests this tidbit and cracks open a peanut. The wind is blowing off the lake, and the sky is blue and clear. The sun is shining. We are on our fourth official date. So far, we have: hung out at the penguin habitat at Lincoln Park Zoo, gone bowling, and played three rounds of miniature golf at Par-King. (I won two of them.) In between, we've talked, met for coffee. Lately he's started calling me late at night. Ben used to do this when we were going out—call me to tell me good night. With Ethan, we talk until I start to drift off. The deep, even sound of his voice soothes me. I don't sleep much these days, so what little I get is generally in the hours right after we finally hang up.

Sometimes I feel like we're pushing our luck with all this acting like two regular people in a relationship. In the dark after we've finally ended our nightly phone call, I lie in bed and wonder how many coffees, how many rounds of mini golf, before we meet our quota of normal. You have magic powers and your grandmother is a bipolar rusalka, I tell myself. And Ethan's not exactly the poster boy for normal either. Eventually the cartoon anvil is going to fall on our heads.

But then I find myself watching out the window for his car. And when he kisses me, I press myself against him and feel a ridiculously hopeful pleasure as his tongue tangles with mine and his hands—oh God, he has wonderful hands—stroke my back, my arms, my face, skim my sides, his thumbs massaging at the curve of my breasts. I run my hands under his shirt, his skin warm against my palms, the familiar tingle flickering through my fingertips as they graze that lion tattoo near his shoulder.

Except here's the problem. I have no idea what's going to happen to me even a day from now. When I took the power Baba Yaga offered, I did more than just enable myself to save Ethan's life. I gave up my own. At least I think I did. I owe the witch now, and I'm not sure what she wants or when she plans on collecting. If I end up trapped in Baba Yaga's forest as payment for our bargain, how much worse would it be to go there feeling the way I do about Ethan? How could I live forever knowing what I'd lost?

Again, I remember last night's dream. David asking me if I'm sure about Ethan. The truth? There are moments when I'm positive that I don't know everything I need to know about him. But the person I'm most unsure of is me.

As for Ben, well, it's still unresolved. I don't love him. I never have. But when someone almost dies in a witch's forest because of you, there's a certain sense of obligation. Tess says I need to untether him. But she's not the one who's going to have to tell him to stop waiting for me to change my mind. This doesn't make me like myself very much. But it hasn't forced me into action either. Turns out that when it comes to Ben, I'm a head-in-the-sand kind of girl.

"I'm with your father on the lights," Ethan says. He passes the peanut bag to me. He's wearing jeans that hang just the right bit of low on his hips and a white polo shirt and sandals. His hair is a little shorter than it used to be, but the bangs, even when they sort of part in the middle, still fringe his eyes. It still looks good on him.

I try not to hyper-focus on the fact that Ethan had probably been to Wrigley before there were night games. These are the kind of moments that most girls don't have to deal with. Girls whose boyfriends—yes, I guess that's what he is now—weren't immortal for like a hundred years and now aren't. Girls who aren't me.

"I like night games," I say. "But sometimes my father would let us cut school for a day game. That was always the best." I don't add that he stopped doing that after my brother died. Or that since last fall, we haven't done much of anything as a family except deal with the fallout of my crazy life—something that Mom and I still haven't found the right time to fully explain to my father. He still thinks the jewelry store where Mom works was hit by another unfortunate freak lightning storm. Or possibly a gas-line explosion.

I push these thoughts aside. It's a gorgeous day. We're at a Cubs game. I'm wearing a new pair of khaki shorts and a gauzy, slightly sheer pink short-sleeved top with a pink lacy bra underneath that shows just the right amount. Other than the potential that the Cubs will lose this last game of the series to the Phillies, there will be no gloom-and-doom pondering today. No supernatural wackiness allowed.

"Hey," says Ethan. "I thought we were sharing." He snatches the peanut bag, then drapes his arm around my shoulders and pulls me close. The clean scent of Ethan's soap mingles with the smells of the peanuts and beer from the guys behind us, who are on their third round already, and the hot dogs that the kids in front of us are shoving into their mouths. Baseball makes me happy.

I let Ethan kiss me even though I'm not big on public displays of affection. Our lips are salty from the peanuts. He nuzzles the side of my neck and traces his fingers down my bare leg, rubbing his thumb just under the bend of my knee. I shiver pleasantly. Kissing is something that Ethan does very, very well.

"You taste like peanuts," he says into my ear. The feel of his mouth makes my stomach tighten and sends tingles to every part of my body. God, I love baseball.

Ethan kisses me again, and I forget about the peanuts. His lips graze lightly against mine and the feathery feel of his mouth on mine sets off sparklers low in my belly.

When the world begins to dip and shift and bend, at first I think it's the kissing. Damn, I think. This is one spectacular kiss.

"Anne," Ethan says. It takes me a few seconds to register the alarm in his voice. Has something happened to the peanuts? Has he had some kind of mystical premonition that the Cubs are actually going to pull this out and win?

The plastic sack tips off his lap. Peanuts tumble out, bouncing on the concrete and falling under the seats of the hot-dog-eating kids in front of us. The sounds of the ballpark stretch out as if in slow motion—like how a siren wail changes as the ambulance streaks by. Everything contracts. Like paper cranes, I think suddenly. Our world is folding like we're pieces of origami art.

"Hold on." Ethan grips my shoulders, and I feel the hard pressure of the chair arm against my belly as he clutches at me. The world tilts again. Wind roars in my ears.

"Ethan." The word draws itself out for long seconds, then seems to catch on the wind and disappear. My stomach dips. Nausea rises in my throat. So much for baseball. *You suck, baseball. Just like the Cubs.*

Above us—I think it's above us—I hear an all-too-familiar howl. *Are you kidding me?*

"Guess she's a White Sox fan," I say. I think it's a pretty clever comment, given that possibly we're going to get swooshed away by Baba Yaga before the game even starts. The wind swallows my sentence. So much for humor under pressure.

"You have promised me, girl." Baba Yaga's voice thunders in the air. "The past, the present, the future."

My eyes squint in what's now become a gale-force wind, so I can't even tell if the rest of the baseball fans at Wrigley are being treated to my witch's display of crazy. Maybe they aren't. Maybe it's only the Cubs fans. Or our section. It's possible that the Bleacher Bums are staring at us, wondering why we're flailing in a whirlwind.

I hang on to Ethan, my hands grabbing at his neck, his back, trying to keep us together. My palms burn as the magic inside me—most of it my gift from the same witch who is now ruining my love of baseball—starts to pulse and ready itself. But what am I supposed to do? I don't even know what's happening. How do I fight against it?

And then, something else. Mingled with the magic that's coming from me, I feel a different power rising from Ethan. But that's impossible. He doesn't have magic any more. Does he? And if it's his, then why does it feel unfamiliar, dark? Even as I form the thought, the sensation disappears. Or maybe it's just my panic, blocking me from cogent thought.

The wind intensifies. I feel myself slipping from Ethan's arms. I dig my fingers into his shoulders and realize I'm more than scared. I'm pissed.

"No!" I shout into the wind. "No! I know I promised. I get

it. I've bound myself to you. But I'm on a date. We seriously don't have time to do this now."

Baba Yaga doesn't answer. *Bitch*. She doesn't even show herself. Or maybe she does and I'm too busy trying not to get sucked away. My feet scrabble against the concrete and the peanuts.

"I mean it," I yell. "I'll go. Just not now."

The green grass and ivy-covered walls of Wrigley Field disappear. Ethan and I stand in the middle of a park. Grass, lots of grass. Some lilac trees. Huge U-shaped building at the far end. Big white columns. Lots of windows. An iron gate on one side.

In a horrifying rush, we're moved closer. We don't walk; we're just there. My stomach pitches. It's like being in one of those movies with the jerky camerawork. Zoom—we're standing near a tree. Zoom. We're so close to one of those white columns that I can see a trail of ants marching up its surface. Hear birds tweeting in the trees. Smell flowers and heat. Zoom. Back to the park. A pile of dirty snow sits in the shade under a clump of trees.

Zoom. We're at the door—tall, brown wood. Some kind of carvings. Zoom. The park again. My pulse feels erratic. Something pulls me from Ethan. I fumble for his hand. Find it. He grips my fingers so tightly that they lose feeling. Zoom. The world bends. For a happy second, I think we're back in Wrigley again. Scattered peanuts on the ground, suddenly so close I feel like one of those ants.

"Anne." Ethan's voice is faint, like he's not with me at all. But I'm holding his hand, aren't I?

The magic part of me kicks in. I can make this stop. I know I can. I do not have to do what she wants me to. I don't care what I've promised. I'm me. Not her. *No. Oh crap. No.*

Zoom. Back in the park looking at the huge U-shaped building.

I don't know what I object to the most. That I'm being sucked somewhere against my will or that I know where we keep going. Not just a huge building. A palace. A Romanov palace, to be more exact.

My stomach tightens. My breath feels frozen.

"Focus," Ethan says. "If you can focus, I think we can—" His words ride away in the wind. Everything's a crazy blur.

Zoom. Not the park. Not Wrigley. Inside now. Inside Alexander Palace.

She stands there in an inner hallway. My Anastasia. She's young—ten maybe? Eleven. Not quite a teenager. Not yet the girl who Baba Yaga took. But I know her. I've dreamed her, been in her head. I know every part of her. Every molecule. She's in my skin, my hair, my blood.

The door next to her opens. Ethan and I jerk closer. I fight it. Try to bring us back. We pull away, there and not there at the same time.

Okay, not quite what I want.

Still in the hallway, young Anastasia stands very still. A curious look crosses her face. She turns to the door that's opened. Smiles at the person who walks from the room.

I hear myself gasp. Viktor. He's younger too. Thin, his face lean and angular. His eyes dark but not quite scary dark. Not like I've seen them. If Anastasia's ten or eleven, then there was time still. Six or seven years before the end. But Viktor's wearing his Brotherhood outfit—coarse brown robe, a little cross on a leather string around his neck. So close I can feel the heat of his body. Smell something herbal and weird on his breath.

"Baba Yaga. No. I can't go here now. I won't." I say it. I think it. I will it to be.

As suddenly as it all began, it ends. Wrigley Field reappears. If the peanuts weren't scattered all around us, I'd think we'd just had some weird hallucination.

"Did you—" Ethan begins. "Did we just—"

"Yeah." I suck in a breath. "But I'm trying to pretend we didn't. Not working, by the way."

I look around. Beer-drinking guys are still drinking their beer. The hot-dog guy coming down the steps bangs on the metal container and yells, "Hot dogs! Get your hot dogs," just like a whirlwind didn't almost fly us to Russia. On the field, the starting lineup is still warming up. Other than Ethan and me and the peanuts, nothing has changed.

"C'mon." I'm out of my seat, dragging him with me. "I—we—need to leave. Now." Suddenly, I'm not in the mood for baseball.

Guess we should have stopped at date number three.

ETHAN

ANNE'S HANDS ARE STILL WARM, FINGERTIPS GLOWING slightly as we leave the ballpark and come to a stop on Addison. Around us, people are filing into Wrigley Field. Like salmon headed upstream, we walk opposite the crowd, away from the stadium.

Seeing Anastasia and Viktor like that has stirred both memories and anger. I'd known him by then, I think. Just barely a member of the Brotherhood myself. No idea what was in store for me.

"Hey, buddy. Buy your girl a T-shirt." The vendor waves the Cubs jersey in our faces.

We keep on walking, headed east toward the lake. Possibly a dangerous idea. The last time we were at Lake Michigan, things didn't go so well. The rusalki almost drowned me. And that was just the beginning.

"Did you stop her?" Her hand tightens around mine as I ask the question.

"Baba Yaga? From sending us back to the Romanovs?" Anne shrugs. Lets go of my hand. "Maybe."

"Anne," I begin.

"Ethan." She mimics me.

I exhale a sigh through my nose. This is our pattern. I analyze, she ignores. Will she ever accept how powerful she is? I wish she would. It would make all of this easier. Make us easier.

"Yeah," she says. "I think so. It happened so fast. We're there. We're here. Anastasia, Viktor. You saw them, right? Absolutely not where I wanted to spend my afternoon."

We walk another half block, maneuver through the hordes of people headed to the ball game.

I don't expect her next question. But it doesn't surprise me either. "Did you try to do something too? To stop it, I mean. I thought I—"

"No." I don't elaborate. Her tone says she thinks I did. Did I? The flutter of power that surged inside me. I felt it. Clearly she felt it. But how is that even possible? I have so little power left. And what remains has never felt so dark, so unfamiliar.

"It's like a push," Anne says. "Like my mind pushed into hers."

"You stopped her that way? Is that what you're saying?"

"Don't know. I—it wasn't just me. I mean, I think she stopped too."

We walk some more.

At the corner, Anne turns to me. "Damn it. She made you drop all our peanuts, and I'm totally starving right now. Isn't that weird? Or no, not hungry—just emptied out, maybe? Hollow. Does that even make sense?"

It does. "Magic drains. You know that."

Briefly, her eyes narrow—you're lecturing me, they say— but she doesn't comment. Just says, "I get it. But this used more of me. I mean, I made a bullet rise out of your chest back in Baba Yaga's forest. And that felt like my insides were getting sucked out. But this—this was something else. This was like—well, like the magic wanted out but something stopped it. Not something. Baba Yaga. I pushed at her. She pushed back."

"You're strong now," I tell her. "Maybe stronger than she knows."

Anne rolls her eyes. "Doubtful. And what if I am? I'm still bound, aren't I? Stuck doing whatever it is she wants me to do. That part never changes, does it? I can push and push at her, but eventually she's going to get what she wants. Because she's the witch."

This, of course, is the problem. If not for Anne, I'd have died in Baba Yaga's forest. Every time I kiss Anne, every time I look into her eyes, I know I wouldn't be here without her promise to Baba Yaga. No matter how much I love her, this is something I cannot change. Seeing Viktor as he once was just reminds me of how we got to this place. Because I saw only what I wanted to see. Because I allowed myself to be used. And everything that's followed has come from that. Good and bad both.

As though she knows what I'm thinking, Anne links her fingers with mine. "God, Ethan. We're a mess, aren't we?"

We continue toward the lake. Against my palm, her hand grows warmer, then warmer still. I let go when it hits painful.

"Crap. Sorry. I—it's always there, you know. The magic. I'm getting used to it. At least I'm trying. But I hate that it's always just below the surface. Even if I needed it just now."

"Shh," I say. "It's okay." I hook my elbow under hers. Memory flashes. So many years ago, this was how a gentleman escorted a lady. I smile, imagining us together at the turn of the last century, walking arm in arm. I picture us together in London, in Paris, in St. Petersburg.

"But it's not okay, Ethan." Anne slips her arm from mine. "I'm bound to a witch who thinks I can figure out how Viktor is immortal again. Like I can do that? I mean, if the most powerful witch in the world can't figure it out, how can I? And if I do, guess what? I'll probably have to kill him to break Lily's curse. That's the way the story goes, right? Shed the blood of the one who's responsible for the rusalka becoming a rusalka and she goes free. Which normally I wouldn't care about except this rusalka is my birth grandmother. And you know what else? None of this would have happened if I hadn't…shit."

If you hadn't made a bargain to save my life.

I pull her to me again, and this time she doesn't push me away.

"You don't have to do it," I say eventually. "The only one who makes that choice is you. You can let him live. Who knows—maybe in the long run it's more of a punishment than a reward. It was for me."

"He's not you."

"I'm aware."

"So what then, Ethan? Let Lily suffer forever? Let her stay like that now that my mother knows she's alive—well sort of, anyway. How can I do that? I know she's crazy, but she's my mother's mother. God, Ethan—all she wants is a chance to be human again, to talk to my mom face-to-face. To control how she lives or dies. But you know the rules—not gonna happen while he's alive."

I don't have an answer. I don't think she expects one. But I won't lie to her. I will not tell her that taking a life is without consequence—even of someone who would gladly kill you if he had the chance.

Anne breaks the silence. "Do you think that's what Baba Yaga wants from me? Viktor dead? Is that why she showed him to us just now? Will that be enough? Will she let me go? This is so messed up, Ethan. And my life was already messed up enough."

"There's a way," I tell her. "We'll find a way." I work to believe my own words. Maybe there is a way. In all those fairy tales, there is always a loophole. We just have to find ours.

And because words aren't enough right now, I kiss her. She hooks her hands behind my neck and kisses me back. Her lips press against mine, warm, salty, sweet. It will be okay, I think. It has to be. I'll make it okay for her. Whatever the cost. This second chance at life that I've received? It has no value without her.

Anne opens those luminous brown eyes and smiles against my lips. Things will work out, I tell myself. We'll find a way.

And then her eyes grow wide and she sucks in a breath. Her gaze locks behind me to the other side of the street.

I let her go. Whip around.

Half hidden in the doorway of an apartment building is the tall, thin figure of a man. He moves onto the street and rounds the corner, heading south. He doesn't turn his head, doesn't show his face. But I would know him anywhere. So would Anne. My pulse begins to pound in my ears.

Viktor.

"It can't be—" Anne says.

"It is. Hurry." We sprint across the street, dodging honking cars. By the time we get to the other corner, he's gone. I scan right, left. We run another block. Nothing.

"Stop," I tell Anne. "There's no point. He's gone."

"Was that really him? Why would he show himself like that? Maybe it wasn't even him. Maybe it was just some more Baba Yaga hijinks. She wants to screw with my head, right? Well, it's working."

"Seemed real enough," I say. "If he's watching us now, things are going to escalate."

"Tell me something I don't know."

It's a request I can't satisfy. So instead I say, "Remember how strong you are. It's important that you remember."

"And if I'm not?"

"You are. Not just your magic, Anne. You."

"I'm not," she says again. "Maybe I never have been."

"Believe," I tell her, because at this point it's all I have. "Like I told you when this all began. The first thing you must always do is believe."

TUESDAY, 4:18 PM

ANNE

I CAN'T LEAVE YOU ALONE, LIKE, EVER, CAN I?" TESS—A BAG of tortilla chips in her hand—flops down on my bed. Chips scatter everywhere. She scoops them up and stuffs them in her mouth, chewing noisily.

"Nope."

She thumbs chip crumbs off her chin and white sleeveless T-shirt. Scoots back against my headboard, tucking my pillows behind her, then kicks off her silver flip-flops with the tacky flowers in the middle—the ones she wears because they're so heinous she's convinced they make a reverse fashion statement. Her blond ponytail hangs over the back of the bed.

"So what now? 'Cause I'm thinking maybe I need some kind of spreadsheet to keep track." She rolls her eyes, but underneath the snark, there's real concern in her voice. My guilt-o-meter, already running overtime, kicks up another few notches. I hate being the one that she worries about. I hate that she might get hurt—again—because of what's going on with me.

But I called her just now, didn't I? Asked her to come over because I knew she'd fill the room with talking and chips and Tess. Loud. Obnoxious. Perfect. And still willing to hang out with me, even though she almost drowned a few weeks ago in the middle of the Baba Yaga and Lily craziness.

I curl up in my pink beanbag chair—the one I've had since I was five and should probably trash except that some things are just hard to get rid of. Like the navy comforter folded at the foot of my bed. The one that used to be my brother David's.

My bedroom window is open, and the smell of chips mingles with the smell of our freshly mowed grass. If I didn't know better, I'd say it was a normal summer day.

But I do know better. So does Tess, who Ethan probably wouldn't want involved. But Ethan's not here right now. He dropped me at home, said he'd call later, then reminded me to be careful and went on his merry way. Correction: I doubt highly that he was merry. Stupid expression.

"Okay, boss. Tell me what's up. And don't leave out any good parts. If there are any. You know—Russian Romeo's naked chest. Stuff like that. I cut out of work again for you. So you owe me. Miss Amy is going to seriously fire my ass. At least once she finds someone else to teach preschool jazz and tap." Tess crams another handful of chips in her mouth and chews noisily. When I make a face, she opens her mouth and sticks out her chip-coated tongue.

"You never change, do you?"

"I know, right? That's what you love about me."

I fill her in. She interrupts only twice: first to ask me to repeat the kissing details—Tess loves the play-by-play—and second to ask me if what I have on is what I wore—it was, and she approves, especially of the lacy bra. Tess is a fan of the subtle peekaboo.

"What do you think Anastasia and Viktor were going to

talk about? So weird, right?" she says when I'm done telling her about our little flashback to the Alexander Palace. "She still believed he loved her like a sister. Maybe you should have stayed. Maybe he would have said something that—"

"No way." My stomach tightens. "I hate that we were there at all. Watching Viktor look at Anastasia, just knowing what was going to happen…Besides, who knows if that was even how it actually was. Even Ethan doesn't know how all this works. I don't even know for sure how we got back. For all I know, we could have overstayed our welcome and been stuck there."

"You went into Baba Yaga's forest last fall without knowing how you'd get back. And that worked out."

I snort a laugh. "Oh, right. That worked out just great."

"Well, okay, there were a few glitches. The last time when I ended up there with you, well, that was a mess, I know. Huge, scary witch in her freaky chicken-leg house." Tess shivers.

"But I mean it." Her expression turns serious. "Don't you realize that if you keep running from this, it's just going to keep running after you? I mean there's Viktor, spying on you from across the street. Not good, Anne." This is the first time since we've been back from the forest that Tess has acknowledged that none of this is over.

"Maybe I want to run. Maybe I should run. God, Tess, can you even believe we're having this conversation? We're supposed to be talking about what colleges we're going to apply to. Or whether my new jeans make my butt look fat. Not magic and witches. Or how I need to kill my crazy ancestor to free my equally insane grandmother from her mermaid curse."

Tess scoots off my bed and flings herself onto my pink bean-bag chair next to me. The ancient stuffing sags beneath us. "Do you want to run?" She looks at me, her eyes still serious and intense. "'Cause if that's what you want, then I'll try to help you."

"And exactly how are you going to do that?"

"Don't have a clue," she says evenly. "But if you could save my life, then I guess the least I can do is figure out how to help you, right? Or are you too pig-headed to let me do that?"

She punctuates her response by poking a finger repeatedly against my forehead, right between my eyes. I guess she didn't get the memo that I'm sort of a witch now—and a bitchy one at that. I could possibly turn her into a frog or something if she pisses me off too much.

But it's impossible to stay angry, even if maybe I should. If I'm horrible enough, she'll stay away and be safer than if she keeps hanging with me. And because it upsets me—the power inside me, the earnest look on Tess's face when all I want is for us to just goof around and keep pretending that my life hasn't changed in dangerous and scary ways I can't control—the thing inside me bubbles up without me asking it to.

The two candles in their little glass holders on top of my bookcase flicker to life, flames burning taller than if I'd just lit them with a match. The cool breeze fluttering at my curtains amps into a strong wind.

"Shit." I close my eyes, breathe in, and concentrate. Feel the wind settle.

When I open my eyes, Cinnamon Sugar and Vanilla Sundae are burning peacefully again.

"Holy crap." Tess shakes her head. "I so need to let you have your way with Neal. Don't you, like, owe me some free vengeance or something for almost dying out there when I went to save your boyfriend from the mermaids?"

Neal is Tess's ex. It's taken her three breakups to keep it that way, but I think this time it's permanent. As for the other part, I don't remind her that the only reason she followed Ethan that day a few weeks ago was because she didn't trust him.

"So if I don't run," I say, "you'll really help me?"

Tess nods, serious again. "Been with you this far, haven't I? Why would I leave when it's just getting interesting? Besides, who else could you possibly tell all this stuff to?" She grins. "Well, except for Ethan. But he's not your best friend, is he? And speaking of Mr. Stealthy, where is he anyway?"

I hesitate. Do I really want to tell her that I don't know? That I was still so freaked out about seeing Viktor—past and present versions—that I chose not to ask?

She guesses at it without me saying. "It's okay," Tess says. "It's probably better if he doesn't tell you everything. Safer, even. You know I don't—"

I put a hand—gently—on her shoulder. "I know." Neither of us has to finish our sentence. I know she doesn't trust Ethan. Which is exactly why there's one detail I've left out— that I'm pretty sure that somehow Ethan has power again. When I asked him about it, I think he lied. Tess, it seems, is not the only one with doubts.

Tess nibbles on a chip. "Doesn't Baba Yaga know it's summer vacation? I don't want to bend my brain like I'm back in calculus class. We do enough studying all year long. Tell her that the next time you see her, okay?"

"Oh, right. I'll be sure to…"

"Sure to what? And why do you look like you just saw a ghost? Is there one in here?" Tess whips her gaze around the room.

"Give me a second." Her talk of school has popped last night's dream back into my head.

"It's like school," I see David telling me. I'm lying next to him on his hospital bed. Is that what I dreamed? *"Like when you're cramming for a test. You have to read everything you didn't get to during the semester. Especially the little stuff that you might think isn't important."*

I hoist myself from the beanbag and grab my laptop from my desk. We've been so preoccupied—me, Tess, Ethan—that we haven't been thinking straight.

"I've got it all wrong," I say. "I've been waiting for Baba Yaga to do something like she did today. Both Ethan and I—we've been treating this like all we can do is wait for the witch to send me somewhere or for Viktor to appear or whatever. But you're right. I need to stop running. We've figured stuff out before. We can figure it out again. I dreamed about David last night, Tess. He talked to me. Said I just needed to know what to see."

She's the first person I've told about these new dreams—the ones of my brother that I've been having now, night after night. I thought I was done dreaming about him, like I was finished dreaming about Anastasia. But I guess I was wrong about that.

"You think your dream was real? And what's with the laptop? You and Blue Eyes going to email each other? Maybe talk about how the Cubbies probably lost after you left?"

"We're going to research."

Tess furrows her brow. "Research what?"

I open the laptop and power it up. "Everything."

"Well, in that case, I'm going to need some more chips."

Tuesday, 5:02 PM

Ethan

I'VE BEEN THE ONE TO REACH OUT, BUT STILL I FEEL MYSELF tense as he walks into the café on Armitage, a tiny storefront sandwiched between two antique shops. Meeting here meant coming back into the city, but somehow it feels safer—as though the distance from the suburbs will protect Anne if this goes badly. It's a foolish illusion, but I hold it to me as Dimitri—heavier now than when I'd seen him last—settles his bulk in the chair opposite me at the small table.

"You're looking well, Brother." He holds out his hand, and after a moment, I clasp it. The greeting startles me. Viktor's betrayal destroyed any connection to the Brotherhood I might have still felt. The risk of what I'm doing stands out in clearer relief as we shake hands; this is the man who kidnapped Anne. The man who would have gladly killed me last fall—if I had been able to die.

But he, too, was betrayed. We have spoken now and then, never in person. He has sworn that he has no further allegiance to Viktor—the man who lied to all of us. I do not know if I believe him. But I've chanced this meeting nonetheless. If I'm to go after Viktor, I need allies. And Dimitri is where I've begun. There are others scattered throughout the world—only a handful of us became immortal during the Revolution—but I have not seen or spoken to them in decades. I had no need. I was Viktor's right-hand man. And Dimitri sat at his other side.

"And you?" I ask him. "How is the world treating you these days?"

He smiles slowly. His face has changed some since the last time I saw him. Like me, Dimitri is aging again. He was at least ten years older than I was in 1918. Soon, I think, he will turn thirty. This time, it will show.

"It has been, well, an adjustment, has it not? Or perhaps our current condition was what you wanted all along, Ethan. To be like everyone else, counting down the days until we are no more. I have come to terms with it, but it is different, no? This newfound mortality of ours. We can break now, like the rest of the world. It has taken some getting used to."

I shrug. Take a sip of the tea I'd been drinking while waiting for him to arrive. Annoyance ripples over me. At Dimitri for considering only himself. At myself for realizing that I've thought the same thing. And because of this, I find myself saying, "Is that all you have to share with me? That you're still too good to just be human? Perhaps I was wrong in asking you here. Maybe there is nothing for us to discuss after all."

Dimitri signals the waitress before he responds. "Is that how it is, then, Brother? So be it. I will not question your motives if you will not question mine. We will have our meal. Talk like old friends. And if I don't quite believe that you are as selfless as you would like me to think, then that is my business. It won't alter what we decide here."

Like his use of my former title, his words catch me off guard. He's right, of course. Here is the truth I learned in my second visit to Baba Yaga's forest: like Dimitri, sometimes I miss not being able to die.

"Coffee," Dimitri tells the waitress. "And eggs over easy. Bacon, crisp. And rye toast, two slices, dry. Butter on the side. And potatoes—you have hash browns, yes? Make sure they're well done. And jam, if you have some."

If she's put off by his dismissive tone, she hides it well. The two piercings in her left eyebrow move slightly as she scribbles his demands on her order pad.

"Can I get you something else?" she asks me, and when I tell her no, she tucks the order pad in the white apron that's tied around her black pants and black shirt and strides to the kitchen.

"Americans," Dimitri says after she's gone. "They need direction to make a proper meal."

I choose not to respond. We have more serious matters to discuss than his general disdain for the world or the condition of his rye toast.

"Thank you for meeting me," I say instead.

Dimitri dismisses my attempt at polite small talk just as he'd dismissed the ability of the waitress to bring him an acceptable meal. "Have you seen him then? Alive?"

"Very much alive. And still a threat—to all of us."

The waitress returns with a mug and the coffeepot. We pause until she's filled his cup—"to the brim," he directs her—and then he responds.

"To the girl, you mean." He grins at me. "If only you could have seen his face the day he realized that you'd actually found her. You know he never believed you had it in you, Etanovich."

"Ethan. I haven't been Etanovich in a long time. Won't be ever again. And yes, I'm certain he was surprised. But that's in the past. It's what's going on now that concerns me. As I told you on the phone last night, she—"

"Yes, yes, *Ethan*. You told me. And I have decided to believe you. What is my alternative, really? I should have been dead long ago. It is not much of a stretch to accept that your little Anne has made a new bargain with Baba Yaga. Or that she wants to save a rusalka you say is her grandmother. Which would make the rusalka Viktor's descendant, yes? Oh, this gets quite tangled, Brother.

"But here is what intrigues me. Viktor has found a way to regain his immortality. Fascinating, yes? The hag took him away to her hut, kept him in God knows what condition, and yet somehow he walked out of that forest and made a bullet rise from his chest. This is what you've told me. What I've stayed up all night considering."

"And?" I sip my tea, now gone cold. Dimitri stirs more sugar into his coffee. We watch each other—like two chess players considering our next moves, trying to anticipate what the other might do.

"You tell me, Ethan. And what? Why are we here? What would you like me to do?"

I hesitate. The waitress returns, sets the plate of food in front of Dimitri. He nods, then pokes a fork into the eggs. The yolks flow onto the plate, pooling around the potatoes and bacon. He takes a bite of his dry toast. Chews. Then scrapes a small bit of butter onto the remainder with his knife.

I hesitate, then: "Figure out how he's gotten back the immortality the rest of us have lost. And what he plans on doing now that he thinks himself invincible again."

Dimitri's dark eyes glimmer. "I thought that was little Anne's job. And so, Brother Ethan, what does this mean? Do you love her now?"

Inside me, the small bits of magic that have inexplicably returned rise dark and angry. I push them back. Set my cup on the table. This is neither the time nor the place to reveal what I still don't understand. I sacrificed my power to Anne as we stood together in Lake Michigan. Now magic once again stirs in my veins. I wish I knew what it was. Or whose.

I look Dimitri in the eye. "You wouldn't be here if you didn't want to be. You, me, Anne, the witch—we all need to know how to stop Viktor. If that frees the rusalka, then that is a good thing. You and I both understand what it is to be bound. What you've done or haven't done over the years—I'm not asking for a confessional here. All I'm asking is that you help me find a way to end this."

Even as I say the words, I know it's not that simple. Anne has bound herself to Baba Yaga. Stopping Viktor won't change that. But it's a step in the right direction.

Dimitri forks more egg into his mouth. Lays two slices of bacon on his toast and eats that as well. Takes another swallow of coffee, then dabs his mouth with his napkin.

"You are not an innocent in this, Ethan," he says. "You killed a man, remember?"

"He would have killed me if he could have."

"So what then, collateral damage? His name was Anatol, by the way. If he had a last name, I never knew it. I—but that's history, eh? Here's what you really want to know. I think that Viktor wants what he's always wanted—to live forever. To show the tsar and the rest that he managed to achieve what they could not. Power. Money. Life eternal. It drives him now as it always did. The things most men want even if they cannot admit it. This is what I believe."

"Just that?"

Dimitri laughs. "Is that so little? Immortality is not enough to make a man kill? To motivate a man to figure out how to escape the Death Crone?"

"Maybe," I say. "But it's never served us well to underestimate him."

Dimitri nods. "Perhaps." But I see in his eyes that perhaps there is something else. Like the strange new magic floating in my veins, something very dark.

"Are you with me, then? You'll help? If you betray me, I will come after you. So I need you to promise. After all, I don't know what you want out of all this either. But for now, I'm choosing not to ask."

"I like a happy ending," he says. "Let's leave it at that."

Tuesday, 5:58 pm

Anne

HERE'S WHAT WE KNOW AFTER TWO HOURS OF RESEARCH: the world still thinks Anastasia died with her family. Baba Yaga appears only in stories and on fairy tale sites. And rusalka curses may or may not be lifted by avenging the death of the rusalka and shedding the blood of the person who attempted to kill her or caused her to leap into the water in the first place. As for the Alexander Palace, home of my doomed Romanov ancestors, we've stared at tons of pictures of the rooms and grounds, but it's not like some piece of text said, *Hey, the secret clue you're looking for is right here.* Nothing to support the things I saw with Ethan during our little time-travel visit that may or may not have been real.

Here's what we don't know: everything else.

Tess stretches her legs into the sitting version of a split and rests her chin on her elbows. "You know, I'd sort of forgotten since we looked at all this last fall. These stories don't end well, do they?"

"They're not that bad. Vasilisa gets the better of Baba Yaga in her stories." Vasilisa, the girl whose stepmother sends her to Baba Yaga's forest to get rid of her but whose magical doll helps her. The girl who manages to get out of the forest alive.

Her story ends; mine seems to keep spinning out with no end in sight.

"Yeah, well, you over-identify with that one." Tess grins. "But the rest of them?"

She scrunches her nose. "Lovers killed. People ripped apart. Some guy who dies when he gets hit on the head with an egg, if you can believe that one. A bad wife sitting in the dark. Some of them just end with the narrator drinking beer. I mean those Grimm brothers weren't always happy either, but this stuff is rough. Except I guess we already knew that. But maybe we just don't understand all the rules or something. Isn't that what Professor Olensky kept saying last fall? That we have to see everything like a story?"

"Except that he was wrong, remember?" The image of the professor's dead body flickers through my mind and I work to push it away. "The way to the forest wasn't through a story. It was me. My blood. Even that stupid lacquer box turned out to be just a prop. I didn't even need it the second time, did I? I just bled on all of you, and zap, there you were."

Almost dying because of me, I don't add. But Tess knows what happened. I don't have to say it.

The thought makes us silent—so silent that we both jump when there's a tap on my bedroom door. "Anne?" my mother says. "Your father's going to be home soon. He's bringing home Chinese. I told him to get enough for Tess."

She opens the door and walks in, but just a few steps. Even though we're talking again, and she knows I've got a Destiny— definitely with a capital *D*—she still seems hesitant to come into my territory or ask questions to which she might not want the answers. Our cat, Buster, slips in with her and, after one slight meow, leaps onto my bed where he immediately curls up, a soft gray ball of fur, and closes his eyes.

"Can you stay, sweetie?" Lately my mom is skittish around Tess. Almost like she's worried that she might have to ask Tess something like, "How are you, honey? Any residual effects since you almost died in the freak tsunami my daughter caused in Lake Michigan while trying to save you from the evil mermaids, one of whom is my birth mother?"

Better to discuss our takeout order.

"Will there be egg rolls?" Tess looks at Mom hopefully.

Mom smiles. "I'll text Steve and make sure he gets extra."

"Then I'm staying."

"You done for the day?" I ask her.

Mom nods. "Just a phone call to a vendor for that show at the Merchandise Mart next month. Honestly, I don't know how much longer I can keep things going. Maybe it would be best to just put it all in storage until…"

We all let her sentence hang there. No point in finishing it. With her boss, Mrs. Benson, still MIA and the Jewel Box basically smashed to pieces again because of me, my mother is keeping the business going by selling the remaining jewelry out of a makeshift store in our living room. A couple of folding tables, a small cashbox, and a handwritten inventory sheet—this is how Mom is conducting business. Mostly people make appointments, but lately they've started to drop by whenever they feel like it.

Mom worries that the neighbors will complain that we're running some kind of home pawn shop. That isn't going to happen now that I've put a protective warding spell around our house to keep out negative influences, but I've kept that fact to myself—mostly because I'm not totally sure I've done the spell correctly. It's entirely possible that I've cursed the jewelry to disintegrate once it leaves our house or something.

Mom pauses to run a hand over David's comforter and then straighten it—a long slow silence for all three of us—and then says, "Ethan isn't coming back tonight, is he? I don't think your father ordered enough if he is. So I'd have to call him and—"

"It's fine, Mom. I'm sure there'll be enough either way."

My tone is sharper than I want it to be. Mom deflates and goes silent, then closes the door behind her as she leaves.

Tess purses her lips.

"What?" I ask irritably. "Did you want to talk about Chinese food some more? Well, neither did she."

On my bookcase, the two candle flames flicker, then burn taller and brighter.

"Settle down there, Sparky," Tess says dryly. "It's tense with you two. I get it. What else did you expect? I mean seriously, you don't see me having discussions about magic with my mother, do you? Speaking of which, yours isn't going to say anything to her, is she? I mean I figured that this was all too weird, and it's not like they'd start talking about it over a glass of wine or something, but—"

"I think you're safe, Tess."

"Well, good. 'Cause you don't want me to panic or something."

I shake my head. Tess rarely panics. Sometimes I wish she would. It might make her less likely to do things like try to save Ethan from rusalki all on her own.

I turn my attention to the laptop. Press Save and close our useless list. What was I thinking? I wonder. That it would be like last fall, and we'd research and suddenly figure out the answers? I'm silly for thinking that any of this is easy. I should know better.

I've left some pages open, reduced on the toolbar, and I start to close those out too.

"You talk to Ben lately?"

I stop what I'm doing and look at Tess. She narrows her eyes, which is never a good sign. There is only one topic that is a problem for me and Tess, and this is it.

"You know I have." This is true; I'd gone for coffee with Ben a few days ago. *"We're not going out anymore," I told him. His answer had been, "That can change."* And then somehow I'd promised to go to a Swedish film festival at the Art Institute with him. Ben's got this thing for movies with subtitles. Personally, I don't get it.

But there I was agreeing to see some movies that will probably be about people in boots and hats looking cold and depressed. Like winter in Chicago, only in Swedish. And since the Jewel Box is destroyed again, I don't even have a summer job as an excuse—unless you count the time last week when I helped Tess teach the preschoolers basic ballet steps at Miss Amy's. Which definitely does not constitute gainful employment.

"And?"

"And nothing. Well, something. I'm going to this foreign film with him. But it's nothing. We're not—"

"If you're not, then why are you going to the movies with him?"

I shrug. I don't seem to have any answer that makes sense. "It'll be okay. I just can't—it's hard. I mean it's my fault that he—plus, he's Ben. He's so—"

"So in love with you?"

I frown. "So exactly why are we talking about this?" Even as I ask the question, I already know the answer. Ben is safe. Ben is normal. Ethan is everything but. Tess knows it. I know it. Everyone knows it. Only it doesn't make things easier. It doesn't change how I feel—which is still not in love with Ben.

Tess reddens—a slight blush that works its way up her neck to her cheeks. "Well," she says, then stops. I look at her more carefully.

"What? And why are you turning red?" A thought comes. Ben and Tess? Is this possible? And how do I feel about this? Suddenly I feel awkward.

Tess sighs. "I saw him at Java Joe's the other day. I needed a jumbo latte before tap and jazz. It's like herding cats with those girls. I am seriously never having kids. First one needs her shoelaces tied. Then another one has to pee. Then there's the twins—Lacy and Hannah. I swear, if I let them, they'd be rolling on the studio floor ripping each other's eyes out. I've never seen anything like it. They—"

"Tess. Focus. Ben?"

"I'm getting there."

"Get there faster."

"He's still freaked out, Anne. I think half the time he wants to pretend that none of what happened a couple of weeks ago really happened. I mean, let's face it—that's what everyone else around here keeps doing. A witch flies over Second Street in her mortar, steering with a giant pestle? Just a thunderstorm. A horde of crazy mermaids crash into the Jewel Box? Probably some kind of hail or once-in-a-century winds. You've said it yourself. It's like last fall. The truth doesn't make any sense, so they come up with something that does. Do you know Ben's quit lifeguarding? That's why he was in Java Joe's. He was applying to be a barista. Ben was captain of the swim team, Anne. And now he hates the water. He can't even look at the pool anymore because it makes him think of Lily and everything else."

Like how the mermaids almost killed him. Like the look on his face when I agreed to Baba Yaga's bargain so I could bring Ethan back to life.

My chest tightens. My heart feels like it's struggling to beat in too small of a space. He hadn't told me. Of course he hadn't told me. I keep making it clear that I don't want the same thing he does. Why would he tell me something that makes him look even more needy?

"Shit. Why didn't you say something?"

"I just did."

"I mean before now?"

She hesitates, then blurts out, "Because what good would it do? It's just going to make you feel worse. He'll get over it. I really think he will. But you've got to stop sending him mixed messages. If you want to be with him, then be with him. But if you don't, then—"

"I get it, Tess. Ben good, me bad. I get it."

"That's not what I mean and you know it." Her brows furrow. "You're just myopic about some things. You think you owe Ben. But did it occur to you that maybe he thinks he owes you? That now that he's been through this whole life-and-death thing with you, maybe he feels like he has to protect you or something? You can't just keep going for coffee with him and kissing him and…"

"He told you that?" I gape at her.

"Maybe. Well, not the whole psychoanalysis part. I figured that out on my own."

I wait for her to tell me something else because clearly there's something on her mind, but she doesn't.

In the silence, it occurs to me that just possibly I haven't been the most observant person lately. And that when it comes to boys, even less. Oh, I've had some legitimate reasons like, um, running for my life every five seconds. But she's right.

"It's not like we're talking behind your back," Tess huffs. "It's just that he's so messed up. So what am I supposed to do? Tell him to bug off?"

"No. God, no."

"My point exactly. And besides, against every law of nature that makes sense, you love Mr. Hey I Used to Be Immortal But Now I'm Just a Doofus from Russia Here to Make Everyone's Life Miserable. If you'd just admit it, it would make things easier."

"I don't know if I love Ethan."

Tess rolls her eyes. "I adore you, Annie. But you are seriously delusional."

Maybe I am. Do I love Ethan? If things would just calm down for five seconds, maybe I could figure it out. Like that's going to happen. I have a destiny. Calm is off the agenda.

On my bookshelf, the candles are still burning very bright. I point a finger at the Cinnamon Sugar one and concentrate. The flame leaps high and straight, almost to the ceiling. If I wanted to, I could make it touch.

"Hello? Pyro? What are you doing?" Tess's voice pitches high, waking Buster, who jumps from the bed and pads over to stare at me. It also startles me. Would I have really done that?

"Don't know. That's the point, isn't it? I don't know what I'm doing." This is not entirely true; we both know it. I do know—sort of. Or rather, the power that's inside me now—it knows what it wants. It just seems to be waiting for me to understand what I'm supposed to do with it.

I concentrate on the candle; the flame flickers out. A thin trail of dark smoke winds its way through the air. Dripping wax puddles at the base of the candle.

Tess flicks her gaze from me to the candles and back again. "You can be really scary. Did I ever tell you that?"

"Sorry. I'm just—you know what? I think we're done here. You thirsty? 'Cause I'm parched. I need Diet Coke, and I need it now." It's a lame attempt at changing the subject, but it's all I've got in me right now.

Satisfied that the candles are done bursting into wild flame, I turn my attention to the laptop, close the pages still open on the toolbar. And pause on the last one. Alexander Palace. Huge columns. Pretty walkway. Acres of private park. Just like it used to be. Just like Ethan and I saw it earlier today. Anastasia's house.

I hate even looking at it. But I can't pull my gaze away.

"She lived there, Tess." I tap the screen and my finger leaves a smudge. "Anastasia and her sisters and brother and mother and father. She walked in that park. I saw her do it. I felt her do it. Just like I felt her die. He betrayed her. Her whole life betrayed her. And what did I do? I brought her back and then let her die anyway. Big help. No one stopped Viktor from using her then, not even Ethan. So how am I suddenly supposed to know how to stop him from whatever it is he's doing now?"

Tess puts her hand on my shoulder. "Anne, please. I'm sorry I brought up the Ben thing. I thought you'd want to—I'm sorry."

I realize that if I look at her, I'm going to cry. I'm relieved when I hear the sound of a car pulling into our driveway. My dad's home, probably with the Chinese takeout. Enough of my personal pity party. We'll go downstairs and eat egg rolls and fried rice and whatever else he's brought. There's time still before this all comes apart. This morning I stopped Baba Yaga from sending me wherever it is she expects me to go. After all, part of this power inside me is hers. It makes sense that I could fight back.

This is my big, bold plan—to eat pork with garlic sauce—when the world starts to bend and fold right here inside my room. Tess screams. The fur on Buster's back stands on end. He hisses.

"You are hesitating too long, girl," Baba Yaga hollers, hovering in her mortar at my window, impossibly large and impossibly half in and half out of my room, the wall somehow bending with everything else to accommodate her. A red scarf—her babushka—covers her head. Her skin is brown and wrinkled, and her eyes glow like two huge black orbs, a skull where each pupil should be.

Her mouth twists in a grimace as she bares her iron teeth. "You have all this inside you now, tucked away, and what do you do? Nothing. Are you still the girl who bargained with me in my forest? That girl was strong. That girl did not let go of what she wanted. But you? You sit and wait. You play with your magic. Tomatoes on a vine. Candle flames. Such a child you are. Such a silly little girl. You know you feel it stirring inside you. You called me to you with it, girl. Even if you do not understand how."

Buster launches himself at my witch. He swipes at one of her huge hands with his paw. Unfortunately, Buster is declawed. So he doesn't really do much damage before the hand swats him across the room. He hits my carpet with a smacking sound and lies there looking dazed and angry.

"You've got your own cat," I scream at her. "Leave mine alone."

"Yeah," Tess adds in a pause between my screams. "This isn't your forest. You need to go away."

"The barriers are broken, girl. Did you not understand what you have promised? What you are? What you will become? But first, you have a job to do. And you must begin it now."

There's a sound like rushing water, and Tess grabs my hand. The world contracts again. I think I'm screaming, but I'm not even sure of that. And then, Baba Yaga still looming in my window and the world swirling like a kaleidoscope, I hear the sound of Ethan's voice in my head.

"No," he seems to be saying. "No. Anne. Wait. I'm coming. I need to be with you. You can't—"

If he's really saying something and not just a figment of my terrified imagination, he doesn't get the chance to finish. Because the world contracts even smaller, and then we're gone, Tess and I, tumbling through blank empty space and rushing noise.

Tuesday, 6:18 pm

Ethan

I FEEL HER PULL AWAY FROM ME. FROM EVERYTHING. I'D thought the link between us severed as I passed my magic to her in the lake. But I was wrong. Somehow, it's grown stronger. Strong enough that I can feel her fear. See her clearly for a brief second or two. In her room with Tess and the witch, the Alexander Palace on the computer screen behind her. In my mind, I call to her. Ridiculously, I tell her to wait. To hold on. Only what can I do? She's there, and I'm here, just steps outside the café, with Dimitri.

"What is it?" he asks. He stares at me like I've gone mad. "What do you see?" He looks around us as though something will be there.

"It's begun," I tell him. "I'm not ready to help her." And in my head: *will I ever be ready?*

"Then I would think you should do something about that, Brother," he tells me. "Or perhaps you already have. I am no fool, Ethan. You are not completely without power now, eh? There is something left?"

I hesitate, but then I admit it. "Something new. Like what we had, but not exactly. I don't understand it yet. But it's there."

He watches me, eyes dark, then darker. "I do not like liars,

Brother. If you want my help, then do not withhold the truth from me again."

I let him have the last word. I have no plans to apologize. No further promises. Our pact is what it is. Either we hold to it, or we don't. I have no patience to argue with him.

"Explain," he says eventually.

"Forward and backward. The past, the present, the future. The witch has sent her somewhere. Russia, I think. But I don't know how to reach her. I thought I could help her control how she went into this. She—we—stopped it this morning. I thought…"

Panic rises. How could I have let her out of my sight today after what happened earlier? After all we have been through, one thing has never changed. I am still quite the *zalupa*. Or perhaps our Russian word for *dickhead* gives me too much credit. Baba Yaga was tricked by us once. I doubt she will be so foolish ever again.

"You're telling me that Anne is somewhere in Russia at some time possibly past, present, or future, and you have no idea how to get her back?"

I nod.

"And she's alone?"

I sigh. "No," I tell Dimitri. "She's with Tess."

A Really Little Village Somewhere in Russia, Definitely *Not* This Century

Anne

"I THINK I'M GOING TO PUKE." TESS LEANS OVER AND DOES just that. Wipes her mouth with the back of her hand. "Gross."

The world has stopped gyrating. But my room is gone. We're half sitting, half lying in the middle of a dusty road. I have dirt in my mouth. When I spit, the blob of saliva looks dusty too.

Done puking, Tess shoves her hair out of her eyes and looks around. So do I.

Here's what we see: Little wooden houses in the distance. A horse-drawn wagon bouncing up the crappy dirt road just beyond where we've landed. Trees. Possibly a small farm, if I squint.

We are in big trouble.

Tess catches on quickly. "We're not in Baba Yaga's forest, are we?" she asks in a voice that mirrors the panic growing inside me. "Oh, my God, Anne. What the hell just happened? And explain to me why I continue being your friend."

My heart is pounding so rapidly that I figure I won't have to come up with an answer. I'll just die right here of some kind of coronary incident, and Tess will have to figure it out on her own. Which possibly would be the better scenario.

"Russia." I stand, brush dirt off my clothes. "It's Russia. I mean, we're in Russia. I think. Or maybe it's called the Soviet Union. Or one of the places that ends in 'stan. You're the history person. The Ukraine, maybe. Belarus? Do you see a primeval forest? It could be Poland. Shit. I guess it depends on what year it is."

"Year? Did you say *year*?" Tess's voice hits a range somewhere between screech and glass breakage. Over on the dirt road, the horse and wagon plod slowly by. Luckily the guy in the peasant outfit is too busy shooing away a cow to pay attention to us. Or maybe he does see us and figures we're just a figment of his imagination. Maybe Tess's screaming has rendered him spontaneously deaf. Anything is possible at this point.

"I'm pretty sure," I say. I try to sound calm. And like I know what I'm talking about. I *think* we're in Russia. But I've only seen it in books and on the Internet. For all I know we could be in northern Wisconsin. Maybe people still ride in wagons as you get closer to Canada.

"Well," I continue, trying to stumble my way to something that sounds plausible. "None of this looks anything close to where Ethan and I were for those few seconds this morning. But it does look like Russia. At least I think it does. Plus, what Baba Yaga told me, remember? The past, the present, the future all mingling? So I guess this is the past? Maybe I'm wrong. Maybe the Alexander Palace is behind that clump of trees?" My explanation comes out like a question. Not good.

"There is no palace here, Anne. Do you see a palace? There's grass and trees and dirt and that guy and his wagon. And oh yeah, I threw up a little on my new white shirt. Fabulous. You and Blue Eyes go to the palace. You and *I* are stuck in the middle of Russian nowhere. And I *so* hope you have a plan for how to get us out of here."

I think this over while Tess brushes some more nineteenth-century or possibly twentieth-century—since didn't they still ride around in wagons in the early nineteen hundreds, especially in rural wherever we are?—dirt off her jeans. They're her favorite pair, a sort of skinny but not too skinny dark gray that make her butt look phenomenal. Now they're here with her, and neither of them is looking happy about it. If jeans could talk, hers would say, "Get me back to the mall."

"I don't know why we're not at the Alexander Palace," I say as Tess finally gives up on the dirt brushing. "It doesn't make any sense."

"Oh, but the time-travel part—that's just fine?"

"You're not helping, you know. What I mean is if Baba Yaga sent us here, then why? If she's decided to get this journey thing going, why show me one place a few hours ago but then have us end up somewhere else?"

"Because she's, oh, I don't know, a crazy witch?"

"That's not an answer."

"It's good enough for me. And speaking of crazy witches, Glinda, you're the one who's all powered up these days. Can't you, like, just zap us back home? I mean isn't that the point? She gave you extra mojo and now you owe her?"

Tess has a way of boiling the complex down to the basics. Except it still doesn't answer my question: why here? What is it about here, wherever here is?

I blow out a breath and try to calm down again. "Think, Tess. We need to think."

"We need to get out of here."

"And that's not going to happen if you keep bitching."

"Well, I wouldn't have to if you'd only—"

"Ethan." Maybe it's my annoyance at Tess's refusal to shut up that makes the fog of paralyzing fear lift just the tiniest bit. I'd heard him, hadn't I? Just as everything began to go all wonky, and we swirled around and ended up here.

"Ethan what?" Tess looks to her left and then her right. "Is he here too? Because that would be—"

I place my hand over her mouth. "Just shut up for two seconds. Please." I close my eyes. Tess stays silent. And then I remember.

"I heard him! Just as we were starting to get sucked away. His voice was in my head or something. He was telling me to hold on. He said he needed to be here with me. Only then the connection or whatever it was just broke."

"Well, that explains *everything*, Anne."

We stand there glaring at each other. Tess digs her cell phone out of her pocket and looks at the screen hopefully. She presses every button. Her forehead wrinkles.

"No service, no bars."

"No kidding. I—do you feel that?" The ground has begun to vibrate beneath us. I feel it in my feet, then my legs, then inside me like the too-loud bass of a passing car. We look toward the road as they appear. Horses and riders. At least a dozen.

They careen around the bend of the dirt road where that wagon had been, riding fast, then faster. The riders are men, all of them. All with big fur hats and wearing pants and a tunic top that looks military. And every single one of them is holding a sword. Make that a terrifyingly huge, curved sword.

Cossacks. I know it as I see them. Know it because they're part of the story that Ethan had told me when I first met him. That day we ran to his loft and he told me the story of how he ended up in the Brotherhood. *Cossacks.* The men who killed his family.

My heart begins to pump wildly in my chest. Actually, wildly doesn't even begin to cover it. Some vague, tiny piece of me says, "Hey, Anne, don't you have some sort of magic witchy powers that can stop the crazy Cossacks with their Huge, Pointy, Scary Swords?"

Except I'm not a witch. I'm just Anne who doesn't know what the hell she's doing and is probably going to die here before she figures it out. I resort to the only answer that makes sense right now.

"Run," I tell Tess. "Run. Now."

There's a grove of trees in the distance—not quite a forest, but maybe good enough. It's far, but maybe we can make it. We run as fast as we can, but the ground is rocky and uneven, and clouds of dust fly as our shoes slap the dirt. My whole body vibrates with the sound of the horses coming up behind us.

"Oh my God." Tess glances behind her. "We're not going to make it."

She stumbles. I try to grab her, but it's too late. She slams into the ground, right knee first, and skids. Her face smacks the dirt. When she rolls over and tries to sit up, I can see that her hand is cut and bleeding, and there's a long gash over her left eyebrow. Blood streams down her face and into her eyes.

"I'm okay," she says, even though clearly she is not okay at all. She tries to stand. The horses are gaining on us. One of them shouts something in Russian. My heart pounds with each horse hoof.

"Do something," Tess whispers.

"I'm trying. Crap. I can't think. I don't—"

"Anne! We're going to die!"

Since this does not seem the best option for either of us, I make an attempt.

"*Ya dolzhen,*" I say, slipping into the Russian that Ethan taught me to begin a spell. *Ya dolzhen. I must.* Then I freeze. I must what? What do I need to do? Stop them? Put a block around us somehow? What? Damn it. It's all happening so fast. I can't think. I need to think. I need to—

"Oh my God," Tess says over and over. "We're going to die. They're going to kill us. I'm going to die—again."

"No, we won't!" I scream. I try again. Start to imagine a wall around us. I'm panting, breathless. Fear prickles every molecule of my body. Like how I felt at the lake when Tess and Ben almost died. Like how I felt when Ethan actually did. My body shakes. My hands glow white, then blue, then—

When they ride right through us and around us, it's like we're not there at all. I can feel the heavy weight of the horses, smell wool and body odor and dirt. Their swords swish through the air. They're all shouting in Russian. One guy laughs. The harsh sound of it crinkles the hairs on the back of my neck.

Only we're not dead. I haven't done anything. This much is clear to me—at least not anything that would have worked. But we're not dead. We're there and the Cossacks are there, but somehow we're not together. It makes no sense. But it's like we each exist in the same space but not at the same time. We can see them and hear them and even feel the ground shake because of them, but somehow they don't know we're here.

I sink to the ground and wrap my arms around Tess. I'm

not sure if I'm crying or laughing. Probably both. Tess is still bleeding. But we're not dead. Okay, we're still in Russia and clearly not in our own century and I have no idea how to get us home, but we're not dead.

"What just happened?"

"Don't know," I tell her. "But I'm good with it." I watch the Cossacks ride toward the trees. One of them shouts what sounds like a command, and the horses all turn toward the right. But they're still headed away from us. I figure I need to stop Tess from bleeding before we continue our analysis of the time-space continuum.

"What do you mean you don't—"

"Hold still," I order her. "Seriously. You're bleeding pretty bad."

This time I'm calm enough to actually accomplish something. Methodically, I set to work. I place my hand over the cut on her eyebrow. It's deep, probably requiring stitches.

"Gross," Tess mutters. "Are you touching my bleeding head?"

"Shh. Just let me do it. Don't be a baby."

The familiar humming buzz fills me. I'm less panicked now so my body seems to be more willing to understand what to do.

"Feels hot," Tess says.

"Don't talk." I press my hand more firmly to her forehead. Feel the wound shift and move. And heal. When I take my hand away, her forehead is just sweaty, not cut. I do the same with her hand. Make her roll up her jeans and use both hands to heal the abrasion on her leg and knee while I'm at it. The thing inside me pulses. Even the blood that's dripped down her face disappears.

Tess studies her healed hand. She brings it to her forehead, her fingertips feeling for the wound that's no longer there.

"Holy crap," she says. "You actually did it." She grins at me and shakes her head. Then: "You don't look so good."

I'm halfway between witty comeback and wanting to vomit when I glance toward the woods.

The Cossacks are in motion again, heading past the trees. And then from behind us, cutting across the grass from the same direction the Cossacks had come, a man comes running. He's headed toward them, shouting something, shaking his fist. For the first time I notice a curl of smoke in the air, growing thicker by the second.

They can't possibly hear him, I think. But one of the Cossacks turns his head. Gestures to the others and points to the running man.

In that instant, something seems horribly familiar.

"They didn't see us, did they?" Tess is saying. "How is that possible? This is crazy, Anne. We need to—"

"Get up." I haul her by the armpit. "C'mon."

"What? No. Where are we going?"

I pull her toward the farm. And the Cossacks. The running man continues to run.

"No. Are you freakin' insane? Give them another chance to realize we're here? No way."

"Then stay here. I'll be back." I don't tell her the rest of what I'm thinking. I just start running. She's right, I think. I'm crazy. But I have to know. I have to see. I know she's going to chase after me, and I know this isn't a good thing, but I can't stop myself.

When it happens, it's just as horrible as Ethan had described it to me. Worse, because I'm here to see it.

The Cossacks wheel to a stop, point their swords in the air. Their horses paw at the ground like they want to get going again. The running man reaches them. As one, the Cossacks point their swords at him.

Someone shouts something I can't make out and probably couldn't understand even if I did. I smell smoke. I flick my gaze behind me. That curl of smoke drifting toward the clouds is growing thicker and blacker. Something is on fire. I'm close enough now that I can hear the running man choke out a sob.

Tess catches up to me. She grabs my arm and yanks me back. "Jesus, Anne. Stop. What are you doing? They're going to kill that guy. He needs to get out of there."

She's right, of course. They are. Even as I think it, another person runs from where the lone man had come. He's smaller and thinner, and as he gets closer, I see that he's a boy, maybe nine or ten years old.

I'm sure then what's about to happen. Fear and bile rise in my throat.

"*Otets!*" the boy calls out. Then, "Papa!"

"Papa? It's his dad." Tess is still clutching at me.

One of the Cossacks raises his sword. "No!" I scream along with the boy. "No. *Nyet!* Don't!" Does he hear me? Does it matter?

The Cossack shouts something, and the riders make a circle around the man so that he can't escape. I'm screaming at them again and so is Tess, but when they break the circle to ride off, the man is lying facedown on the ground. One of the Cossacks waves his now blood-smeared sword in the air. Even from where I am, I can see that the man on the ground is dead. A red stain begins to spread across the back of his shirt.

The boy—I can see for sure now that he's a boy—reaches the dead man and throws himself in the dirt next to his father.

The Cossacks don't stop, just ride away laughing. All except one. He wheels his horse around. Trots back to the boy and his dead father.

"No," I scream again, even though I'm sure that none of them can hear me. "Leave him alone."

Except one of them does hear me. The boy. He stands and turns to the sound of my voice. Looks directly at me. Then shakes his head and looks back at the Cossack.

The Cossack leans down and yanks him by the shirt. Pulls him into the air so his feet are dangling, then spits in his face. He leans in closer and says something to the boy. He points a finger at the dead man on the ground and shakes his head. Then he lets go. The boy drops to the dirt. The Cossack rides off.

I stand there watching. My body shakes like the world is made of ice. The boy looks at me again. His eyes are an amazing blue. A blue you couldn't forget once you saw it, and I think I've seen those eyes enough to remember.

"Holy crap," Tess says. "That's Ethan, isn't it? Oh my God, Anne, is that why we're here? So we can watch his dad get slaughtered?"

I nod. It's impossible. Except it feels real. It is real. Little Ethan with his blue eyes. Ethan, whose story I already know. He'd found his mother and sister dead, slaughtered by the Cossacks. He'd tried to stop his father from going to avenge their murder. And then—now—he watched his father die.

Should I say something to him? What's the protocol here?

"So, um, why can he see us—or at least you—and the crazy Russian horse guys can't?"

I'd have attempted an answer, but I don't have to. Because suddenly the world shifts and folds, and the last thing I see are those blue eyes staring at me, clearly seeing me and wondering who the hell I am.

My room materializes around us. Outside on the driveway below my window, I hear the slam of a car door and then inside, downstairs, I hear my father walk in, close the front door, and say, "Chinese takeout is here. Who's ready for egg rolls?"

"Egg rolls?" Tess mumbles from where she's flopped on my floor. "Does he not know we almost just got skewered by some back-in-the-day Russian crazies?"

Outside, I hear another car screech to a stop in the driveway, and then the front doorbell starts ringing over and over like someone's desperate to get inside.

"Anne!" Ethan is shouting when either my father lets him in or he just walks in without waiting, neither of which I can see. I hear him bolting up the stairs and the sound of my father saying something—possibly that he should have called first because there aren't enough egg rolls.

He races into my room and hugs me to him. Presses his face into my sweaty hair. I wrap my arms around him and hold tight. My heart doesn't want to slow down. I breathe in Ethan—all solid and real. His hands rest on the small of my back. Somehow this makes me feel safe and edgy at the same time.

"Hey!" Tess says. "What about me? I almost got shish-kebabbed too. And by the way, you were one skinny little boy, did you know that?"

I ease out his grip and study his face. The eyes are the same as the boy we just saw. No way could I ever mistake them.

"I felt it," he says. "I don't understand. But I knew it was happening. I—" He turns to Tess. "What do you mean, little boy?"

"We saw you," Tess tells him. "You were a little boy. Your father—" She stops. Claps her hand over her mouth.

"Are you guys okay up there?" I hear my father on the stairs. We've got like three-and-a-half seconds before he gets up here. My father, who unlike my mother, has no clue about the magic wackiness I've been up to.

I cut to the chase. "We ended up in old-time Russia. We saw the Cossacks kill your father. We saw you." My heart pounds again as I say it. Suddenly I'm aware of how horribly intimate that moment was. Something that was Ethan's own private memory. Now it's my memory too.

Ethan goes very still. His face pales, and those blue eyes look grim and dark.

"The one Cossack," I say quickly. "He said something to you, Ethan. Before he dropped you to the ground and rode off. You never mentioned that to me before. Did that happen? Did he really tell you something?"

Ethan looks startled. "He said he would kill me," he whispers. "But that he'd been told not to. I thought he was lying. I thought he was afraid of me. Later, I always imagined he just didn't want my blood on his hands. He'd killed my entire family. What did I matter at that point? But what if that wasn't it at all? What if he really had been instructed to leave me alone? That would mean—"

"It would mean that maybe your father was murdered on purpose, not just someone's whim. It would mean—"

68

My own father now stands in my door, watching us all like we're escaped criminals or something. Buster wanders back in and starts rubbing on my leg and purring. I notice for the first time that there are still a few drops of blood on Tess's forehead. It's the first proof since we've been back that this whole thing really happened. That I haven't just been hallucinating or something.

"Later," I say quickly.

"Hey, Mr. Michaelson," Tess says cheerily.

"Are you bleeding?" My father points to her forehead.

"Am I?" She touches her hand to her forehead, then wipes the smear of blood on her jeans sort of casually, like it's a speck of dust or something. "You know your daughter. She's a wild one. We got hungry waiting for those egg rolls. She fought me over the last tortilla chip. But I ate it. Good for me, right?"

My father narrows his eyes.

"Food's on the table," my mother calls from downstairs.

"How did you get back?" Ethan asks quietly as we head for the door.

"Wish I knew," I tell him. "Maybe it'll be written in the fortune cookie."

WEDNESDAY, 12:42 AM

ANNE

DINNER LASTS AN ETERNITY. EVENTUALLY, TESS AND Ethan and I convene in my room and talk. We lounge on the floor, Ethan's back against my bed, his legs stretched out, while Tess and I share the beanbag. My stomach is full from an overload of shrimp fried rice.

"I'm sorry, Ethan," Tess says. "What they did to your dad, to your family? I don't know how you live with that."

And this is how I know that Tess is ripped apart by what we've seen in our trip to the past: she pries herself out of the squishy beanbag, knee-walks to Ethan, and pulls him into a hug. He looks shocked—it's not just me who knows she's no Ethan fan—and gently wrestles himself free when she doesn't let go soon enough.

In the end, we realize that we don't know anything. Did Viktor have something to do with the death of Ethan's family? Maybe. Maybe not. Was it my power that brought us home? A little, I think. I'm tired of not being sure.

"You need to stay with her," Tess decides for Ethan. She's squashed back against me in the beanbag, and I can smell garlic pork on her breath. "I'll stay too, if you want. But you need to be here. If she starts to disappear again, maybe you can stop it this time."

"I don't need a baby-sitter," I grumble. I've eaten too much Chinese food, and my fortune cookie read, "You live in interesting times." My mother picked at the food with her chopsticks and watched Ethan and me with a worried look on her face. My father insisted that Tess eat the last egg roll. Now Ethan looks conflicted about the prospect of spending the night in my room. Not exactly the reaction a girl hopes for.

"Really," I go on. "I'll be fine." In the end, we all decide that this is probably not the case.

So after my mother's fifth pointed "It's getting late" visit to my room, Ethan and Tess say a noisy good-bye and I walk downstairs with them. We make a point of shutting the front door loudly, and then Ethan and I sneak into the kitchen and he waits in the darkened mudroom off the back door in case Mom or Dad decides they need a late-night snack.

From the bottom of the stairs, I yell, "Going to make some hot tea. Either of you guys want any?"

They both yell back, "No," and eventually I hear them close their bedroom door.

We sneak up the stairs.

"You really don't have to do this," I whisper, except I know that I don't really mean it. "We both know we're not safe until this is over. It's part of the deal."

"I'm staying," Ethan says.

At which point it occurs to me that there are two of us and one bed.

It occurs to him too. "I'll sleep on the floor," he says.

"There's the beanbag." I point to it like he won't be able to figure out where it is unless I do. "Sorry about the pink. It's pretty girlie, I know. You can take the bed. I'm good with the beanbag. When I was little, I used to—"

"Floor's fine. Trust me, I've slept on worse."

I'm sure he has. All right then, mister, it's the beanbag for you.

In my bathroom, I change into shorts and a tank top. When I come out, Ethan—still fully dressed—is stretched out on the floor, his head on the pink beanbag, his bare feet brushing against my bed's white eyelet dust ruffle. In no way does this diminish his hotness factor. Not that I plan on telling him.

"You know," I say quietly, because my parents' room is just down the hall. "This isn't exactly practical. I mean it's not like you can spend every night here until this is over."

"This isn't every night, Anne. It's tonight. I'll stand outside, if that's better for you, but I'm not leaving. Not tonight."

"Pretty firm on that, aren't you?" I huff.

"Yes." He crosses his hands behind his head, elbows sinking into the beanbag. The edge of his polo rides up, and I catch a glimpse of flat, tan stomach and a thin line of hair that disappears into his jeans. A herd of butterflies flutter in my stomach.

I switch off my lamp and climb into bed.

The darkness somehow makes him feel closer.

I close my eyes.

In the dark, I hear Ethan's slow and even breathing. Has he fallen asleep? Is he just pretending? Why have I agreed to this? I mean, it's not like his presence has stopped me from a whole series of near-death experiences. In fact, he's brought most of them my way by just existing.

No way am I going to sleep while he's breathing down there.

So here's what I'm thinking. If I wanted to, I could lie down next to him. If I wanted to, I could tell him to lie down next to me.

If I wanted to.

Do I want to?

Does he want to?

We spent the night at his apartment only a few weeks ago, but that felt different. Possibly because I was in a panic about my magic getting stronger. Also because technically I was still with Ben and that made things awkward. And definitely because a rusalka who turned out to be Lily, my birth grandmother, appeared in Ethan's shower.

Or as Tess described it the other day when we were reminiscing about Crap That's Gone On Since That Day We Saw Ethan at the Ballet: "I think there's a clause in your magic contract that guarantees you stay a virgin. You could be the poster girl for our health-class abstinence-only policy."

Here, now, in the dark of my room, it's different. Good, different. Nice. That butterfly herd starts doing dips and turns.

"Ethan," I whisper.

"Hmm," he says, clearly not asleep. "What?"

"Nothing," I say. "Do you need anything? I can get you another pillow or something."

"I'm good."

Wonderful conversation.

We lie in the dark some more. The question I really want to ask sits on my tongue.

"You knew," I say, deciding that I might as well just throw it out there, because eventually I'm going to say it and we're lying here in the dark with nothing better to do. Okay, there are lots of better things we could do, but I'm not quite ready to do them. "You knew that Tess and I had gone back in time, didn't you?"

He's silent for long enough that I actually peek over the side of the bed to see if he's been stricken mute or suddenly disappeared or something. Moonlight is filtering through the thin curtains at my window, the angle of light casting part of his face in shadow. He looks up at me. A muscle in his jaw tightens, just slightly.

"I knew when you were gone, yes. I knew that you were being pulled away. And that I wasn't there to stop it."

He sighs through his nose. So what does this mean? That he still feels responsible for everything that happens to me? That's sweet. Romantic even. But misguided.

He may have set things in motion that day we collided with one another at school and the spark of power sizzled through me. But I'm over blaming it on him. Way over. It's *my* destiny. Not his. But now there's this.

"Like felt it?" I ask, and my stomach knots just the tiniest bit. "Or really knew? 'Cause I heard you in my head. Or at least I thought I did. You were telling me to—"

"I told you to wait. That I needed to be with you."

As if we're still on the same tightly connected wavelength, we both sit up—me in my bed, him on the floor. Somehow this makes me even more conscious of how close he is. That it's after midnight and we're in my room. Together.

And both aware that we've been linked to each other since the beginning. Been in each other's dreams. Felt each other's emotions to some extent. But what's happening to us this time is different. It's more specific and more intense.

Intense enough that I ask, "So, um, is this the first time that this has happened for you? I mean with me, I guess."

Ethan laughs. "As opposed to what? The hundred other girls chosen to save Anastasia from Baba Yaga?"

I hang over the bed and invade his personal space. "It's not funny," I whisper. "Doesn't this freak you out? Me reading your thoughts and you reading mine? And when will this occur? All the time? Or just in certain situations? Because let me just say that of all the superpowers I could ever wish for, knowing what someone else is thinking is totally not one of them. I think all sorts of crap that I don't want anyone to know. Don't you?"

In my stomach, the tiny knot blossoms. *Can* he read my mind all the time? Or only when I'm in danger? And as I seem to be in danger most of the time, what does this mean? Plus, how long has he been sneaking peeks into my head? Only this time? Or has he been entering my brain at will? Like just now during the whole "Where are we going to sleep?" conversation—did he catch me wondering about what it would be like if we both shared my bed? All the stuff I tell Tess—has he been listening in?

And what about Ben, who Ethan is fully aware I still talk to? Is Ethan somehow tuning in to that too? That stupid moment after coffee when I kissed Ben, a reflex kiss really, did Ethan see that in his head? Or worse, feel it? The creeper possibilities are endless.

Annoyance and nerves do a jittery dance inside me, and because I don't know how to make them go away, I kick off the covers and plop down on the floor next to Ethan. He startles a little—like he's part surprised and part not.

"Have you?" I say, continuing my runaway train of thought.

"Have I what?"

"Been spying on my brain this whole time?" Does this explain what I felt at Wrigley Field too—that weird sense that Ethan has powers different from what he had before?

"No." He sounds indignant that I'd even suggest it. "But it was distinct. I heard you. I sensed you. I didn't see you, exactly. But it was almost like that. I just, well, knew."

He shifts toward me and cups his hands gently around my face. My nerve endings give a pleasant little shiver. "What about you?" he asks. "Have you been reading *my* thoughts?"

The question throws me. Have I? I know it's not something that's come consciously. "No," I tell him. "Not like this."

"Then like what?" Ethan eases closer, traces his fingers in light circles down the small of my back. It is a highly distracting move.

I fumble for the right words. "Since that first day at school," I say, "there's always been something. We both know that. But since we came back from Baba Yaga's forest this second time, it's intensified. Not just feelings or images. This time I heard words. Whole sentences. It's so much more specific."

Knowing what someone else—what Ethan—is feeling, thinking—it unsettles me. Like right now, does he sense that there's a piece of my brain registering the presence of his hands on my back? They feel warm and solid, both sexy and comforting.

"Don't be scared," Ethan says. His hands stop circling and rest low against my back—a nice pressure. "I'm here."

His words make my worry spill out. "But doesn't it bother you? Me being able to look into *your* head? What if you have stuff you don't want me to know about?"

It's just barely a breath, but I hear Ethan hesitate. "Everyone has secrets, Anne. I've been around a while. I suppose I've got more than my share."

"Secrets you want to tell me?" Ones I want to hear?

He eases back to look at me. Raises one dark eyebrow, his face still half-shadowed in a slice of moonlight. "Then they wouldn't be secrets, would they? But even then—I trust you."

Do I hear hesitation in his voice again? Maybe it's just my imagination.

"Come here." He pulls me tight against him, kisses my mouth. I don't have to be a mind reader to realize that he's done talking. My own thoughts vanish—other than a fleeting idea that possibly he's seducing me, and that I'm good with that. Or maybe he really does have secrets and figures if he distracts me enough, I'll forget about mind-melding and just let him have his way with me.

Which is totally working until just as I kiss him back and our tongues touch and every nerve ending in my body sets itself on fire, I do see into his mind. Or maybe he's seeing into mine. At this particular second, it's impossible to tell the difference.

I just know that he's in my head—that skinny little boy he used to be, with those huge blue eyes watching his father die.

"Anne," Ethan says. "Do you—"

"Shh," I tell him. "It'll fade." I mean the vision, not the kiss. *Bad vision. Shoo.* I want to be in the present, not the past. I scoot into Ethan's lap and wrap my legs around him. He smells insanely good. *Take that, you stupid vision.*

For a second it even works. My senses shift into overdrive— the smoothness of his skin, the firmness of his muscles, the thick, wavy texture of his hair. The blue of his eyes, wide open and watching me. He skims his hands up my back and his thumbs graze my sides. *Oh crap, that feels good.* He nuzzles my neck, presses tiny little kisses along my jaw. My body has never been so happy.

Another image flashes, as bright and real as if it were in the room and not just in my head.

"Shit." Pressed against me still, Ethan freezes.

I suck in a breath. Narrow my eyes. "You're kissing me and thinking about someone else?"

"No. I—"

"Well, she's not in *my* memory bank." In our mutual heads, the girl with the long dark hair smiles. I scoot away from him. This particular peek into his brain is a definite buzz kill.

Dark-haired girl is not alone. Ethan, dressed in dark wool pants that belt at the waist and a silky cream-colored shirt, is holding her hand. His hair is still thick and longish, but it's slicked back somehow. He looks, well, smitten. Fabulous.

In our heads, he kisses her.

Seriously? Out. Out. Out.

I squeeze my eyes closed. And when that doesn't work, I dive back into my bed and pull the covers over my head.

"Anne," Ethan says. He sits down on the side of my bed. I shove him off and he hits the floor with a thud.

"Don't say a word," I tell him from under the covers while the Ethan in my head strokes the girl's hair. "Unless it's a suggestion about how we get this to stop. Because I am completely grossed out right now."

"Tasha," he says. And then I remember. Tasha. The girl he told me about. The one he'd loved. The Russian girl living in London who he left when she realized that he wasn't aging.

That month after month while she got older, he was staying the same.

I peek out from under the comforter. The Ethan in my head kisses Tasha again. "*I love you,*" he tells her.

Three words that neither of us has spoken to the other. Will we? Do we? Hard to say when I'm stuck in a brain loop watching him make out with someone else.

"Am I causing this?" I ask him, trying to look just at him and not at the images in my head but failing miserably. "Is it us together? Something else?"

Ethan's forehead wrinkles. Maybe that's why we're together—both clueless. Things finally get romantic between us, and suddenly he's sucking face with another girl in my head—and neither of us can figure out why.

"*I have a surprise,*" Head Ethan tells Tasha. Her eyes widen and she smiles at him. "*I'm taking you to the ballet. A friend of mine gave me the tickets.*"

"*Friend?*" She smiles again, but I see true curiosity in her eyes. "*You've never introduced me to your friends. I'd love to meet them.*"

"*Not them,*" he tells her. "*Just one. His name is Viktor.*"

"*Is this Viktor as mysterious as you?*" Dark-haired Tasha laughs. "*Because you are still quite the mystery, my darling.*"

"Darling? She called you darling?" Comforter wrapped around me, I slide out of bed again. I step to face Ethan as if somehow closing the distance will stop the vision. It doesn't. Even in the darkened room, I can see him blush, a hint of red that spreads up his neck to his jaw.

"We were in love."

I nod like I get it, which basically I do. In my head, after all, it's still the Jazz Age. It's not like he was cheating on me with her.

"*You'll have to judge for yourself,*" Head Ethan tells Tasha. "*At the ballet.*"

"*I will indeed,*" Tasha tells him. "*But I'm certain I'll adore him. He's a chum of yours. I trust he'll be quite wonderful.*"

Wow. She is *so* going to be disappointed.

My Ethan places a hand on my arm. His eyes are distant, like he's trying to remember something. "Is that how it was?"

"I don't know," I snark. "You were there, not me."

The Ethan in my head smiles at Tasha. But I can see that he looks a little uncertain. So possibly he wasn't totally in the dark about Viktor. Or maybe that Ethan wanted to keep the Tasha thing a secret. I look over at him to confirm any of these ideas, but he's still lost in what we're seeing.

"*It's* Giselle," past Ethan says. "*Not as good as the Bolshoi version, I suppose, but I think you will enjoy it.*"

Tasha laughs. "*We're in London, Ethan. Not Moscow. This is why we talk in English, no? To, what is the word? Adjust. We'll have to manage. I like it here. The English are not Russians. They take their tea with milk, and their language—it doesn't have quite the passion we are used to, yes? But I can play Rachmaninoff and Liszt and Chopin, and I can teach. It is not so good in Russia anymore. Not since the Revolution. You know it. I know it. And I would imagine your friend Viktor knows it too. He is Russian too, yes? You have not said. But he must be, if he wants to join us. Giselle is so delightfully tragic.*"

"Da. *Yes. He is one of us. An acquaintance.*" He kisses her on the forehead again, and it feels weird to watch them together like it's real time even though it's totally in the past. His lips press against her skin, and my own forehead tingles in response. Is that even possible? How can I feel what she's feeling when she's not exactly real?

Tasha smiles at her version of Ethan. "*This is what you always do, dearest, isn't it? You distract me with kisses when I want to get serious. But you—you are always serious underneath, yes? Something sad, I think. Something you want to say but never do. So this Viktor—did you know him back home?*"

Tasha waits for her Ethan to answer the question while my Ethan and I stand eyeball to eyeball, linked to this memory or vision or whatever it is of the past. His past. Tasha's past. A past that I'm suddenly feeling like it's my own.

Tasha's Ethan nods and looks sort of miserable, which makes total sense since he's explained to me that he never did tell her. He had this huge secret—about being immortal and having pledged to save Anastasia and being part of Viktor's secret Brotherhood—that he didn't ever share with her. How would I feel about that, I wonder? I think I know Ethan. But do I? Has he changed since then? If he had that moment to do over, would he react the same way? Or would he still keep his secrets?

"*A family friend,*" Tasha's Ethan says. "*I've known him since I was a boy.*"

"*Ah,*" Tasha says. "*Well, then. I know I will adore him. And he can tell me stories about you.*" She laughs again and smiles broadly. Her teeth are straight and even. She looks stunning and perfect in a way that I've never been and probably never will be. "*I would imagine that you were a lovely little boy. So serious and earnest.*"

She grins when Ethan in the past looks sort of embarrassed. "*See? I am right, am I not? My earnest young man.*"

Both Ethans—the one in my room and the one in my head—look uncomfortable.

"Is this how you remember it?" I ask my Ethan as I try to

get the vision to go away. It's like whispering to someone at the movies. The images and sounds keep playing in the background.

Ethan shrugs. "Maybe. I don't know. It was a long time ago."

That's not enough of an answer, and I think we both know it. Ethan in my head hooks his arm with Tasha's, and like when he'd kissed her, my own arm feels the pressure of his muscles—a phantom arm pressed against mine.

And as he moves with her, the shift happens. Not quick and dizzying like what happened when Tess and I were sucked into the Russian past. This time the change is more gradual.

"Do you feel that," I begin. "Ethan. Do you—"

"Yes. Are you—"

This is all we manage. Two half-completed sentences. Two half-completed thoughts.

One final thought comes to me: if I'm going somewhere, I'm not going in my bare feet.

"Shoes!" I say and shove my feet into the only thing available—a pair of rhinestone-studded flip-flops that Tess gave me for my birthday.

Ethan stumbles into his sandals and grips me tightly. I link my arms around his neck.

We're pulled half in and half out of both worlds. For a few strange moments it's like standing on the Continental Divide— one foot in my room, the other in London in Ethan's past. We waver there, and the room shimmers and bends. There's an Ethan holding me and an Ethan in front of me, and I wonder for one brief hysterical second if maybe they'll multiply and there'll be thousands of Ethans in thousands of moments, like one of those fun-house sets of mirrors you see in scary movies.

I try to stop it, and I think Ethan tries to stop it too, but it's like trying to get the wind to stop blowing. I have powerful magic inside me, but still I'm dragged backward. And there's a flash of understanding that maybe I have to do this. That whatever is about to happen in the past with Ethan and his friend Tasha is something I—we—need to witness.

Like before, the world bends and contracts and folds. Nausea rises in my throat. Even this slower pull makes me dizzy, anxious. My room tilts. Or maybe it's me and Ethan tilting.

I blow out a steadying breath. And let what's happening happen.

London, 1926

Tasha's Music Studio, Evening
Maybe Wednesday, Maybe Not

Ethan

MY SCIENCE EDUCATION HAS BEEN MOSTLY SELF-TAUGHT. I have little knowledge of the time-space continuum. But I know magic when I see it. Even with that, I'm not prepared for how strange it feels to stand here—not in a dream, but in what can only be described as real time—watching myself with Tasha.

Can they see us? They don't seem to. I clear my throat loudly. Next to me, Anne startles. But Tasha and my past self don't react.

"Well, that's good," Anne whispers. "I mean, I guess so. It's like with me and Tess. All those crazy Cossacks just rode right by us like we weren't even—Wait. That's not exactly right. The Cossacks didn't see us. And your father didn't see us. But for one second, you saw me. I know you did."

"Well, let's hope that this version of me isn't that observant," I say.

Anne grins. "Chances are good."

I frown at her. And decide she's probably right.

"*Come, dearest,*" Tasha says. "*We don't want to be late. Wouldn't want your friend Viktor thinking ill of us, would we?*"

I watch myself press a kiss to Tasha's forehead, then take

her hand. The room is suddenly familiar with its burnished wood floor and shining grand piano in one corner. We're in Tasha's music studio—the small but thriving business that was sustaining her. It sat on the first floor of a building near Trafalgar Square, right below the tiny flat she rented. The room smells exactly as I remember—a heady combination of paper and furniture polish and the cut flowers she insisted on keeping in a crystal vase on the small table near the window. It was her one consistent luxury.

She smiles, then traces one long, graceful finger over his-my lower lip. My own lip feels the touch of her fingertip. Like the room itself, the gesture is familiar. So much comes flooding back that I feel almost paralyzed with it. We had been lovers, Tasha and I. I had slept with women before her, although not many. My Brotherhood vows had slipped away slowly, then quicker as the years began to turn and the Revolution seemed farther away. Always there was my search for Anastasia. But then there had been Tasha. And something inside me had changed.

"Ethan." Anne's voice pulls me from my thoughts. I focus on her—those luminous brown eyes, auburn hair pulled back, tiny sprinkling of freckles over her nose. *How long have I been standing here, pondering the past?*

Anne gestures toward the door. "We need to follow them, right? I mean that's got to be the whole point of this. That and figuring out how to get back to my house before my parents realize I'm gone. Although I guess the other alternative is that they realize you're spending the night. I'm not really sure which would freak them out more."

With a jolt, I realize that Tasha and the other me have left the studio. Anne and I stand alone in the room, the perfume of the stalks of forsythia in the cut-glass vase filling the air with their scent.

Anne squeezes my hand. "You loved her. It's okay." But there's wariness in her eyes that I'd rather not be there.

I wrap my free hand over our clasped palms. "I know this is strange. I—"

"Ethan. It's your past. And it might not even be the way it was. We need to remember that, right? Like what Tess and I saw. Maybe we're seeing what was. Maybe we're not. We don't even know why this is happening exactly. So no worries. You loved her. She was your girlfriend. I get it. Lots of people have exes. Except I guess normally the new girlfriend doesn't get quite so up close and personal with the past. Lucky me, huh?"

I let Anne pull me to the door, then stop at the threshold and look back. Memories flood through me. Me leaning over Tasha as she sat at the keyboard. Kissing the back of her neck. Caressing her long hair. Drinking tea with her in the late afternoon. Making love to her as the last of the sun filtered in thin shafts through her bedroom window. And later, leaving her with only a note of apology. But never, ever the truth about who and what I was then.

Love requires truth. Did I love Tasha? I think I did. But not enough. Not in the right ways.

Outside, there's a noise—a car horn and the sound of horse hooves clipping against the pavement. Like me, I think suddenly. Old and new colliding for dominance, both existing in the same space. Even when I'm not magically transported to the past, I'm there anyway, just through my existence.

"Hey," Anne says quietly. Her cheeks look slightly flushed

and it takes a few seconds before she meets my gaze. "Ethan. I know you're thinking about her. But you need to think and walk. We don't want to lose them, right?"

She looks down at herself. "Terrific. My first time in London, and I'm wearing old shorts and tacky flip-flops. Let's hope we stay invisible."

She rolls her eyes, and in that moment it's Anne who's familiar again and Tasha who's the distant memory. What *was* is not important. Only what is. We need the past to explain the present, to understand how Viktor is once again immortal. And I need to figure out how to save Anne from a fate with Baba Yaga that she absolutely does not deserve. Anne to whom I always owe the truth. Anne who I love in a way that transcends past, present, and future.

We head out. The noise and bustle of London envelops us. Tasha and my past self are still visible about half a block from us, walking at a brisk clip.

We follow them, dodging a family pushing a baby carriage and a cluster of uniformed schoolboys laughing and jostling each other. If they see us, they make no show of it. We seem to be as invisible to them as we were to Tasha and my past self.

Anne points ahead of us. "Look. They're turning."

We do the same, and as we round the corner, I get my bearings.

"We're not far from the theater," I tell Anne. "The one where the Royal Ballet performed back then. Assuming that the details of what we're experiencing are accurate to what actually occurred. Actually I don't think it was even called the Royal Ballet then. I think—"

"Doesn't matter, Ethan. Whatever it was, it's where we're going. You guys were meeting Viktor, right? That's the important thing. It's got to be."

She's right, of course. And once again I'm painfully conscious that many things in my past meant more than I ever understood.

The other Ethan and Tasha step from the crooked sidewalk to cross the crowded boulevard to the other side. My gaze stays on them as I take Anne's hand and we step off the curb. Then she's yanking me back as a carriage pulled by two black horses comes inches from colliding with us. The side of the carriage scrapes against my arm as we scramble out of reach.

Anne huffs out a breath. "Can we try not to get killed?"

We dash the rest of the way without incident. At the opposite curb, Anne comes to a sudden halt, a curious look in her brown eyes.

"If I hadn't pulled you back, would that carriage have hit you? The Cossacks didn't seem to be able to touch Tess and me, but is that really how this works? What if it doesn't? When Tess fell, she hurt herself. What if colliding with the carriage is like that?"

I rub my arm. There's a definite abrasion. And thus a clear risk. I work to keep my tone light. "Don't know," I say. "So how about I just watch where I'm going? That should work for now."

Anne narrows her eyes at me, and I know my attempt at humor has fallen flat, but we leave it at that and continue walking.

Is she right? Could I—could she—have been hurt? Somehow we always circle back to the same issue. I can love

Anne all I want, but I can't promise to keep her safe. And I despise how that makes me feel. Just as I despised myself for leaving Tasha without ever telling her the truth.

Tasha, who now walks into the theater with me, even as I follow behind her with Anne. Already I can make out the posters advertising the evening's performance of *Giselle*. The ballet troupe was new then, just starting out. But there's a buzz of excitement in the air from the entering patrons—all of whom seem wholly unaware of our presence.

In front of the doors, Anne turns to me, her voice low. "So does any of this feel familiar? Do you remember going with Tasha to meet Viktor? I know it was a long time ago, but you have to remember something. Don't you?"

"Yes and no. It's not as easy you think. Time is a funny thing, Anne. We don't always know that big moments are big. Certain things—like when Anastasia was taken, when her family was murdered—they're unforgettable. But a random moment of a random day that you had no idea wasn't necessarily random? So much else goes on. So many other memories fill the space."

"Well, start thinking." She flashes a brief smile. "We're here for a reason, right? But it's your past, Ethan, not mine. I may be sneaking peeks into your head, but you're still the one who knows what's real and what's not."

We stand at the wooden doors, ballet-goers angling around us and into the theater. Anne's tone hints at an annoyance I haven't felt until now. Something sparks inside me—rises quickly and with a dark intensity I don't consciously summon. Without meaning to, I read her emotions. They rush into my head, a tangle of fear and confusion and, yes, anger. The ease with which her thoughts meld with mine shocks me.

Anne looks at me sharply. Presses a hand to her forehead.

"Hey," she says, and now it's more than annoyance that I hear. "Don't do that. You're poking around in my head again, aren't you? That is so not fair. Let me make it easy for you. I don't want to be here, but I am. And in case you're wondering, yes, it's totally weird to watch you making out with your old girlfriend. So there it is, okay? You can stop trying to pick it out of my brain."

"I wasn't—"

"And don't bother apologizing," Anne says. "If I wasn't in your head too, I probably wouldn't be so pissed right now."

Oh.

"Let's do this," she says.

I open the door. We step inside.

THE BALLET THEATER, EVENING
MAYBE WEDNESDAY, MAYBE NOT

ANNE

I STOMP BY HIM INTO THE THEATER. IT'S A GOOD THING I'M invisible to everyone else because that way no one will notice when I kick him in the shin. Does he have any idea how creepy it feels to have him dip into my thoughts like he's looking for something in a crowded closet? Okay, I was peeking into his brain too. But I didn't mean to. I just don't seem to have an option to avoid it. It's like the channel is open and neither of us can close it.

I glance at him, but his expression is pretty neutral. Does he know that I'm wondering—for not the first time—what secret stuff he's still keeping from me?

I don't know if he can read everything in my head. *But if you're in there, Ethan, here's what I hate right now: that I know how much you cared about Tasha.* Clearly you guys did stuff together, but I'd have preferred to avoid the video clip. It's one thing to know that your boyfriend had a love life before you. It's another thing to catch him reliving it. Call me petty, but that's the way it is.

And here's what else I hate right now: that I can't think these thoughts in private. Okay, you can't think yours either, but that doesn't make me feel any better. It just makes me scared and frustrated. *I mean seriously, Ethan—I don't want to read your "Hey, we used to have lots of sex" thoughts about your ex any more than you want to know about Ben's post-latte peck on the lips.* Not that those two compare by any vast stretch of the imagination.

Ethan's brows are knitted together. I try not to think that this makes him look cute, which would certainly dilute the "I think this sucks" vibe that I'd prefer to give off.

And then someone bustles past us into the theater and I look up.

It's absolutely beautiful. This is the first thought I have. And the second. And the third.

I forget that I'm arguing with Ethan. I forget how scared I am or how I hate that I'm jealous of this girl who doesn't even really exist anymore. I don't bother to scan the lobby for Tasha and the Ethan doppelgänger. Or for Viktor. For the first time in a long while, I don't feel guilty about Ben or worried about my parents. Or freaked about Baba Yaga and sad for Anastasia and Lily, my rusalka grandmother.

Instead, I let myself just look. I gaze around the old theater—with its curving stage and high ceiling and ornate box seats and balcony—and breathe in what I've missed so very much. Ballet.

The dancers aren't on stage yet, but I can sense them behind the red velvet curtain getting ready. As if I'm back there too, I can see them shimmying into costumes and warming up. Smell the rosin as they rub it into the soles of their slippers. See the girls rising en pointe as they ready themselves to perform.

My eyes fill with tears. My throat tightens. I was never going to be a great ballerina. I'm not thin enough or dedicated enough. I hated what it did to my feet. My talent is only middle of the road.

But I loved dancing. The pure joy of it. I liked how it made my body feel—lithe and limber, as though if I tried hard enough, I could float above the stage. In those months when my brother was dying, I practiced harder. It was the only thing that let me forget that my family was imploding.

And then one afternoon Tess and I went to see *Swan Lake* in a different gorgeous theater and noticed this handsome blue-eyed guy watching me. The guy who turned out to be Ethan. The one who changed everything.

I'm angry with him still, for reasons I can name and some I can't. And I can tell he's not totally happy either.

But I let him slip his arm around me and feel the strange thrill of knowing that we're basically invisible to everyone else. If he kissed me right now, no one would see us. People might sense it—like you sense a ghost or get déjà vu. But they'd go on anyway and walk to their seats and *Giselle* would start, and no one would know that we were standing behind them, his lips pressed against mine. Tess will definitely appreciate this story if I choose to share it with her. This is the kind of stuff she loves.

Ethan's arm tightens around my shoulders. My heart hammers harder—both at the thought of losing myself into a kiss and the realization that he probably knows what I'm thinking. I feel my face grow warm.

"Look," Ethan says, and my thoughts refocus. He gestures.

In the box seats above us to our right, Tasha and the other Ethan settle themselves into plush chairs. The two of them, but no Viktor.

My Ethan's blue eyes scan the auditorium, then his gaze returns to the box seats. He scrubs a hand over his face. If he's sensed my kissing thoughts, his expression doesn't show it. He looks tired and serious, a hint of five-o'clock shadow on his cheeks and chin. Of course, I'm standing in a beautiful old theater wearing shorts, a tank top, and *bedazzled* black flip-flops. It is totally unfair that he looks as hot as always, while I probably look like I fell out of bed and into a whirlwind—which is basically what happened.

"I remember something," Ethan says. His eyes brighten. Still no sign that he read my make-out fantasies.

"Viktor had arranged for the box seats—and that bothered me. It would have been private, but it also called attention. People always want to see who's sitting up there. That wasn't usually the way we did things. We rarely made ourselves obvious."

The auditorium begins to darken. The other Ethan leans in to whisper something in Tasha's ear. In the dimming light, I can see her smile, then tilt her head back like she was laughing. And then they both look behind them as a third figure comes into view.

Even with his face in partial shadow, I have no trouble identifying Viktor. All arrogance, he stalks into the room, and when past Ethan stands to shake Viktor's hand, the light from the stage catches Viktor's face. His dark eyes glitter in a way that makes my stomach clench, and goose bumps prickle my arms and legs.

Next to me, my Ethan links his fingers with mine. "Nothing to be afraid of," he says. "Not from him."

His tone is neutral, pleasant even. But underneath, I feel his anger mingle with my own. Viktor has caused so much hurt, so much damage. I need to use that fear and anger to figure out why we're here and what we need to see.

"Looks like they're staying put," Ethan says. "C'mon." He squeezes my hand. And we head toward the staircase that leads to the box seats.

The music begins as we're walking. Again, I'm reminded of how much I love dance—the grace of it, the stories of the ballets, the feeling that I can almost defy gravity.

"I don't know *Giselle*," I say as we reach the first landing and move to the second flight of stairs.

"Giselle's a girl with a weak heart. She falls in love with a nobleman. Only she has no idea that he's already betrothed to someone else. When she finds out, this weakens her even more and she dies. Her friend the gamekeeper, who loved her deeply, mourns at her grave. And then—this is a tragic ballet—the wilis rise."

"Wilis?"

"They're Slavic. Spirits of—oh." Ethan stops dead still on the last stair before the second landing. He drops my hand. A strange look crosses his face. "I really had forgotten. This is—"

"Is what?" My heart skips half a beat. Isn't going back in time and watching another Ethan with another girl enough without adding in some Slavic folklore craziness? By the look on his face, the answer is a resounding no.

"The Wilis take her. It's another name for rusalka—female spirits who've been jilted by their lovers. They seek revenge on men. They take Giselle. And then they go after her nobleman. Because they think he should die."

My beat-skipping heart moves to racing. "And? Do I want to know?"

We step onto the landing, empty of people except for us. "And Giselle saves him," Ethan says. "It's the inevitable. She protects him and the Wilis can't drown him. She doesn't give in to their hatred. Her nobleman lives, and she can rest in peace."

My mouth goes dry. "Like Lily. Except Lily can't go free without my help. Unless…"

"I don't know, Anne. *Giselle* is about love, about forgiveness. Lily's a rusalka, a wili, yes. But the rest of it…"

I push away the thought. "She forgives her nobleman. She doesn't give in. Lily could do that, right? It could happen."

It could. Anything could, I guess. But I know what he's thinking because I'm thinking it too. What if Lily does forgive Viktor for trying to kill her, for making her so desperate to protect her daughter from him that she gave her up for adoption—so he wouldn't know she existed—and then leaped into the river? Will it be enough to free her from her curse? Or will Viktor still have to die? And my promise to Baba Yaga— what about that? I still haven't found the source of Viktor's new immortality.

"It's a ballet, Anne," Ethan says softly. "Maybe it's just a ballet."

"This whole thing is so twisted," I say because it is and neither of us seems able to untwist it, no matter what we do. "My family is so far from normal it's not even funny. I'm never going to be a regular person again, am I?"

"You never were," Ethan says, his voice husky enough that I shiver pleasantly in spite of my crankiness and confusion. "That's a good thing, you know."

Is it? I can trace myself back through a sea of crazies to Tsar Nicholas himself…and my power to a witch named Baba Yaga. I count off my ancestors, the ones we've discovered since the day Ethan and I collided and life as I knew it changed forever: Viktor, Tsar Nicholas's love child. Their daughter,

Natasha. And her daughter, a woman named Lily—my birth grandmother who Viktor tried to kill because she posed a threat to his plan to stay immortal by keeping Anastasia with Baba Yaga. Lily, my tragic birth grandmother who jumped into the Chicago River and, instead of dying, became a rusalka.

Is she like Giselle? Could she be?

In the auditorium, the music swells. I know the dancers are onstage now. The story has begun to spin itself out. We should be spying on the other Ethan and Tasha and Viktor. Doing what we've been brought here to do—or at least that's what it seems. But now this new thing. My brain hurts trying to make sense of it all.

Ridiculously, I wait for Ethan to tell me not to worry. *Sure, Anne, no problem*, I want him to say. *If Lily does a 360 and forgives him, Viktor will just go away. No harm, no foul. And your nutty Russian mermaid grandmother? She'll sort things out. It'll be fine. But don't worry. No way did mystical forces we don't understand send us back here to connect all this to a ballet.*

Instead, he takes my hand again, his long fingers curling around mine, and we start to the box where the other Ethan is sitting with Tasha and Viktor. His grip is warm and familiar. Soothing. It will all be okay, I think. Stop worrying. Then with a suddenness that swoops my breath away, I read his thoughts again. My hand, still in his, goes cold.

"You went to see Dimitri?" I'm shocked at what I'm pulling from his head. How could he do that? Maybe I'm wrong. I have to be wrong.

Ethan purses his lips together. And when he stays silent for one beat too long, I know I'm not wrong at all.

He tries to blow it off. "This isn't the time, Anne."

"Oh? I think it's the perfect time."

"He's on our side. I'm as sure of that as I can be. We need him. He was Viktor's protégé. He's an asset, not a liability." Ethan says this like he believes it, but something in his eye—a brief flash of wariness—tells me he's not as sure as he sounds.

"Like when he tried to kill us? That kind of asset?" Don't we have enough problems right now without him adding Viktor's best bud to the mix?

I struggle to stay calm. *Think happy thoughts, Anne. Puppies and clouds and Lou Malnati cheese pizza.* We're in no position to argue. We need to be a solid unit until we get back to our own time. Back to where we have a little more control. But Dimitri? Seriously?

"Things changed when we all became mortal again," Ethan says.

"Maybe." I contemplate whether this is really true. "Maybe not. Look at Viktor. He wanted us to think he was a hero when he gave himself to Baba Yaga. But he was only looking out for himself, same as always. Maybe Dimitri just wants you to think he's changed. But really, nothing's different."

I can tell that he's got more to say about the subject, but then some man in a fancy black tux hurries by us down the hall, and both Ethan and I are reminded of where we are and what we're supposed to be doing—which is definitely not standing here arguing.

"When we get back," Ethan says, "we'll deal with it. I should have told you. I was going to tell you. I would have told you. I promise."

Would he? I hope so. And because I don't read anything else in his mind to contradict, I say, "Things have been a bit crazy. I get it." Then I add: "You and me, Ethan. Whatever's linking us is getting stronger, isn't it? Even here in the past. Maybe especially here."

As I say it, I know it's true. Fear prickles my skin. The momentary calm when Ethan took my hand is gone. A single thought reverberates in my head: something bad is about to break loose.

"We'll deal with that too," Ethan says. "It's what we do."

"This whole mind-reading thing sucks," I tell him.

Ethan grins, a calm-before-the-storm smile. We open the door to the box seats and step inside.

If we'd thought things were crazy up until then, we were wrong. The crazy was just getting warmed up.

Theater Box, Beginning of *Giselle*
Maybe Wednesday, Maybe Not

Ethan

TWO STEPS INTO THE SMALL ROOM ON THE SECOND LEVEL of the theater, I know that something is off. The ballet continues to play out onstage. We are still in the past. Only then, things change. Time rips. The past wavers, then flickers into something more immediate—as though it is happening for the first time, not the second. I feel myself falter, try to step back into the hall. But my body moves forward and I take Anne with me.

Do we cause this to happen? Does Viktor? Is it somehow Baba Yaga or our combined powers or some other force that doesn't come immediately to mind? I just know that when we enter, there are two of me—my current self and my past. Anne stands at my side, my hand wrapped around hers, a solid connection, her thoughts flowing into mine as mine ripple into hers.

Viktor is about to sit in one of the plush chairs. Tasha—the girl I loved but not enough to tell the truth—leans slightly toward him, as though when he seats himself, she plans on telling him something.

And the man I once was—who because of magic and circumstance I still fully resemble—sits alert, part of his attention on the stage, part on Viktor and Tasha. He is pulled between two stories, both of which will have tragic endings. Does he—did I—know that then? I try to remember.

What comes to me is this: I sat there looking eighteen because I'd committed myself to a cause that by then I had begun to question. I loved a woman who I knew I was going to abandon. And I had become suspicious of the man whose cause I'd followed blindly, without question. But never suspicious enough. I will regret that forever. I know I am paying for my blindness.

But now, a rush of heat spreads up my arms. Something is suddenly terribly wrong. In one dizzying moment, everything inside me shifts, hard and jagged, like shoving a round peg in a square hole. Not like our journey through time. That was external. What happens now is inside me. I double over with the force of it. Something is attempting to wrench me from my own body. I struggle against it. Try to remain conscious of who I am.

"Ethan!" Dimly I hear Anne shout my name. My vision fogs. She shimmers in and out, or maybe I'm the one shimmering. For one brief moment, I see her panicked face. She says something else. Her lips move, her hands gesture. But it's too late.

I am me. My past self is me. And then in a sickening rush, we become one. I feel the essence of what I am slip away to combine with what I was. Everything I know, everything I've been, starts to ebb.

I fight against it. The dark power whose source I still don't understand rises inside me—angry and harsh. I focus, latch on to its wild, furious, swirling depths. Wrench myself away to hover in and out of both bodies, both versions of me. For that moment, there's nothingness, like plummeting from an airplane through piles of clouds.

Then—something dark and empty. Like a vessel that wants to be filled. That needs to be filled. It slithers through me like oil, pulling any power I can use with it, and everything begins to slip. I struggle to hold on to my thoughts. *I am Ethan who is now mortal. I am Ethan who was betrayed by Viktor. I am Ethan who loves Anne. I am…*

"No!" I say it aloud. Use the word to try to hold back the inevitable. "No." I say again. But I hear my voice fading. Somewhere a thought: my past self will know. Or my current self will. If past and present merge, I'll still know what's happened in between. Those years won't be—

What? Was I thinking something?

I shake my head. Clear my vision.

"Ethan," says a deep voice next to me. "I had no idea your young woman was so lovely. She's quite the treasure, yes? But it seems she is quite in her own world right now. That, my friend, is the power of the ballet."

I look to my left. Tasha stares at the stage. Her brown eyes seem somewhat vacant.

"Tasha," I say softly. My voice sounds unfamiliar to my ears. Odd.

She startles, then turns to me and, after a beat or two, smiles. *My lovely Tasha.* The strange feeling that has washed over me begins to pass.

"Where was I?" she whispers. "Caught in the story, I suppose." She brushes a strand of brown hair off her forehead, then looks at her hand as though it's something unfamiliar.

My mouth curves into a smile, and again I have the briefest sense that my movements are not quite my own. Strange.

Tasha turns to Viktor. "My apologies. I'm not usually this impolite. I just don't feel like myself today. Or perhaps it is *Giselle*. Such a tragic story, no? It took me quite away. You and Ethan will have to forgive me."

"It is quite easy to forgive such beauty," Viktor says. "There." He snaps his fingers. "The moment never happened. We won't even remember it five minutes from now."

For a moment, the fogginess in my head returns, like the feeling one gets upon awakening and trying to remember a dream. I shake my head, trying to clear it. What an odd thing for Viktor to say—Viktor who never forgets anything.

We are not quite human, Ethan, he once observed. *The life of an immortal requires a special level of care. We must look. Learn. Listen. We never know when something will be of use.*

I look up and realize that he's watching us—Tasha and me. His dark eyes glitter in the light from the stage. I know he disapproves of this relationship. Believes that it is foolhardy of me to allow anyone too close. But I do not agree with him. And I think in this regard that he has his own secrets. We all do—the Brotherhood members who are now immortal. Time has had a way of making this occur. Viktor is entitled to his privacy. But so am I.

"Are you all right, Ethan?" Tasha rests one cool palm on my hand and tilts her head to look at me.

"Fine," I tell her. "Never better." And in that moment, this becomes true. The fog that's clouding my thinking lifts. Something seems off still, but I push the thought away. This is Tasha—so beautiful, so talented—Tasha whose long graceful fingers I love to watch as they move, quick as birds, across the piano keys. I will tell her later, I think. I will tell her that I love her. And someday, I will tell her what I am. Maybe soon. Yes. Soon.

Onstage, Giselle starts to go mad. Her lover loves some-one else.

"Tragic tale," Viktor whispers. "To love someone who will leave you."

Tasha leans across me toward Viktor. "But she forgives him," she says with a small, tight smile.

My vision hazes. For half a beat in time, I get the distinct sense that I don't belong here. Images of another place, another girl—pale face, hair auburn, with brown eyes like Tasha's, only deeper—flash through my head. But nothing stays. The mental pictures flicker away like smoke from a lit match.

I struggle to regain myself. Why are my thoughts drifting like this? I am not some idle old man playing chess and drink-ing tea and dreaming of days gone by. Possibly, I never will be.

I am not just Ethan, after all. I am of the Brotherhood. To me there are no coincidences. The magic—the power—that allowed us to save Anastasia by compelling a witch who most of the world think is just part of a child's fairy tale—is real. And the prophecy that teaches of a girl who will release our Grand Duchess—that is real too. I have pledged my life to it. I am what I am because of it. Immortal until I find the girl who will complete our mission. She could appear at any time. In any place. Even here at the ballet.

How wonderful that would be, I think now. To end this. If I found her now, this mysterious girl for whom we've been searching, then it would be over. She would help us free

Anastasia. Bring her back from the dead. Release her from that witch with the iron teeth and enormous hands. Baba Yaga, the mighty Bone Mother who I never believed existed. What has life been like for Anastasia? It is something I cannot contemplate. I chanted the spell. I saw the witch take her. There is no purpose in looking back. I have no regrets.

But what if the girl of the prophecy really is close? The world would gasp in shock. The foolish and short-sighted who believed it was necessary to murder the Romanovs for what Russia has now become, they would see that we have saved them from even more misery—from Stalin and his cronies. Having one of Nicholas and Alexandra's children alive would be a miracle. It would change everything.

It would free me.

The thought startles me. Never have I put my current existence in those terms. Why now? What has changed?

Perhaps Viktor is right. I am allowing myself to be distracted from our cause.

Tasha pats my hand. She smiles. And I let all those thoughts pass.

Theater Box, During *Giselle*
Maybe Wednesday, Maybe Not

Anne

The pain is crazy. Like someone turning me inside out. This is what it feels like when something begins to yank me forcibly from my own body. Memories rush through me as my brain tries to make sense of what's happening. I remember times I dreamed as Anastasia—felt like her, moved like her, cried like her. That horrible moment I morphed into her when I was in Baba Yaga's hut. I know what it's like to be someone I'm not. But nothing has prepared me for what happens next. There's noise and dizziness, and I think it's happening to Ethan too.

I scream his name. And then I'm just screaming. Does anyone hear me?

There's noise and dizziness, and the endless stabbing sensation of being ripped apart and shoved somewhere I don't want to go. And inside me—flashes of questions. Am I making this happen? Is it something in the past? Viktor? Baba Yaga? The questions tumble in my head adding to the dizziness and nausea. And a weird thought—I need to throw up, but I don't know where my mouth is.

It stops in stages. The world settles. The pain eases.

I'm not dead. I'm not gone. Slowly—it takes a lot of effort—I open my eyes.

And see someone else's outfit, someone else's hands, someone else's, well, everything.

Seriously?

I blink. Look again. The other body hasn't gone away. And unless I'm totally hallucinating—which might be the better option here—I'm inside it.

This can't be happening. Time travel—okay. Reading Ethan's thoughts—creepy, but I can deal. But body shifting? *Hello. If anyone is listening, this is where I draw the line.* Especially because unless I'm mistaken—and I don't think I am because let's face it, what girl doesn't play a little compare and contrast with her boyfriend's ex—the body I'm trapped in is Tasha's. Yes, *that* Tasha.

And Ethan is standing next to me—well, her—looking dazed and clueless. But which Ethan is he? My Ethan? Or Ethan in the past?

Calm down, I tell myself. It should be easy enough to figure out. I'll just tell him who I am. If he freaks out, then he's the wrong one. Simple enough.

"Ethan!" I scream at him, not calm at all. "It's me, Anne. I'm stuck in your ex-girlfriend's body. You've got to do something."

Except what comes out is Tasha's voice. And unless I'm totally mistaken, she's not saying what I'm saying. She's chatting about the freaking ballet.

And I still don't know which Ethan I'm looking at.

"Oh my God," I yell at Ethan—present, past, at this point I'd just love one of him to hear me—while below us on the stage Giselle is going crazy because she's been betrayed by the guy she fell in love with. "You're not talking to Tasha. Ethan! It's me. Anne! Something's happened. Something bad."

Only here's what happens: I look at Viktor and say, "But she forgives him." It comes out in Tasha's voice.

This absolutely can't be happening. Shit.

"Ethan," I try again. "We've got a huge problem."

The words echo only in my head. My mouth doesn't say them. Instead it quirks into a small smile.

Ethan smiles back. So what does this mean? Where is my Ethan? If I'm stuck in Tasha's body, then maybe he's stuck in his old body? Does he know? It sure doesn't seem like it.

This is bad. Really bad. My heart should be racing a zillion miles an hour. But the heart in Tasha's body—the one I've invaded like an unwilling body snatcher—beats slowly and evenly. Only my brain seems aware of the switch. The same brain that suddenly seems to have lost its fast-track connection to Ethan's thoughts.

Plus, where the hell is the rest of me? If I'm here in the past in Tasha's body, where's the physical me? My personal body that I had no intention of leaving any time soon. I scan the small room. No real Anne standing at the ballet in her shorts and tank top. Not good. Not at all.

Tasha's hand is resting on Ethan's. In my head, I tell myself to move my hand away. That maybe then he'll notice that his girlfriend is acting standoffish. He'll think, *Hey, why did she do that?* And then he'll investigate. He'll look into Tasha's eyes and think, *Hey, that's not my girlfriend. That's someone else in there.* And then maybe—

Maybe what? What good would that do? And besides, it's not working. My Tasha hand is still on top of Ethan's.

All right. I need to try this another way. Onstage, Giselle is dying. In our box in the balcony, I'm racking my brains for a solution to my out-of-body problem.

Breathe, I tell myself. Just breathe. Figure this out. You are a powerful girl now. You've got witch powers. You can do this.

Shit. I *so* cannot do this. I don't even have my own body anymore. There's nothing for me to breathe with.

And then somewhere—in my brain? Tasha's?—Baba Yaga's voice speaks. Low and harsh, like tires rolling over gravel, but familiar. Insistent.

Listen, Baba Yaga's voice says. *You will know what to do if you listen. Trust yourself. Learn. See what must be seen. Inside the insides, my girl. Listen to what is there.*

Does she really say this to me? It's pretty crowded in my head right so I can't say for sure. Maybe it's her. Maybe it's just wishful thinking. Maybe it's a trick.

But what's my alternative? Sit here in this body and hope that somehow something drags me back out? That doesn't seem to be the most solid plan.

Onstage, Giselle finishes dying. The ballerina clutches her chest gracefully as she flutters to the floor. Is she dying of a heart attack? I would like to be clutching my chest right now, but Tasha doesn't seem to want to do that. Is she in her head too, wondering about the chick who's invaded her personal space?

"Are you all right, my dear?" Viktor leans across Ethan. His breath smells like some weird combo of spearmint, herbal tea, and incense. His dark eyes grow darker, almost black. If I could shudder right now, I would. In my head, I do.

A question in the middle of my freak-out: Does he know? Is he somehow aware things aren't normal right now? Normal, of course, being a relative term for a guy who at this point in history was immortal and knew that Anastasia wasn't dead—and was planning on keeping it that way.

A guy like that would know everything, wouldn't he?

This is what I wonder while I try to calm down and listen. If I'm here for a reason, if this is happening for a reason—and at this point it better be—then maybe the Baba Yaga voice is right. Even if it's just me telling myself what to do. *Don't freak out, Anne. Figure it out. You can do this.*

"*Spasibo, kharasho,*" is what comes out of my mouth.

Terrific. Now I'm speaking Russian.

"Pardon me," I say then. "It is so easy to slip into Russian with both of you here. But I have promised myself that I will speak English. Be like these Londoners. I am well, thank you. There. That's correct, yes?" Well, okay then. At least Tasha's polite enough to translate for everyone. Including me.

Ethan smiles at me. It's such a sweet smile and so familiar that I'm caught off guard. For the tiniest second, things feel normal. It's Ethan—tall, blue-eyed, hair just a little too long. Ethan same as always. Ethan who was kissing me in my room before all this extra craziness began. Ethan who I might be pissed at but who I think I love. Who I know loves me.

He rises from his seat, pulls me up with him. There's an odd look on his face, and that smile, I realize, has never quite reached those blue eyes.

"I…we," he begins. He clears his throat. Looks at me as though he's seeing me for the first time.

Viktor stands too. "We have a few minutes before the second act. Some refreshments, perhaps? The English do know how to make a fine cup of tea. Or maybe such a lovely evening calls for something a bit stronger. Of course, the lovely Madam Tasha can have whatever she desires." He bows slightly, watching me—or I guess watching Tasha—so intently that if I was in charge of my body right now, I'd shiver. In my mind, I do.

Ethan nods sort of blankly. He blinks. Stares at me again.

"Tasha?" His voice rises in a question. "Tasha?"

"Yes, dearest," my mouth says. But inside Tasha's head I'm watching Ethan, who is still standing very still, staring at me.

Viktor's eyes narrow. Slowly, he brushes an invisible piece of lint off his dark suit.

My Ethan *has* to be here—stuck in past Ethan's body. If I'm lucky, he's realizing it. At least I hope he's realizing it.

But now what? How do I get out of this body? How do I let Ethan know I'm in here without also alerting Viktor, who already looks more than suspicious—which doesn't surprise me. My wacky Russian ancestor may be evil and conniving, but he's not stupid. Maybe he doesn't know that two of us are actually four, but he's got to realize that something strange is going on, even by his standards. I see him tilt his head like he's thinking things over. I need to do something—the right something—before he catches on.

As Tasha, I take Ethan's hand. He twines his fingers with hers, and Viktor stands aside so we can walk ahead of him out of the box seats. Down the hall, I can see a small area set up to serve refreshments. In my mind—all that's left of me—I call to him: *Ethan, Ethan, Ethan. Can you hear me? Do you know what's happened?* If he hears me, there's no indication.

My head fills with Tasha—who, it seems, is pretty thirsty.

This is the message her body is giving off. Her throat is dry and she's looking forward to some hot tea. But not with milk, she's thinking. Crazy English with their milky tea and biscuits. She wants hot, black tea with sugar, and she knows she's going to be disappointed.

Her thoughts come to me as images and words—a lot of Russian but some English too. I don't understand every word, but I get the basics. If we get out of this in one piece and back in our own bodies, I'm going to thank Ethan for his love of the whole tea thing. Because without that, I'd be more lost in what Tasha is—

Thinking. I'm not just thinking my own thoughts, am I? I'm hearing hers. At least the ones about tea. Have been hearing them all along. But they've been sort of fuzzy. Like a car radio when you're in between cities and the station turns to static. But the tea craving—it's coming in loud and clear.

If I had my own body, I'd take deep breaths. But I'm just thoughts—hers and mine, and maybe Baba Yaga's too. The truth I haven't said aloud? The witch is always inside me now, some essence of her lingering in my cells wherever I go. I guess she hangs out even when I'm basically just a parasite brain in Ethan's ex's body.

Listen, says the voice that's not me and not Tasha. Listen.

I listen. It's not easy—I'm walking as Tasha and holding Ethan's hand, and Viktor is making small talk about how perhaps we might prefer a small glass of sherry instead.

"Perhaps," my Tasha mouth says. But she keeps on thinking *tea*. This chick is definitely thirsty.

We settle on tea—no big surprise. Tasha's happy when she

sips from her cup. The tea is strong and dark, and somehow I can taste it along with her. Feel its warmth going down her throat as she drinks.

She drains the cup. I keep listening. Honestly, it's a better option than blind panic.

Viktor blots his lips with a white cloth napkin. Ethan continues to look confused. Is he as helpless as I am? I hope he's figured out that he's trapped in his former self.

He stares at me for a while, then studies his teacup like it's going to give him an answer. If we get out of this situation, I plan on telling him that the next time he feels that something fishy is going on, he needs to be a little more decisive. Even if he doesn't know what the hell is going on. *Don't get sucked in by random tea drinking.* No wonder it took him close to one hundred years to find me.

"The second act is even more tragic," Viktor says. "Wouldn't you agree?"

He touches me-Tasha lightly on the arm. It's a casual motion, just sort of neutral and friendly. But on my-Tasha's other side, Ethan stiffens slightly as Viktor's hand makes contact. It's a small series of events, but there's something in it that makes Tasha tense. Her emotions flood my consciousness. She's happy, nervous, scared, excited. The feelings rush through my brain.

And then—well, then it's like getting zapped by lightning. My mind dives below the small-talk and the thirstiness and Tasha's disgust with English tea.

"It's sad," my Tasha mouth says. "But is that truly tragedy? Giselle is no longer with her lover. But she protects him in the end. She doesn't stop loving him. It frees her from the Wilis.

Although I prefer to think of them as rusalki. That German poet—Heine, I think—he took the idea from us. Still the end is the end. Love conquers all. Not so bad, perhaps."

And in her head I hear: Except, of course, for the loyal gamekeeper who loves Giselle and is thrown to his death by the rusalki. Or Wilis. Either way he is just as dead.

She shifts her gaze—my gaze—to Ethan. Her heart, so steady all this time, skips a beat, then speeds up. *You should never have trusted me, dearest. I am not what you think. But you will have to figure that out on your own. You are a smart man. Not like the foolish gamekeeper. But so worried about your own secrets that it never occurs to you that I might have a few of my own.*

What? Is she kidding? Oh my God. She's not kidding. Did Tasha somehow betray Ethan in the past? Is that what I'm supposed to find out? Not about Lily, then, but Ethan?

We—Tasha and me—take a sip of her cup of tea. Her hands are steady on the cup, but her heart is still bopping around in her chest. I feel her lips curve into a smile as she looks at Ethan.

And when the teacup tips and tea splatters her skirt, I know she does it on purpose. In that moment when Ethan's eyes follow the spilling tea, I see Viktor flick a finger in the air. It's a tiny motion, barely noticeable unless you're me and working your butt off trying to figure out how to get out of a body that's not yours.

The cup falls from Tasha's hands, drops to the little table, and cracks into pieces. One tiny shard of teacup flies up and slices into the thin white skin on Tasha's wrist. I feel the cut along with her. Quickly, she presses her other hand to her wrist, applying pressure.

"Oh, how clumsy of me," Tasha says. In my head, I'm hollering, *Hey, she meant to spill that tea! And Viktor made the cup break! They're both playing you!* No one hears me.

Ethan looks immediately concerned. "Let me see." He pulls her hand away, his palms warm and soothing against her skin. I can feel her wrist pulsing. At first it looks fine, but in an instant, the sides of the cut separate. A thin line of dark red blood oozes to the surface.

"It's nothing," Tasha says. Her heart is pounding now. She's definitely nervous—and I think it's about more than just the cut.

Viktor gets into the act. "That needs attending." He reaches over Ethan and presses his cloth napkin to the cut. "You're bleeding. You wouldn't want to develop an infection. Ethan, I do believe there is a small first-aid station on the lower floor. Shall I see if I can find some bandages?"

I know Ethan's response even before he gives it. And in my head I'm telling him not to fall for this. She's hiding something. Walking away right now is the absolute worst thing he can do.

Except that if he goes, maybe I'll hear the truth from Viktor and Tasha once he's gone. My invisible heart starts pumping faster.

"Stay with her," Ethan tells Viktor. "I'll be right back."

He presses a quick kiss to Tasha's forehead. "You won't even know I'm gone," Ethan says. His gaze catches Viktor's as he stands up, and for a few beats, I feel what I've felt before— that he's sensing something isn't right. That he's not himself.

Does he know that he shouldn't leave? Is he—like me— trying to get out of a body that doesn't belong to him?

Go, I tell him with my thoughts that I wish he could read right now. *I know you're conflicted, and I know you suspect something's*

up. Which is good because you're right. They're up to something. But go. If you do, maybe they'll confess something while you're gone.

Does Ethan somehow hear me? I don't know. But he does what I want. He looks back at Tasha only once before he disappears down the stairs.

Tasha and Viktor watch him go. Her emotions shift from relief to fear to something I can't quite put my finger on. If I had my fingers right now, that is.

"Well done," Viktor says quietly. He smiles one of his creepy little smiles and places Tasha's hand over the napkin pressed to her cut wrist. I sit inside Tasha's head wishing that I could will her hand to smack him in the face.

"The cut is deep," she says. "Deeper than I thought. Did you do that on purpose?"

Viktor chuckles. "Hardly. Just a little over-enthusiastic. My apologies, my dear. It will heal."

She huffs out a breath and I feel her forcing her pulse to settle. She's only moderately successful. "It would heal better if I were one of you."

Viktor taps a finger to his lips. "Shh. That, my dear Miss Levin, is not public conversation."

Tasha swallows. I can taste bile in the back of her throat. "But it is what you have promised, yes? I keep an eye on Ethan and you help me bring my father to England. And if I distract Ethan long enough, you make me one of you. Immortal. I don't ask any other questions about your motives. You don't ask me any other questions about mine. But we made a deal, Viktor. And it seems I've now signed my piece in blood."

If I had my own jaw, it would be on the floor. She knew. She knew what they were. And Viktor promised to make her like them. Or at least that's what she believed. Because Ethan told me he saw her years later. And she was old. Whatever Viktor promised her, it never happened.

She smiles, and I know she's forcing her tone to be light and sort of humorous. She's terrified of him, but she's trying not to let on that she's scared.

Viktor returns her smile, but he doesn't answer her question. "I need him to think only of you, my dear. For the next month or so. Until I'm certain about something. You need not concern yourself about what. But I need Ethan out of the way. And you, my dear, are indeed the beautiful distraction."

Tasha nods. Her heart speeds up again, and I can feel her pulse in her neck. Her mind is racing—so many thoughts I can barely keep up. Lots of them are about Ethan. About bringing him home with her after the ballet. About how she's like Giselle. She's willing to stick it to the loyal guy to get what she wants. And if I'm not mistaken, she's also kind of happy that Ethan's hot so being with him is easy. At least he's not heinous looking. He doesn't scare the crap out of her like Viktor does.

But what she says next, her words rushed because surely Ethan is about to come bounding up the stairs again with a bandage, is this: "How is it possible? You have promised, and I believe. Truly, I do. But for the price of this cut in my flesh, you must tell me. How? How is it that you and he never age? Will I be like that too?"

Viktor's eyes darken. Go ahead, I think. Tell her. I'm really curious to hear you explain that one in three and a half seconds. Are you going to tell her about Anastasia? About Baba Yaga? About the ancient magic? Go on, Great-great-grandpa

Viktor, my crazy-as-a-loon ancestor. Tell her how it's done. And if I ever get to speak to her face-to-face rather than being trapped inside her head, I'll tell her how I stopped you. 'Cause I bet even if you knew that was coming, you'd leave it out.

"There are ways," he says eventually. "Old ways that I cannot, that I will not, speak of. But your own eyes tell you it is real. Your Ethan looks the same as when you first met him. He will look the same tomorrow and next month and next year and the year after that."

"You tell me only what I already know. Tell me what I do not." I feel Tasha struggle to keep her voice even and firm.

Viktor hesitates. One dark eyebrow arches. Does he find her question funny?

"You are the one who is in my debt, Miss Levin. Not the other way around. But I do appreciate a certain amount of arrogance. Especially in a woman. So I will say this. Only one other has ever discovered what I have. His name was Koschei and—"

"That's a child's story." Tasha interrupts him. "A man who figured out how to hide his soul and live forever. It's a folk tale for schoolchildren and old women by the fire."

"Believe what you will. But I repeat. There was one. Now there are two. He had his way. I found mine. That is all I will say. Even if I told you the rest of it, you still would not believe. Ethan was like that too. But he knows differently now. Those of us who were there, we know."

Tasha's voice lowers to a whisper. "Who were where? You tease me with this, Viktor."

I know she's not going to break him. He's playing with her.

I scream this in my head as Ethan returns with bandages, tapes up Tasha's wrist, and then they all walk back to their seats because the second act of *Giselle* has started.

And me? I'm still trapped in Tasha's head. It's an angry place in there right now. She's definitely pissed at Viktor and not really happy with Ethan either, because he's fussing over her and I think it's making her feel guilty. Which it should, since she's lying through her teeth to him. Plus, she's worried about this Koschei story—not the one Ethan has told me, something I need to remedy once I'm just plain Anne again—and she's got this sixth-sense thing brewing that Ethan's not quite himself.

Onstage, the wili mermaid ladies dance around Giselle's lover, trying to lure him to his death. I'm more than over-identifying with this ballet. Enough is wrong in my world right now without adding vengeful mermaid visuals.

Close your eyes, I tell Tasha. Seriously. I don't want to look at this anymore. Close your damn eyes.

She blinks.

Hey. Did I—

A tiny sliver of hope rises. If I can hear her, feel her emotions, maybe—

Close your eyes, Tasha. Go on. Do it.

Tasha's eyes flutter shut for a few beats, then snap open. I feel her forehead wrinkle. She looks at Viktor, then at Ethan. She touches a finger to each eyelid. Her pulse picks up the pace.

All right. She can hear me. Sort of. I think.

Stand up, Tasha. Stand up.

Slowly, like she's not sure why she's doing it, Tasha rises from the red plush chair.

If I had my body, I'd do a happy dance right now. Way happier than the creepy mermaid ballerinas on stage.

"Are you feeling ill?" Ethan's up now too. He takes Tasha's hands in his. The feeling of his hands is at once familiar and foreign. I have so got to get out of her body and back into mine. If I'm holding Ethan's hand, I'd like him to know it's me.

But at least I think I'm headed in the right direction. I'll get her moving. Get her away from Viktor, maybe. When she and Ethan are alone, maybe then—

Distract him. Viktor's directive echoes in Tasha's head.

"Yes," she says slowly. "I am just not myself, I'm afraid." And then what only I hear: *Has Viktor done something to me?*

The music from the orchestra pit grows louder. Giselle's forgiveness has saved her lover.

"Take me home," Tasha says to Ethan. "I need to go home."

Viktor smiles. He leans in to Tasha and whispers in her ear. His voice sends shivers down my nonexistent spine. "Remember, my dear. Whatever it takes. Your Ethan will be more than willing, I am sure."

She makes no indication that she heard him, but I know she did.

Giselle has freed herself from the Slavic mermaids.

"We'll all leave then," Viktor says. "Giselle is about to go to her grave anyway." He presses a hand lightly to Tasha's arm, just below her bandage. I feel the rough sandpaper of his fingers on her skin. "Take care, Tasha. You wouldn't want to hurt yourself again."

He looks at her with those dark, glittery eyes. I hate, hate that he and I are related—that I share any tiny molecule of DNA with him.

When we all stand, Viktor pats Ethan on the shoulder. Ethan startles, jerks away slightly. In my head, I hold my non-existent breath. Is Ethan about to notice that something is seriously wrong? No. He tucks his hand under Tasha's elbow and two separate sensations hit me: the comfort of Ethan's familiar hand and Tasha's racing pulse.

"Let's take you home," Ethan says. Trapped inside her, I have no choice but to go with them.

Tasha's Flat, After the Ballet
Maybe Wednesday, Maybe Not

Ethan

Something feels off. It has since intermission. And because it does, I mutter a protection spell under my breath as we enter Tasha's flat. Use the magic Viktor's Brotherhood taught me to ward the windows, the doors, the chimney. We will be safe now that we're inside. Whatever it is that wants to toy with us—if there is something—it will not follow us inside. My powers will keep Tasha safe.

"Did you say something?" Tasha asks. She has busied herself lighting lamps, and the warm glow of the electric lights bathes the room. For both of us, this is still a wonder—my own flat has only gas lamps, but Tasha's building is newer and her landlord prosperous. Electricity is the wave of the future. Soon everyone will have it.

"Just thinking aloud," I tell her. "I'm sorry. You're not the only one who is not yourself tonight. Perhaps we should have stayed in. Then you could have avoided that cut."

She shrugs, tosses her gloves on the small settee, and crosses the room to the piano in the corner, where she sits on the bench and runs her fingers lightly across the keys. Chopin, "Etude in C Minor." One of her favorites. And a private joke, since Chopin wrote it after Poland failed in its revolt against Russia. She plays the first few measures, then looks back at me.

"Come," she says. "Sit next to me while I play."

Viktor has not joined us. "Another time," he said. "When Miss Levin is feeling better. It would make me uncomfortable to impose."

And then the oddest thing: a voice in my head saying, *He's lying. Don't trust him.* What in the world would make me think that? A curious evening this has turned out to be.

I'm about to do as Tasha requests and join her at the piano, then find myself digging through my pockets for a cigarette instead. A habit I've picked up over the last few years since the Revolution. These days I rarely find myself without a pack.

It's a quick and easy diversion for those moments when questions become too pointed. Vodka works the same. People rarely dig any deeper than "international trade, an old family business" if I offer them liquor and tobacco. In the States, it works even better—or at least for now until their government repeals that ridiculous Prohibition that none of them adhere to anyway.

"On the side table," Tasha says with a laugh. "What would you do without me, my dearest?"

She continues with Chopin as I pick up the slim silver case and extract a cigarette, then light it and inhale. I blow out the smoke, a ring of gray haze that hovers in golden lamplight.

In that instant, I have the distinct feeling of being in two places at once. No. That's not quite it. Rather, it is as though I am watching and being watched. Yes. That is closer.

"Dearest." Tasha's voice rises above the music. "You must look at my wrist again. Assure me that the scar isn't too deep.

No need to play the gentleman anymore. Your friend Viktor has abandoned us. It is just you and me and my beloved Chopin. Or would you rather stand there smoking? You know how I despise it."

Her fingers stop suddenly, pull back from the keys. She turns to me again, her face pale in the soft glow of the electric lamps. "How rude of me," she says. "Smoke if you want. I don't know why in the world I said that."

Again, that unsettled feeling, the sense that something is hiding beneath the surface. Tasha smokes more than I do.

Still, I stub out the cigarette in the bronze ashtray on the end table. Seat myself next to her and press my lips to her neck. Her perfume filters into my nostrils, but something unfamiliar too. Something that smells of rainwater and peppermint.

We sit like that for a while, the notes of her music somehow still echoing in the air.

"Make love to me," she says. Her face, so close to mine, is very pale. She strokes a hand through my hair, then eases back to study me.

"Ethan," she says. "Ethan, do you see me?"

Such a strange question, I think, as I press my lips to hers. Pull her to me and feel her breasts against my chest.

For a moment, I think she is going to withdraw that request. Tell me to have another cigarette while she plays more Chopin. She will not take me to her bed. Perhaps for now that would be best. This is what I find myself thinking. That she is not herself and neither am I and perhaps I should leave. Yes.

Tasha slips from my embrace and rises from the piano bench. Extends the hand with the bandaged wrist and pulls me up to her.

No, I hear us both thinking. And something else—something new and dark: yes. I hesitate only a beat, then I crush my mouth against hers.

TASHA'S FLAT, AFTER THE BALLET MAYBE WEDNESDAY, MAYBE NOT

ANNE

H OLY CRAP. *THIS IS NOT ABOUT TO HAPPEN. ONLY I* think it is.

Hey, there, I scream into Tasha's head. *Seriously, missy. Stop touching him. Back away from the lips. I don't have time to deal with this. I have to get out of your body and get Ethan back to normal and tell him that you're a snake in the grass and that there's this story about some guy named Koschei the Deathless that maybe we ought to research, in addition to the whole Giselle-rusalka thing. So stop it.*

She doesn't listen to me.

We head toward her bedroom. I get her to pause a couple of times. Ethan in the past doesn't seem bothered, just like he didn't notice how wrong things were when I got her to tell him to stop smoking. My God, how clueless is he? He just keeps kissing her.

Are you in there too, my Ethan? It's me you want to kiss, not her. And if any other touching goes on, I want it just you and me. Things are a little too crowded right now. Don't you know that?

He kisses her some more, and I feel each of those kisses like he's kissing me. I think I start to cry, but it's only in my head. I hate that when he touches her I know how good it feels. I hate that this is happening.

Be present, the voice that may or may not be Baba Yaga's,

booms in my ears. *Do not be a frightened little girl.* And then: *Daughter, it will be fine. No matter what. You are strong. Just as I am.*

It isn't particularly comforting.

Ethan kisses her lips, her nose, her cheeks, her chin. He trails kisses down the sensitive skin of her neck to where her cleavage is shoved up by the fancy dress. She gives a small moan of pleasure. I hate her for that. Luckily she's got a lot of clothes on. It's going to take him a while to unpeel all those layers.

Tasha reaches up and unpins her hair.

Or maybe it won't take that long at all.

He kisses her again. And again. And so many times that I lose track. He rakes his hands through her hair. Her tongue flicks against his finger as it traces her lips.

Ethan lifts Tasha's hand and kisses the center of her palm. It's familiar and horrifying all at once. You kissed my hand like that, Ethan, I shout at him. You have to snap out of this. You have to remember. You have to—

The memories pound in my brain. Ethan and me, making out in his apartment the night the rusalka—my crazy grandmother Lily—showed herself to us in his shower. We'd run our fingertips over each other's faces, and I'd wondered if people could memorize the feel of one another. That if time and circumstance made something happen, you'd just know. You couldn't forget.

He has to remember. How can he not remember? Was it important only to me?

Touch his face, I tell Tasha. Touch his face and open your eyes.

He kisses her so deeply that if I had breath, it would be taken away. She kisses him back, opens her mouth so his tongue can explore. I try to stop her from making a low, sexy sound in the back of her throat, but she does it anyway as Ethan's teeth graze her lower lip. I hear her thinking—*God, I hate her*—that she's doing what Viktor wants. She's distracting Ethan by letting him love her.

Open your damn eyes, Tasha.

She opens them.

They kiss again, a deep kiss that I want to be mine alone. Time feels like it's standing still.

Ethan's blue eyes—eyes I know, deep as oceans—look into Tasha's. His hands are everywhere, his body pressed to hers. I stare through Tasha's eyes, willing him to somehow know I'm here.

"Ethan!" I shout. "Ethan. Please." He needs to hear me. My Ethan would hear me. That's been the whole problem, only now I need it to happen.

He hugs her. His grip is very strong. She doesn't seem to mind. Her hands stroke his back, and even through his clothes, I knew when her fingers reach that lion tattoo on his back, the sign of the Brotherhood that has never left him. My own fingertips feel the heat of it just as Tasha's do.

"Ethan," I say again in my head. "Ethan."

Something shifts. In those blue eyes—there's—

Ethan.

"Anne?" he says. "Anne."

I'm sobbing now, and this time I think he can hear me.

"Ethan," I say again. "Thank God."

The world contracts and folds.

And just like that, we're us again, and then we're gone.

Chicago,
The Present

WEDNESDAY, 12:45 AM

ETHAN

LEAVING WAS TUMULTUOUS. RETURNING IS JUST SUDDEN. One second we're in London in the past. The next we're back in Anne's room, my arms around her, our lips pressed together in a kiss.

She pushes me away with a force that reminds me exactly how strong she is. For a few beats we just stare at each other. There are no words for what I feel right now. Shame. Anger. Fear. Sorrow. Nothing makes sense except maybe violation. If I hadn't realized when I did—

I clear my throat. "That was—"

"I know," she says. Her eyes are huge and tears slip from them. She blows out a breath, wipes her nose with the back of her hand.

"You know I'd never—if I'd understood sooner, I'd never have…God, Anne. I tried to hold on to who I was. But everything melded together. And then I heard you. I saw you. In Tasha's eyes. It wasn't her. It was you. I don't understand how it happened—any of it. I'm so sorry. My God, I'm—"

"I thought you'd never know me. It took you so long. I—shit." She makes a sound that's half laugh, half sob. "That was crazy. Was it real? I mean if you hadn't figured it out—if I hadn't been able to…"

She doesn't have to finish. We both know how it would have been. If somehow after that we'd come back, things would never have been the same. I would never have been able to forgive myself.

I move to wrap my arms around her, but she holds up a hand. "Don't. I—just don't. Give me a minute, okay?"

I nod. Then glance at her alarm clock. We've been gone mere moments. Impossible. But like everything else that just happened, it seems to be true.

"My God, Ethan." Anne sits on the edge of her bed, then stands up again and paces the room. "They were playing you. That whole time. He wanted her to keep you distracted so he could go do something. Make sure you didn't find any potential girl who could save Anastasia, probably. That's why she wanted you to—well, you know. He promised to make her one of you. Immortal."

Her words shock but not completely. In the moment that I'd recognized her in Tasha's eyes, everything else had come to me too. In a rush, it washes over me. Tasha. Viktor. Total and utter betrayal. The last things in my former life that I thought were true—they were all a lie. Everything she and I shared together. Everything I have felt guilt for all these years—leaving her, never telling her the truth—it was all a lie. How stupid can one man be?

"It was a long time ago," I begin, grasping for some way to make sense of how I never knew. "I suppose—"

"Suppose what? And lower your voice. My parents are asleep down the hall. Are you going to justify what she and Viktor did to you? Say it was okay because it was a long time ago and you—what? Still believed that everything was goodness and light?"

Anne strides to the window, and I follow her, the moon full in the sky behind us. "How long did you go on justifying what you helped do to Anastasia? That it was okay because you believed that you could restore her to the throne or whatever? I mean, I know it's Viktor who had the plan. I know he screwed with your head—in more ways than you ever knew, obviously. But Jesus, Ethan. Didn't you ever once think that something was off? When that evening happened in real time—without us guest-appearing in other people's bodies—didn't it seem suspicious?"

She grasps my hands in hers. "I love you, Ethan. At least I think I do. But it scares me. Not what just almost happened with me along for the ride. That was totally gross and unsettling, but I'd have dealt with it. Somehow. But how could you love someone who didn't love you back? How could you not know?"

The words tumble from her, each one an indictment. *You didn't know. You didn't know. How could you not know?*

And for the first time, I realize—really understand—my complicity in Anastasia's destruction. She is dead and gone now, and would have been in any case. But what I did? It made it worse. It took everything from her. I am as guilty as Viktor, perhaps even more because it's clear that I had opportunity after opportunity to figure out what he was doing. To stop him. To help Anastasia sooner. So many days, so many minutes, year after year, she remained at Baba Yaga's. And I—I let it happen to her.

Just as I let Tasha betray me. Blind to the truth. Over and over and over again.

And once again, even in the past, I've hurt Anne with the

consequences. I think of meeting—was it just yesterday?—
with Dimitri, something I've yet to fully tell her about. I hear
his voice. *You are not an innocent in this, Ethan.* Yet another accurate indictment of my past mistakes.

"We need to talk about the rest of it," I say. "Giselle,
the Wilis—"

"And Koschei. Viktor talked to Tasha about some guy
named Koschei the Deathless. Do you know that story?"

"Koschei? Of course, everyone knows…" I stop mid-
sentence. A chill passes through me—and in my head, I see
shadows. Fragments of images—a hand clenched into a fist,
colors, faces, too blurred to be familiar. For one horrible
moment, I think we're about to travel again. But it's not that.
Not at all. Inside me, the dark something that's been simmer-
ing starts to rise.

In my head, a voice. *No one can destroy Koschei. No one.*

Anne lets go of my hands. "Your eyes," she says. There's
fear in her voice.

"What?" I shake my head. Focus on Anne.

"Look." She drags me to the mirror over her dresser. We
stand together and stare into the glass.

My blue eyes grow darker, then darker still. But that's only
part of it.

Reflected in the mirror, Anne's eyes glow just as dark as
mine—and in the center of each, a tiny skull.

Wednesday, 1:03 am

Anne

Your eyes," I say again because it's slightly less crazy-making than saying "our eyes," which obviously would be more accurate.

Except I can explain mine. And if I concentrate hard enough, I can probably make them go away—at least for now. But what explains his?

Ethan presses his hands to his eyes. Pulls his hands away and looks back into the mirror. It's like he's wearing Prince of Darkness contacts.

"There's something," he says. "Inside me. I—"

Panic gives my own insides a healthy smackdown. I want to stay put. I don't want to go anywhere again. I sure as hell don't want to be shoved inside some bimbo with an evil agenda. Can't we stay just us?

"Focus, Ethan," I say and struggle to keep my voice calm. "Maybe it's just a leftover of what just happened. Like some sort of mystical fallout or something. Travel through time— eyes go black. You know. Probably happens all the time, right?"

He offers up a grim smile, and I try not to let my growing panic eat me alive. We're home at least. That's got to count for something.

I smile back encouragingly. "Maybe I can help," I say. I reach out and clasp his hands in mine.

An electrical storm ignites. My magic, his magic—he has magic again and a lot of it—entwine, combine, explode. My body vibrates. I think my eyes roll back in my head.

The magic sizzles between us, in us, around us. Ethan's face lights with it. His eyes darken more, the irises disappearing. Memories—mine, his, someone else's?—slam into me over and over. Lily in the river drowning, the rusalki swimming toward her. Ethan's father, dead on the ground. Viktor offering food to a skinny boy with blue eyes. David dying. Anastasia screaming as Baba Yaga grabs her. Viktor on the speeding El train, holding a gun to my head. Tasha Levin smiling at Ethan as they sit at the piano. Me—with Anastasia—holding the matryoshka doll between us just before I sent her back to die.

And then more. A ballerina dancing Giselle, protecting her true love from the Wilis. Anastasia sitting on the edge of a quilt-covered bed in Baba Yaga's hut—holding the matryoshka. She opens it and pulls out a smaller version of the same doll. Opens it and pulls out another. Opens it and suddenly I'm seeing inside it—an endless cavern of space that makes me feel like I'm falling. Viktor's face looms up from inside, leering and smug.

I gasp, trying to get air down to my lungs. I need to breathe. I can't breathe. I can't think. *God, I—*

I rip free of Ethan's hands. My own hands are glowing—blue, white, blue. Sizzles of power flickering from my fingertips. And something new this time—dark veins surfacing at the tops of my hands, running down my fingers and up my arms to the elbow. For a few beats, my hands look larger, coarser. Impossible. But it fades before I can even be sure it really happened.

"I need—" I manage. But I don't know what I need. I'm dizzy. I can't breathe.

I yank open the door.

"Don't follow me." I scramble down the stairs with no plan other than to put distance between us.

I'm thirsty, I realize. Terribly thirsty. What do people drink in times of blind panic? Not Diet Coke.

I skid into the kitchen, skim my hand along the wall, and flip on the small light over the sink. No sense turning on the overhead. I'll take my full-on freak-out in the dark, thank you. Stray flickers of light continue careening off my fingertips.

They illuminate the pantry as I scan inside. Brandy. People drink brandy during a crisis, right? There's a bottle on the back shelf. Mom bought it last week when she decided that the best way to cure her "My daughter is a witch; my birth mother is a crazy mermaid" blues was to attempt to flambé desserts. Her Cherries Jubilee had been more scorched than jubilant.

I'm reaching for it when I hear a noise. I try not to be annoyed. I don't want Ethan right now. I want my swig of brandy and possibly a good cry and maybe a sandwich. On top of everything else, I'm suddenly ridiculously ravenous. Like side-of-beef-on-a-roll hungry.

I turn.

My mother—dressed in a thin, white sleeveless nightgown—is sitting at the breakfast-room table, her head in her arms.

My heart knots itself into a hard little ball, then swoops into my throat.

"Mommy? What's wrong?" I stand where I am, suddenly afraid to move. But also afraid not to.

She doesn't answer.

Somewhere in another room, I hear footsteps. Fabulous. I still don't want Ethan down here. I'd rather not add to the situation by letting my mother know that it's one in the morning and I've got a boy in my room. Man. Whatever.

"Mom." The white tile is very cold under my feet as I move to rest my hand lightly on her shaking shoulders. Against her bare skin, my fingers feel the outline of each vertebra. A shiver works its way up my own spine. When did she get this thin again? "Mom. What's wrong?"

She raises her head but doesn't look at me. Instead, her gaze tracks out the sliding glass door into the backyard.

No.

Pulse thundering in my ears, I walk to the door. Press my face against the glass. The moon is very bright. So it doesn't take me long to see. Our sprinkler is on. In the moonlight, I watch the arc of water move back and forth, back and forth. Close enough to the house that stray droplets hit the window— tiny pecks of sound. *Pop. Pop. Pop.*

Standing in the spray of water, her face lifted to the night sky, Lily holds out her arms. Her rusalka body is impossibly gaunt, her ravaged face etched with thin dark lines that cling to her cheeks like seaweed. The sleeves of her gown are gone, and her bare arms look pale and brittle. Underneath her tattered lilac gown, her mermaid's tale swishes in our grass.

My heart—that tiny knot—freezes. Now? She chooses now to come back here?

And then I see him.

Next to her stands my brother, David. He's dressed in the outfit we buried him in—khaki pants and his favorite maroon polo shirt and the stupid brown dress shoes he hated. I cried when I saw that was what my father had packed in the bag we had to bring to the funeral home.

"You should have brought his Doc Martens," I remember screaming. But really, it was just a pair of shoes. That our elm tree is visible through his clothing is my only relief because it means he's not real. Oh God, make that be true.

"I thought it was a dream," my mother says. She moves to stand next to me, and briefly I see her reflected next to me in the glass, insubstantial as a ghost. "I heard a noise. Your father's still sleeping. She came to me." Mom is crying audibly now, huge choking sobs. "Lily came to me. She brought your brother. You see them, don't you? I don't have the magic like you do, but she came to me anyway. She knew what I needed. No one else knew. Just Lily. See?"

"Mom, no. Don't look out there. Please. Don't. It's only going to make things worse. Trust me. It's a trick of some sort. Please."

She slips her arm around me, presses herself close. Her nightgown is damp.

"Mom, have you been outside? Were you out there with them?" I don't know if it even matters. But suddenly I feel as violated as I had inside Tasha's body. My family is being ripped apart. And it's not going to stop.

My mother nods, a barely perceptible jerk of her chin. And it occurs to me to wonder why she'd come back inside. Why, if they were out there—her mother the mermaid and my brother come back from the dead—she would leave them and come to cry at our kitchen table.

"She says you could take me to the past," Mom whispers. "That you have that power. Do you, honey?"

Her tone is oddly normal, like she's asking me if I can pick up milk at the grocery store. "Lily says you could take me. I wouldn't have to go for long. I just want to see him before. When he was well. You don't know that things are going to change, you know? You have no idea how precious every second is. You're just going along and making dinner and nagging him to do his homework and trying to get through your own life.

"That day your brother came home and told me he had that lump under his arm, you know what I was worried about? That one of our jewelry shipments hadn't come in. Your brother was standing there telling me there was goddamn cancer under his arm, and you know what I was thinking? I don't have time for this. I have two customers who expected certain pieces to wear to events and now I have to find some way of making them happy. That's what I was thinking."

In the glass, I see that Ethan is now standing a few feet behind us. I turn—put my finger to my lips. Still, relief floods through me. I'm glad he didn't do what I asked. Suddenly, my mother knowing that he's spent the night is the least of my worries.

"Can you?" My mother turns her gaze to me. Tears sit on her lashes. "You have to do this for me, Anne. I'm your mother. And I'm asking you. Please."

I try to swallow, the knot in my throat grown to a boulder. "Mom. Mommy. No."

Despite myself, I flick my gaze outside again. Lily snakes her arm around David. He beckons to me, a slow twist of the wrist. It takes every ounce of strength I have not to run to him. The way his hair curls a little at the nape of his neck, the broad familiar shape of his hands, the little mole at the corner of his left eye, like one tiny freckle. The tilt of his head as he looks at me. This is not David, I tell myself. But everything I see screams at me that it is.

"It's not real." I force myself to say what must be true. "Mom. She wants something. She's tricking us. She's making us see something that's not there. He's not there, Mom. David's dead. He's not coming back."

My mother reaches up and I think she's going to stroke my hair. Instead, she slaps me, sharply, across the face. I gasp. Grab her wrist harder than I mean to. She cries out, a sound of real pain. In the glass, I see Ethan move forward. Again, I hold up my hand. We need to let her say what she needs to say.

My mother seems oblivious to the fact that she's just slapped me. Her voice rises. "You can, can't you? You can take me to the past. Please, Anne. Just for a few minutes, a second or two. Let me see him. I thought it was Lily I wanted to see. I thought that was what would make me happy. But it isn't that at all. I have a mother. Your Grandma Ellen. I was wrong. I don't need Lily. But I need my son. I want my son. Please, Anne, he's your brother. I'm not asking you to bring him back from the dead. Just let me see him in the past. How could it hurt?"

I shake my head. How do I even begin to tell her that the past isn't always what you think? That even if I did what she asked, it wouldn't make things better. It would only open old wounds and confuse things. I've seen the past, I want to scream. I'm probably destined to see more of it. And if I had any choice right now, I'd never go there again.

"No," I say softly. "I won't do that, Mom. You don't want it. Trust me. You have to understand. You don't want it."

"Don't tell me what I want!" My mother's hand rears back again.

Ethan crosses the distance between us with one long stride. In the dim light from the sink, I can see that his eyes are blue again. But the darkness flickers just underneath.

He grabs Mom's arm. "Mrs. Michaelson. Laura. No. This isn't you. Stop it. Leave her alone. You have no idea what you're asking of her."

If Mom has been unaware of his presence in the room up until now, that little mystery is over.

And here's the thing about mothers that I totally get now: even when they're wacked-out by grief and eating disorders and rusalka birth mothers with crazy agendas who make them see their dead sons and ask their daughters to do the impossible, they're still mothers.

"Anne?" Ethan still gripping her arm, my mother turns her attention to me. "What is Ethan doing here? It's the middle of the night. Has he been here all this time? In your room? With you?"

On the periphery of my vision, I see Lily and David edge closer to our house. She moves with him gracefully through the arc of sprinkle spray like some sort of creepy water ballet.

"Let me explain," I start.

"Are you sleeping with my daughter?"

The question doesn't come from my mother. It comes from my father, who has chosen this moment to come downstairs and join the party. I sense immediately that our previous plan to "keep Dad out of the crazy loop" has just failed.

My father steams across the kitchen wearing boxer shorts, an ancient U of I T-shirt, and a dumbfounded expression. His hair stands up in messy little clumps.

But at least he's asked a question to which I can give an honest answer.

"Daddy, no. No."

The look on his face tells me that he doesn't believe me. The look he gives Ethan is just plain dangerous.

"Steve," my mother says as Ethan lets go of her arm. "Go back to bed."

Like that's going to happen. My hands start to do their glow thing again, and my pulse races off the charts to the kind of territory where doctors bring in the crash cart and charge up the paddles.

Lily and David press their bodies to our sliding glass door. Lily's rusalka tail beats rhythmically against the glass. *Thud. Thud. Thud.* Her dress is so destroyed that most of her body is visible. Almost naked mermaid breasts flatten against the glass. She stretches her mouth into a hideous grin, all pointed teeth and flecks of seaweed.

"Answer me, young man," my father goes on. This is bizarre on so many levels that I don't know where to begin. For whatever reason—most likely situational blindness brought on by his assumption that Ethan and I were having sex in my room—my father has yet to acknowledge that there's a mermaid with her boobs smashed against the sliding glass door. Or that the ghost of David is holding her hand. If we all live through this, I am going to need years of therapy.

"It's not what you think," Ethan observes helpfully. Then to my mother: "Laura. It's going to be all right. You have to believe me. We'll figure this out. We'll stop it. But you have to trust your daughter. You have to trust me."

My father frowns. His hands clench into fists. "What the hell are you talking about? What the hell is going on down here? And if you've laid a hand on my daughter, I'll—"

"Come out to me, granddaughter," Lily says, her mouth leaving puckered dots of moisture and seaweed on the sliding door. Her voice is gravel and water and misery. Double-paned safety glass is obviously not sound-proof. "Will you listen to a man rather than to your flesh and blood? Do as your mother asks. Give her what she wants. Perhaps then she will forgive me."

My father looks like a cartoon character. His mouth forms a perfect O. His eyebrows rise higher than I thought possible, and his face drains of color. A vein on the side of his neck begins to throb.

He looks from the window to me to my mother to Ethan, then repeats the circuit, his mouth opening and shutting like a fish out of water. He tilts his head and stares out the window again, and his eyes fill with horror and tears.

"Dad," I say. "You need to sit down. We need to explain."

I'm not sure exactly what "we" are going to say. But we'd better start talking. That much is clear.

"Explain?" my father says sort of blankly. He walks to the window and places his hand on the glass. The ghost of David lifts his own hand in response.

"It's not real, Daddy. It's not David. It's Lily. Don't look, Daddy. Just turn away. We'll get her to stop. I'll make her—"

"Lily?" my father asks. "Who's Lily?"

Outside, Lily lets go of ghost David's hand and lifts her arms skyward again. Our sprinkler system goes crazy. Sprinkler head after sprinkler head bursts through the ground, spewing water.

"David," my mother moans. "Oh, sweetie. Oh, my baby. My poor baby. I couldn't save you. But your sister—she'll take me to see you. I've asked her for just a few minutes. Just one ordinary day. Oh, honey. I've missed you so much."

"*What the hell?*" my father yelps. He must believe that what he sees isn't real. Otherwise he'd never focus on the sprinkler and not on the reanimation of his dead son and the specter of a crazy Russian mermaid. This is what I tell myself. He is, after all, Steve Michaelson, tax attorney. Jogger. Occasional tennis player. As we've kept him in the dark, he has no frame of reference for what he's seeing.

"What is this?" Dad's voice cracks. "Some kind of cruel joke?" He looks at me like he's seeing me for the first time. "What does your mother mean about you?"

"Last fall," I say. "Daddy. I—God, where do I start. Daddy, Lily is—"

"Monster." My father isn't even listening. He puts his hand on the door.

"Daddy, no!"

But he's already outside.

ETHAN

COME BACK, DAD!" ANNE SHOUTS. "IT'S NOT SAFE OUT HERE."
But he strides toward Lily, and we have no choice but to follow into the erratic spray from the sprinklers.

"Do as she says," I tell Anne's father. "Anne's right. You're in danger. We're all in danger if you don't come inside."

The rusalka laughs, a throaty sound distorted by the throb of the pulsing water. She points at me, her jagged teeth shining as she smiles. "You're the one who's dangerous, Ethan. I can feel it pushing off you in waves. If my Anne is not careful, she'll end up like me. And then where will she be? Swimming and swimming. Trapped. As I am.

"And you, Ethan, your problems will have just begun. If you don't let my granddaughter help me, you will never escape him. Do you not understand what is going on inside you? Are you that naïve?"

"I will never end up like you." Anne's hands are glowing again, lighting the space around her as she takes her father's hand and tries to stop him from reaching Lily.

"Granddaughter?" Mr. Michaelson's voice rises in confusion.

"Later, Dad. Just go inside. Please. I'm begging you. You and Mom both. I know this is all so weird, but Ethan and I can take care of this. It's not David. Believe me. Go in. When it's over, I'll explain."

"Foolish girl," says the rusalka. She runs a skeletal hand over the boy's head. The thing that she has made to look like Anne's brother.

"You're the fool," Anne says. "For thinking that you can manipulate me like this and get away with it. If you want me to help you, then let me help you. Don't appear to my mother in the middle of the night. And if you want me to believe that you're on my side in all this, then don't parade whatever that is around like it's my brother. You leave him out of it."

"Aw, Anne," the David thing says. "C'mon. She was just having a little fun. Where's your sense of humor, sis?" He grins, and then one tiny crack shows in the façade—like Lily, his teeth are far too sharp to be human. Mr. Michaelson gasps. Behind me, I can hear Anne's mother sobbing.

We need to end this. Now.

Lily cocks her head. Water pounds against her almost naked body. Her hair whips around her in the pressure from the sprinklers, dark strands of hair curling like snakes.

She smiles at me. Licks her bottom lip. Raises her arms to the sky.

Above us, there's a crack of thunder and then lightning sheers a jagged finger through the night sky. The mild breeze turns into a brisk wind.

Lily's body straightens and grows taller, thicker.

"Whoa." The David thing's eyes grow wide. His tone admiring.

Lily's hair shortens. Her features shift and morph. Her lilac gown becomes jeans and a blue collared shirt.

Ben Logan stands in the rain where Lily had been. Anne inhales sharply.

"What's happening?" Ben rubs his eyes as the sprinklers pelt against him. "Anne. How did I get here? I was—did I drive here?"

"Is that Ben?" Mrs. Michaelson pushes past me toward her husband. "Anne. You can stop this. Please. Make it stop."

"She's mine, dude." Ben's gaze fixes on me. "You know that, right? She may think she loves you, but she'll figure it out. She belongs with me, not some freak like you. I can read your head, you know? Just like she can. Maybe better. So I know she's seen your spicy little past. That Tasha chick was a trip, right? And you are one stupid bastard. That's what Viktor liked about you, you know? That you were dumb like a pile of rocks. If you jumped into my pool, you'd sink to the bottom. And I definitely wouldn't save you."

"Ben" holds out a hand to Anne. "C'mon, Annie. Give me a kiss. Even your parents like me better. Make 'em a lot happier than knowing that you let freak boy put his hands, well, you know."

My anger rises too swiftly to rein in. As if in reaction, Lily morphs again. Ben disappears. The rusalka stands in front of me, her wet hair snaking around her in the wind.

She hisses, an inhuman sound. "I thought to make it easier. To give you truth in the body of a boy who loves you. But no matter. I do not have much time here. Viktor watches me, you know. And the witch—she watches too. They want what they want and I am their pawn. But they still fear me. Stories within stories, Anne. Secrets hiding within secrets. How many times will you hear and still not understand? I cannot do any more.

You think I lie, granddaughter. But I do not. This man is not what you think. Ignore me at your own peril. I have told you. Baba Yaga has told you. Even your own brother comes to you to tell you what you need to know."

The magic—my regained power from sources yet unknown—swells with my fury. It fills me—flows into my veins, my arms, my hands. I curse at her in Russian as my mind conjures a spell that I do not consciously remember learning.

"*Atebis rusalka! Paslushayte! Vy dolzhny ostavit! Vernut'sya k vode rusalka!*" *Listen. You must leave. Go back to the water, mermaid.* It is not a request; it is a command—an imperative backed up by a magical push. And before that, the universally rude suggestion of what I'd like her to do. I leave out her name. Names conjure a presence. Names bring forth their own power. I want her powerless. I want her gone.

The magic takes physical form. Stronger than the lightning that's searing the sky with its jagged edges. The stream of light burns as it pours from my fingertips—white, then blue, then dark as ink. With a shock, I realize I'm smiling. My magic plows into Lily and lifts her into the air. Beneath her gown, her tail morphs into feet and then back into tail. Still dangling above the grass, she doubles over in agony.

Only then do I realize that maybe I can't control this.

Worse: something inside me likes it.

"Ethan!" Anne screams and shakes me. "Stop it."

"I'm trying." But the magic streaming from my hands and slamming into Lily tells us both otherwise.

Lily crashes to the ground, tries to push herself upright, then stumbles—over feet, then tail, then feet—and smacks against the elm tree. She is not human, not alive in any true sense of the word, but still a long gash opens on one of her pale, thin, naked arms. Blood pools along the cut, mingling with the sprinkler water.

The magic skips across my hands. Somersaults through the air and hits the elm, stripping the bark straight down to the ground. The smell of burning wood fills the air.

Anne gasps. "Damn it. What is this? You're going to burn down my whole neighborhood." She grasps my hand and I feel her own power join with mine. Her magic feels familiar, feels like Anne, but riding underneath it, the witch's power deepens the burn. Magic, ancient and primal. The thing inside me slithers around this new power source, twists itself tight to take what it can.

Anne doesn't have to tell me that my eyes darken. Everything inside me feels wrong. Everything inside me feels invincible.

"Ethan. Ethan. Whatever this is, you need to snap out of it. I'm going to try to help you. I think I can help you. Let me help you."

The link between us tightens like a fist. Like before, images come: Viktor at the edge of the Chicago River, staring at a heavy, woolen coat as it sinks. Anne kneeling next to Ben in Baba Yaga's forest. Baba Yaga at her table, slicing Anne's hand and watching the blood drip. A young Viktor talking to Tsar Nicholas while Anastasia stands at her father's side. Anne bending over to kiss me as I lie dying on the forest floor. My eyes open. I sit up. I smile.

"Focus on that," Anne says. "Just you and me, Ethan. Ignore the rest of it." She cups my face in her hands. Forces me to look into her eyes. I'm burning, I think. Whatever's inside me is burning me alive.

Somewhere Lily is shrieking.

Somewhere there's smoke.

This isn't me. This magic swimming in my veins is not mine. I force it back—will it to shut down. Turn off. Stop.

"Push it back," Anne says. "I'm going to help you push it back."

And then, a voice that is Anne but not Anne, a voice deeper and more ancient: *So I will it. So let it be.* Her lips have not moved, but the words echo between us.

The magic pulls back. Then back some more.

"Let her go," Anne says. She sounds like herself again. "Just let her go."

There's a settling inside me. Like a compartment opening and shutting something away. Slowly, Lily falls to the ground.

The sprinklers shut off.

Lily and the boy disappear.

"What the hell was all that?" Anne's father pushes a wet hank of hair out of his eyes. He looks at Anne. "What have you gotten yourself involved in? And you, Laura." He turns to his wife. "You knew about all this? What? It's not enough that I'm losing you a little day after day. You think we don't notice that you've stopped eating again? For a while I thought you were better. But you're not.

"Do you think that you're the only one who lost your son? I lost him too. We all did. But I went back to work. I hurt every day, do you know that? Sometimes the pain of it is unbearable. But I didn't get caught up in some craziness—whatever this is. Have you let our daughter put herself in danger too? My God, Laura. I thought I knew you. I don't understand any of this."

"Don't blame her, Dad." Anne unlinks her hands from mine. "When we tell you the whole story, you'll understand. It's complicated. I know it all looks crazy—it is crazy—but it's not Mom's fault. It's…it's not anybody's fault. It's just what is. The world isn't always what you think, Dad. There's stuff people don't see. And it's not make-believe. It's real."

"No." Mr. Michaelson shakes his head, a sharp motion. "That's not possible. This guy here that you've been seeing, doing God knows what with while your mother just turns a blind eye, maybe he's the cause of it. But no. We've had enough trouble in this family. Whatever this is, whatever hallucination or illusion or goddamn trick, it's going to stop.

"You will not see Ethan again. He is not welcome in my house. You will spend the summer with your mother, helping her with her work. You will finish your college applications. And in the fall, you'll go back to school. All this running around and keeping secrets—it's over, Anne. I will not have this family destroyed."

"Mr. Michaelson," I begin.

He steps forward, fists clenched at his side. "Shut the hell up. You are not—I repeat, not—welcome here. Leave. Now. If you have any decency, you'll go. My daughter is off limits to you. Understood?"

"Daddy!" Anne's voice is shrill, her face pale. "You need to let us explain. It's not what you think. Ethan isn't the cause of what's going on."

A muscle ticks in his jaw. "I don't need an explanation. Your mother is sick. Your brother is dead. Whatever is causing the rest of it—I don't give a damn. We were getting better until Ethan showed up. And now we're not. When he's gone, we'll be better again. Problem solved. No further discussion needed."

"But Mom—"

"Your mother is going inside to lie down. You are going up

to your room. And in the morning, when we've all had a little sleep, we'll figure out what to do. I've been telling myself that this would all resolve itself. And for that I'm sorry. God, Laura, I'm sorry. But after tonight—we're going to do things my way. End of story."

"You need to listen to your daughter," I say. Under my skin, I feel the magic skip across my veins. I could make him believe whatever I want, I think, and find myself horrified at the thought. Do I have that kind of power? Why?

He splits my lip when he hits me. Blood trickles down my chin.

"Daddy, no!" Anne shoves her way between us.

And here's what goes through my mind: he's not entirely wrong, her father. I am the cause. Even worse, right now, I don't even know if I trust myself.

"Stop it, all of you!" Mrs. Michaelson, her face streaked with tears, grips her husband's arm.

"I'm sorry we didn't tell you before, Dad. We just thought it would be easier if you…Tell him, Mom. You're part of this too. You can't just let—"

"You need to do what Steve says, Ethan." Her voice is flat. "It will be for the best."

Around us, the wind picks up again. Anne's hair blows behind her. Her fingers flex, simmer with light.

"Don't," I say quietly. "It will be okay."

I tell her parents that I'm leaving. Walk to the back gate.

"Fine, then," Anne says. Her voice cracks, then steadies. "You guys want to pretend that what you just saw isn't real? Okay with me." She joins me at the gate.

"If you leave with him…" her father says. The threat hangs

empty. I can see in his eyes that he has no idea what he will do if she goes.

"I need to give them some space," Anne says softly. She touches a finger to my split lip. I feel the cut draw into itself and close. "I don't know what else to do right now. Plus, in another second my dad is going to realize that he's standing out here in his boxers."

Ten minutes later, the moon still full in the sky, she meets me at my car, backpack in hand. Her father stands at the window, but he doesn't stop her. I don't know if this makes him strong or weak. I don't know what I'd do if I were him. I like to think I'd make her stay.

"This is probably stupid," she says. "I mean, are they even safe if I leave? She could come back, Ethan. Lily could come back. God knows what she might convince my mother to do. Something worse than just make her see my dead brother. But I don't want to be here right now. I can't spend another minute watching my father pretend that all my mother needs is to gut it out."

"Do you want to stay?"

She hesitates. Then says, "No."

I don't tell her that I'm surprised at her answer. Nor do I judge her choice.

Together, we do another warding spell around her house. Her magic is potent; I can feel it everywhere. It should be enough. It needs to be enough.

The power that has come back to me thrums in response. Soon, I will have to uncover its source. But not right now.

Protections in place, we drive down the quiet street, no particular destination in mind.

Wednesday, 2:41 am

Viktor

Like Baba Yaga and the rusalka, I watch them. It is a risk to do this in person, but it sweetens the pleasure—the frisson of fear that I will be caught. More often though, like now, I do not need the physical proximity.

Magic, time, Fate—their combined potency affords me certain privileges. The witch can see things that were and that will be. But I can see what is. Blood connects me to Anne and thus to the foolish man who has no earthly idea what he is up against. Oh, he suspects. But he will not catch me. And even if he does, it will not matter. That is how clever I am.

In the witch's hut it was not only time that worked differently. It was everything. The rhythm of our days, the progress of the sun and moon, the beating of my far-too-human heart. All of it altered. Not good or bad, just not the same. Maybe it was the movement—the chicken legs in almost constant motion—carrying Baba Yaga's hut into the farthest corners of her forest, deep inside the woods where no one could find us.

Almost no one, that is.

I was Baba Yaga's prisoner, but I still had my eyes. I watched her: always, always I watched. And when she peered into the skull in her fireplace, I watched then too. She could see things—and not only what was. She could see what had been and what was to be. Even when my body was broken and my skin burned from her touch, I knew that this was something I could use.

This is the difference between those who succeed and those who do not. Even when I wished for death, I plotted what I would do once I was free. The irony, of course, did not elude me. I was there because I had compelled her to protect a Romanov. Viktor, the bastard son, suffering and profiting from the birthright that my father denied me right up to his bloody end.

In the visions in the skull, the future was murky, changeable. The fire would sputter and the flames grow huge, then diminish to embers. The vision would shift, small pieces altering its fabric. People were not always predictable. The future was, I learned, mere guesswork—witches and diviners and powerful magicians could see into it, but they could not control it. They could not force it into being. They could only look and meddle and hope that their influence had the desired effect.

Free will, I came to understand, was exactly that. Even the mighty Baba Yaga could not make someone do something he didn't want to do. Even what she did to me there in the hut. On some level, I came to her of my own volition. If my tenure in her world turned me mad at times, so be it. History is full of madmen. Most of them are sane enough.

My great-great-granddaughter Anne complains that she has no choice. She is young. She does not understand that everything is a choice. Even that idiot Ethan—so easy to manipulate—even he knows that in the end, his actions are still his own.

But the past, ah, that is another story, and one that took me a long, long while to understand. Even I, who uncovered the secrets of the ancient magic, who found the way to compel the most powerful witch who ever was, even I did not understand that it is in the past that true power lies.

It is risky, but it can be done. Still one must work carefully and with great precision—like a surgeon cutting just the right amount and at just the right level of pressure. Too much and the future sits in peril. Too little and what is the point? I have always admired those who could take another life in their hands and not quaver as they held the knife and made that first incision.

In another life, I think, I could be such a person.

Perhaps someday, I will give it a try. Why not? I have all the time in the world.

In the hut, here was my question. The magic to do what I needed was possible. The flexibility of time was mine for the taking. But where does one hide a soul? Koschei had his hiding place. So did that crazy bastard Rasputin. I needed mine.

I promised myself that I would not squander this knowledge like they did—Koschei and Rasputin—who grew careless and carnal and allowed those desires to make them vulnerable to attack. Rasputin was, in the end, just Father Grigory, a greasy-bearded magician with a taste for young girls. Had he not been murdered, I think someday I would have killed him myself. There was no truth to the rumors that he and Alexandra were lovers. But if he had had his way, he would have added Anastasia and her sisters to his list of conquests. I felt no remorse when they pulled him, dead at last, from the river. Once, I thought I might learn magic from him. In truth, he should have desired to learn from me.

I thought about this for a very long time—or so it seemed to me. I was not Koschei and certainly not Rasputin, but I was also not Ethan, who has always believed in love. My Irina, the dancer who thought she had won my heart, was beautiful. But she was also a curse. The revelation of Tasha Levin's unfaithfulness has shocked Ethan. Foolish Tasha, who believed that I would make her immortal. Why would she want to live forever? To play Rachmaninoff until she got the notes right? To remain young, firm, vibrant? A waste of a gift.

Irina was not unfaithful. It was I who left her. But she had her secrets nonetheless. I did not know she was pregnant. I did not know when she gave birth to my daughter and set in motion the bloodline that must end with Anne. A small piece of me regrets this, but power does not exist without sacrifice. Certainly my willingness to be Baba Yaga's captive was proof of that.

One day, crouched in the bed that had been Anastasia's, I realized the solution. Silently—no sense in letting Yaga in on my revelation—I laughed at the simplicity and perfection. Why had it taken me so long to understand? Perhaps because it was so perfect, so fitting to the thing I would place there. My soul would be safe and I would be alive for as long as I chose. I could reclaim the power that would once again show history that I had bested my father. If someday I found living tedious, then I would extract it. Return my soul to my corporeal body and make myself vulnerable once more. And like an ordinary mortal, eventually I would die.

For me, free will could control even that.

So now I knew where to hide my soul, but Yaga watched my every move. I needed to be patient.

Here is something else I learned in the forest: even the strongest of witches feel loneliness. Yaga missed her girl. I believe she had come to see Anastasia as her own—if not a daughter, then at least a companion. The years are long, even in a hut that defies time. It must have been a relief to have someone to bring her hot, sweet tea. To listen to her stories. To fill the spaces in time.

Certainly I was quite the disappointment in these regards.

And so I waited. Let the witch's longing squeeze around her no-longer-beating heart. When the ache grew unbearable, she would float the skull into the fireplace, mutter the words that needed to be said, and watch.

Anastasia sitting at the edge of her bed, the matryoshka doll on her lap. Anastasia sweeping the wooden floor of the hut. Anastasia sitting by the fire while Yaga rocked and rocked, her long skirt brushing the floor, the *koschka* threading its way around her ankles, licking crumbs of brown bread from the floor with its sharp, pink tongue.

These visions soothed my Yaga, but not always. Some days, she went deeper. Conjured up memories that she had not shared directly, the ones she had extracted as she stroked Anastasia's hair with her huge, brown, gnarled hands.

Always with the familiar images, Yaga remained vigilant. Sometimes she even forced me to sit at her side, as though we were companions at a show. But the visions of times she herself had not experienced—these took more from her. Required a fuller concentration. She became less and less aware of my presence. Her huge gnarled hands reached out to the fire, and the vision shimmered and expanded. For brief moments, the scene expanded, past and present melding into one. Anastasia walked outside the palace with her father, so close and real that I could feel the heat of their bodies, smell the snow swirling in the air around them.

The wooden floor beneath my feet grew cold like the ground in St. Petersburg. Yaga's back to me, I took a step from where I sat on the bed. My bare feet touched hard earth. Snow and ice burned the skin of my soles. Startled, I stepped back and was in the hut once again. Baba Yaga turned from the fire, her dark eyes shining with excitement, and seemed shocked to find me there. She had not noticed that I had stepped into the vision.

I knew then that it could be done. I could slip into the past and return, and if the vision was compelling enough, it was quite possible that she would not know. A risk? Yes. But one I was willing to take.

It did not take long for Yaga to conjure the vision I needed. This did not surprise me. My half sister Anastasia had come to the hut full of fear and grief, but until the witch forced her to see the truth, she also came with trust in me. I had promised her that her family would be safe. That she would give herself to the witch and that her sacrifice would protect them. Only much later did she learn that this was a lie. Her head was filled with thoughts of me. It was only a matter of waiting for the right memory to flicker into the fire.

When it did, I made my move. In two blinks of Yaga's dark eyes, I placed my soul where no one would think to find it. And even if someone does—well, I took care of that too.

Then I waited. If I misjudged Anne, I would live forever in the hut. This was part of the risk I took. Would the rusalka convince her to let me free? Surely Anne understood that Lily wanted only vengeance. Here is what I believed: that my great-great-granddaughter would allow her hatred for what I'd done to Ethan to guide her actions. She was of my blood. Her power might come from Yaga herself, but blood is strong. I hoped this would prevail.

I was, of course, disappointed. But rusalki are evil things. Lily made sure that Anne had no choice. I was fine with that too.

A lesser man might worry now. Like Yaga, Anne has found her way to the past. But I am not a lesser man. I am the Deathless Koschei reborn in my own body. Endless lifetimes spinning out in front of me.

WEDNESDAY, 3:30 AM

ANNE

I CRY FOR THE FIRST FEW BLOCKS. THEN I TEXT TESS. I'M not surprised when she doesn't respond. It is, after all, three in the morning. Normal people are in their beds sleeping, not almost having sex while in someone else's body, confronting cranky Russian mermaids, and getting kicked out of their house. People who aren't me.

Ethan lights a cigarette and smokes half of it, blowing smoke out his open window. I choose not to complain. The "I could die from secondary smoke" discussion is not where I want to expend my energy right now.

"We need to get some sleep," Ethan says. We're in Evanston now, headed in the general direction of his apartment, but neither of us has committed to actually going there.

"We need lots of things," I say. It comes out much sharper than I mean it to. Probably I should apologize. But even talking is an effort right now.

Two more blocks.

Ethan breaks our more than cranky silence. "Pancakes."

"What?"

He points. A neon IHOP sign blinks in the dark about a block ahead of us. "Do you want pancakes?"

"What?" I repeat. Is he actually offering to take me to break-fast? At 3 a.m.? In the middle of a crisis of legendary proportions?

"They have lots of syrup choices. Do you like syrup? I don't think we've ever discussed it."

Syrup?

Ethan pulls to the curb near the IHOP parking lot. The look on his face says that he is serious about the syrup question.

"If I take you home with me right now," he says quietly, "we'll both be uncomfortable. I want to take you home. I want you to sleep in my bed, and I want to hold you and keep you safe. I want to be there when you wake up in the morning. I want to brew you a pot of tea and make you toast with butter. Then I want to spend a day with you. We'll walk by the lake and go to a museum, and later we'll walk some more and we'll talk. The sun will shine and we won't be run-ning and you won't be scared. That's what I want to do. But as none of that is going to work right now, I think we're left with pancakes."

It is the sweetest, most romantic thing he's ever said to me. It's the most romantic thing anyone has ever said to me. Possibly that anyone has ever said.

"You want to take me for pancakes?" Maybe it's a trick. Some Baba-Yaga- or rusalka- or Viktor-induced delusion that's going to go poof as soon as I agree to IHOP.

But Ethan nods and shifts the car in gear. In no time at all, we're walking into the brightly lit IHOP, being seated at a booth and handed menus. We order pancakes. Buttermilk all around.

"They used to have more choices." Ethan points at the four little syrup pitchers tucked against the wall of our booth. "I liked boysenberry. But I suppose it really was wasteful to put all that out on each table."

I gape at him again. He is not a person who I imagined having syrup preferences. Or going to IHOP. Or eating pancakes.

"I'm a purist," I tell him since it seems rude to let him chat about this all on his own. "Maple syrup. Warm. Maybe a dab of butter." Maple is not represented in the four little pitchers of syrup tucked against the wall of our booth.

The tired-looking waitress wearing green and white Nikes brings our pancakes and a pitcher of maple syrup—sufficiently warm. She leaves a big pot of coffee on the table after filling our cups.

For a while, we eat. Pour warm syrup on warm, dense pancakes and fork them into our mouths. Ethan reaches across the table and wipes a dot of syrup off my chin with his napkin. I gulp two cups of lukewarm coffee. Somehow it makes me feel a little calmer.

Maybe we'll just stay at IHOP forever. *If we kept ordering pancakes, they wouldn't kick us out, right?*

Cup of coffee poised at his mouth, Ethan looks at me. A crooked smile plays at his lips.

I had forgotten that we were reading each other's thoughts. Correction: I've been too freaked to read his since we got back from the past. But I guess in his head, I'm still coming in loud and clear.

"Not always," Ethan says, which answers my question even without me asking it. "It comes and goes."

So we can't even count on that. *Wonderful.*

I eat another pancake. Chew and swallow. Chew and swallow. Ethan pours us both more coffee. He shakes a sugar packet—two quick flicks of the wrist—rips it open, and stirs the contents into his mug. Two booths over, a heavy-set middle-aged guy places an order for blueberry waffles.

I set my fork on my plate. Ethan looks up from his coffee. I don't want to ask. But I also don't want to wait to read it in his thoughts. I want him to tell me. If he tells me, then I can trust him.

"Whose magic is in you, Ethan? Even a few weeks ago, you didn't have that kind of power. When we were stuck in Baba Yaga's forest, when you basically died and I brought you back to life, there was nothing like that inside you. But now there is. And it doesn't feel like you. Not at all."

"You ask like you're sure I have an answer."

I shrug. The truth? I have my own answer. I've had it since I was trapped in Tasha's body. I just didn't understand until now.

Ethan leans into the booth, his eyes very serious. They're regular Ethan blue now, not dark and scary. A tired look crosses his face.

"I think," he says very slowly, "that it has to do with Viktor."

"Just think?"

His lips quirk in that signature crooked, self-deprecating smile. "I can't be sure. But yes, I think the power has somehow come from him. And I don't have to read your thoughts to know that you agree."

The pancakes in my stomach threaten a reversal. "I'm part of Viktor, Ethan. I'm his blood. Your magic, it's always felt clean to me. Lily, she's just sad all the time. Baba Yaga's power feels ancient. When I use what she's given me, I feel linked to things that go back so deep I can't even imagine. But Viktor's magic frightens me. And not just because he's tried to kill me with it. There's just a darkness. Like he's so furious all the time. Not like you. When we've linked our power together, it's scared me, but it's always felt right. This just feels angry. Like Viktor."

Ethan drums those long fingers of his on the Formica table. Purses his lips.

"But why?" His question sits between us, heavy as the congealing maple syrup on the remains of our pancakes. "If we're right, why make me more powerful? Doesn't that make me a threat? He knows Lily wants him dead. He knows we want to strip his abilities. So why would he give me more power?"

"Distraction, maybe? He's big on that, remember? That's what he convinced Tasha to do to you. So maybe it's like that. Only this way, he doesn't need to get anyone else involved. He just shifts some mojo to you somehow and then bam—you're so distracted trying to get rid of it that he can get away with whatever it is he wants to get away with."

"Maybe. But it doesn't explain how he managed to come back to life after Lily shot him. I don't understand it. You don't understand it. Even Dimitri—"

I narrow my eyes. We still haven't dealt with the whole "Why did you go see Dimitri and not tell me, and can you really trust him?" issue.

My phone, resting on the table near the holder of flavored syrups, scoots closer to the strawberry pitcher as it begins to vibrate.

Tess.

Tess? At four in the morning?

"My brother woke me up," she says when I answer. "He's doing this internship, remember, the one where he shadows a heart surgeon at Rush downtown. He has to be there at five.

And his car wouldn't start, so can you believe that he just walked into my room and started pawing through my purse for my car keys? Like that would be okay even if it wasn't dark thirty in the morning?

"So I'm like, 'What the hell are you doing?' and he's like, 'I need to get downtown. The freakin' trains aren't even running yet.' So I let him take my car. And then—because now I'm totally wide awake, I check my phone. And there's your text. Oh my God, Anne, what's going on?"

It is such an insanely long monologue that I lose track halfway through, refocusing only as she finally takes a breath.

"I can't explain it all over the phone. Can you meet us?"

"Us? As in you and Ethan?"

"Yes, Tess."

"I'm on my way." Beep. She ends the call.

I redial her number.

"I said I'm on my way."

"Not home." I give her directions to the IHOP.

"Tess," I say before she can hang up on me again. "You don't have a car, remember?"

"Not a problem."

WEDNESDAY, 4:53 AM

ETHAN

I F I LIVE ANOTHER TEN LIVES, I WILL NEVER UNDERSTAND women. Or perhaps it's just Tess I'll never understand, and Anne's undying loyalty to her. It is beyond rational comprehension. So I don't even try. I finish my pancakes, down the rest of the coffee in the pot, and wait for Tess to arrive.

"She's worried about me, Ethan. I need to tell her what's going on. Do you really expect me to do all that in one phone call?"

Obviously yes is not the appropriate answer.

"Why put her in danger again?"

Anne scowls. "She's already in danger. Just knowing me puts her there. What would you rather I do? Not tell her and let Viktor or Lily or Baba Yaga attack her or something? You're right. She's not safe with me. But she's in more danger on her own. At least if she's here, we can try to protect her. I couldn't stop Lily from getting in my mother's head, and that was right in my own house. Wards. Protection spells. They only go so far. Plus, let's face it, I…"

Her words trail off. She's staring at the entrance to the restaurant. I follow her gaze.

Tess all but flies into IHOP, Ben behind her. Ben Logan. Anne's lifeguard. Well. This is going to be interesting.

"Shit." Anne's face blanches.

Tess slides into the booth next to Anne. Ben—understandably—chooses to remain standing.

"Move over, Ethan." Tess gestures with her hand like I'm a puppy in need of direction. "Go on, Ben. Sit down. Ben gave me a ride because Zach had to—oh wait, I told you that on the phone, right? But anyway, Ben saved the day. Didn't you, Ben?" She smiles widely at Ben, who's still standing at the edge of the booth, clearly weighing his options.

"Ethan." Tess tucks her blond hair behind her ears and frowns at me. "Let's not have a pissing match. Move over. Ben can't just stand there."

"Tess." Anne finds her voice. "Maybe we should—"

"Tess and I went out last night." Ben nods his head like he's agreeing with something. He cracks his knuckles.

I slide over. "Join us," I say.

"After she left your house," Ben goes on, "we went for coffee at Java Joe's." His neatly groomed brows knit together as he looks at the empty spot on the brown molded-plastic bench. Then his gaze shifts back to Anne and Tess as he folds his tall frame into the booth.

"I was going to tell you," Tess says. "But it was late and I was exhausted from the whole Russia thing and that third egg roll wasn't sitting well and besides"—she points at me—"Ethan was spending the night and—"

"He spent the night?" Ben directs the question at Anne like I'm not an inch away. I clear my throat. Debate whether it might not be worth it to summon up a little dark magic. What would Viktor do? Invisibly choke the life out of Ben until he fell face forward into Anne's plate?

"Ethan!" Anne snakes a hand to grip my arm. "Play nice." She shifts her attention to Ben. "And yes, he was at my house. To protect me. Which, okay, didn't exactly happen. But neither did anything else."

She blushes prettily. But her eyes flash with annoyance, then curiosity. "Are you guys going out now? I mean, besides the coffee?"

Tess looks at Ben. Ben looks at Tess.

"Maybe," Tess says. "Maybe not. Ben and I have discussed my need to be more choosy with my affections. Are you going to eat that pancake? Do you think we can get more maple syrup? I mean who actually uses those other ones? I don't know why they put them out except maybe for the stoners to stare at the color at three in the morning."

"Tess," Anne says slowly. "You came here because I asked you to, remember?"

Tess breaks off a piece of pancake with her fingers and places it into her mouth. She wrinkles her nose. "It's cold."

"Tess," Anne says again.

"Tell her," Ben says. Something's off about his tone.

"You have enough to worry about." Tess breaks off another bite of pancake, then drops it back on the plate.

My heart shifts rhythm. "Tess. Ben. What's going on?"

"Who else could I call?" Tess says. "Ben's the only other one, you know. He was there with us. Who else can I tell? If I don't tell you, then it has to be Ben."

"The only one you can tell what?" Anne shifts in her seat. Tess continues to look across the table at me and Ben.

"The goddamn bastard was in her yard watching her window, Anne." Ben bites off each word.

"Who?" Anne's voice rises. "Who was in your yard, Tess?"

"I wasn't sure at first. I'd driven home and parked in the driveway, and I was thinking that maybe I needed a Coke or something. You know Chinese food—you're always dying of thirst for like hours. Not to mention that I practically destroyed my throat screaming while we were hurtling through time. So I'm about to go in the house, but I can't find my key and my parents are still in Napa checking out this winery they've decided to invest in because they think it will 'bring them closer together.' God knows where Zach is."

"Tess. Get to the point." Anne puts her hand on her friend's shoulder.

"I'm getting there. I think the details are important. What I'm telling you is that I wasn't paying attention. But I felt it anyway. This weird goose-bumpy feeling crawled up my arms and neck. Like someone was watching me. But when I looked around—nothing. So I went inside. And that's when I called Ben."

Ben takes over the story from there. Explains how Tess seemed spooked so he offered to take her for coffee. Dropped her off back home about 11:30. Even came in and checked the house with her. Nothing. Zach had called and was on his way home. So Ben left. And felt the same weird "something" when he went back to his car. Felt it again when he got home. But like Tess, he didn't see anything.

The only thing out of the ordinary was that the door to his house was unlocked, which struck him as strange since his parents are meticulous types. But their car was in the garage and his father was in the den watching television. Nothing amiss as far as Ben could tell. Just a door that someone forgot to lock.

"Here's the thing," Ben says. The waitress has brought more coffee and two extra mugs, and Ben takes a long sip. "It's taken me a long time to come to grips with all this. And"—he turns to me—"don't think that it makes me your buddy. I still think you're dangerous. I think Anne needs to run from you like she'd run from a virus. But she won't. And I can't force her. I'm her friend, not a cop.

"Like I've told Tess, I tried and tried to convince myself that none of that shit really happened. But I couldn't. It's like falling down the rabbit hole. Once you see this whole other world, you can't go back. So the way I figure, I'm stuck with you. You're a damn douche, but I can't just pretend you're going to disappear out of her life. Or that witches and mermaids and guys who rise from the damn dead don't exist."

"Your point?" I hold his gaze and wait for the punch line.

"I'm not going anywhere. If you need someone else to battle whatever this is, I'm your guy. I don't think you have a chance in hell of being able to protect these two on your own. Even if Anne has, well, powers. You do, right? God, this whole thing freaks me the hell out. But I watched you, Anne. I saw you put your hand on his heart and make a bullet come out of his chest. You were dead, dude. And she brought you back to life. I have to believe it because that's what I saw.

"And the other guy, Viktor, right? I watched him get shot and rise from the dead all on his own. He was a skeleton when he came out that chicken-leg cabin. Then boom, he's younger. So if Tess says that's who she saw when she looked out her window, then I believe her. Which means I'm stuck. I can't just go home and pretend this isn't real."

"I did see Viktor," Tess adds. "He was standing under our

spruce tree. You know those wards or whatever you placed around my house? I think they were the only thing keeping him out. But I looked at him from behind my curtain and I just knew that if he wanted to, he could break through. It would be like snapping a twig or something. Then I heard Ben's car in the driveway on the other side of the house. When I looked again, Viktor was gone. But I'm positive it was him. Oh my God, do you think he did something to Zach's car? Maybe that's why it broke. So he'd take mine and I'd be alone in the house. Ben was the surprise. The thing he didn't think would interrupt him. Shit."

We down some more coffee and discuss it further. Fill Tess and Ben in on everything else that's gone on. Our trip to 1920s London. The body shifting—we keep the details to a minimum, much to Tess's dismay. Tasha's betrayal with Viktor. Even the ballet that we'd gone to—the possible *Giselle* connection to Lily and also Lily's appearance at Anne's house. Anne's father's ultimatum.

In the end, we all agree. The threat is real and imminent and classic Viktor. Keep us all distracted while he gets whatever he wants. How far will he go to keep his immortality? And what will he do if we attempt to stop him? Or, Anne asks, if we don't?

We leave out only one thing. The power that Viktor seems to have shifted to me. Neither Anne nor I mention it. But I can feel it prowling in her thoughts, just as I'm sure she can sense it in mine. But without discussion we seem to be in tacit agreement—this is something for us alone. Especially now with Ben in the mix. So far I'm able to keep it at bay. And when I can't…

"Do you think Viktor really will do something horrible if he gets the chance?" Tess asks. "I guess he already could have, right? So maybe he's not so bad? Or is he just afraid that Anne will sic Baba Yaga on him or something?"

"I think," I say slowly, "that we can safely assume that he is not afraid of us. Not even of Baba Yaga. He never has been, remember? He's the man who found a way to compel a legendary witch. I doubt his time with her was pleasant, but afraid of her? I highly doubt it."

"Here's what I want to know." Ben drums his fingers on the table. "What's the dude want? And don't tell me the obvious. Of course he wants to live forever. Isn't that what the bad guy always wants? World domination. Eternal life. Both. We all watched those Indiana Jones movies. Holy ark, holy grail, whatever. It all amounts to the same load of crap.

"So Viktor's twist is he used his half sister Anastasia to get his wish. And made you"—he jerks his chin in my general direction—"immortal along with him. Which, let's face it, he probably expected that you'd be totally fine with. If I were an evil mastermind, I'd be looking for the stupidest minions I could find. The ones who didn't want to complain. Again, nothing new there. Even Julius Caesar surrounded himself with idiots. Or at least that's what he figured until they offed him."

Ben, it seems, has more layers than I'd anticipated. And, unless I'm mistaken, has used his knowledge of both cinema and history to call me a fool.

"So maybe what we saw in the past was really true," Tess says. "He's older than you, right, Ethan? And we already know that he wanted revenge on Tsar Nicholas. Wanted him to acknowledge to everyone that Viktor was his son.

Even Professor Olensky never really thought about why the Brotherhood existed. He just bought into what the legends said—that it developed as this secret-society thing to protect the Romanovs. And Viktor was the bad guy who corrupted the system to get back at his dad. But maybe it wasn't exactly like that. Maybe the Brotherhood was always a cover-up for what Viktor had planned for years. Maybe right from the start he was looking for people who he could use."

The image of my father lying dead in the field, that of my mother and sister murdered in our house, come to me again, as they have so many times over so many years. To believe that their deaths weren't just random violence is a step I'm not ready to take.

Anne rests her hand over mine. Squeezes. "All that doesn't matter, though. I mean not really. True or not—it's old news. He did it. I stopped him. And now I have to stop him again. I don't think anything else is relevant."

"Maybe," Ben says, "I'm your fresh set of eyes here, Anne. I'm not invested in this like the rest of you. But you know how I love movies. And like I said, every movie with a bad guy, well, you have to know his motivation to figure the rest out. Unless it's one of those ones where the bad guy figures he's so invincible that he tells the good guy everything just before he attempts to kill him. I hate those."

The restaurant has begun to fill with the breakfast crowd. Our waitress trudges to the table, hands me the check, and informs us that her shift is ending. Her subtle way of saying it's time to give up the booth.

"What about that Koschei story?" Anne stretches, rolls her shoulders. She leans her elbows on the table. "You never did tell me the rest of it, remember?" She rests her gaze on Tess and then Ben. "When I was stuck in Tasha's body, she and Viktor talked about Koschei the Deathless. She was like, 'Hey, that's just a story,' but he was all 'Hey, it's more than that.'"

"Of course he'd think that," I say. "It's what he aspires to. Koschei is from Slavic folklore. He found a way not to die. As Ben would say, stories are full of people who try to trick Fate. In the stories, Koschei always gets caught. Someone figures out how to kill him. Surely Viktor doesn't want that. And mentioning it to Tasha—it's clear now that he was manipulating her beyond what she may have wanted from him. The name 'Koschei' would scare her. Like Baba Yaga, it's a story, but not a pleasant one. Tasha already believed that he could harness enough magic to give her immortality. So why not pump up the fear by implying that he was as strong as a legendary immortal?"

"Oh, goody." Tess slumps in her seat. "More crazy stories. And here I thought we were maybe on the verge of figuring out something. Do you know it's getting light outside? What time is it, anyway? Maybe we need to just get out of here. This booth is pretty small, you know. I love breakfast food as much as the next person, but we can't sit at IHOP forever. Although it's better than being home and freaking out."

She picks up the coffee pitcher, tips it over her mug. Just one small drop falls into her cup. She shakes it. Empty. "Or maybe we can. Maybe Anne can find a way to hide us in this coffeepot. Then if Viktor or crazy witches or mermaids on a vengeance streak come looking, they'll never find us. 'Cause who would think four people could tuck themselves in a coffeepot? We can put it on the shelf in my parents' closet along with Grandpa Bernie's ashes.

"Did I ever tell you that's where Grandpa Bernie is spending eternity? It's totally gross. But the only thing in his will was that he wanted to be cremated. He never said what he wanted done with his ashes. So now he's sitting in between my dad's golf shoes and a jar of pennies. My dad thinks this is just fine. My mother keeps telling him that if she goes first, she wants us to sprinkle her remains in the fountains at the Bellagio in Vegas. She says that she's not sure where her soul is going to end up, but she'd rather it not be in a jar inside a box balanced on top of a box of old Christmas cards."

"Oh," I say. *Shit.*

Anne looks at me sharply. "What?"

"Koschei. I think maybe it does mean something."

Anne angles her gaze. Her eyes flicker with a mixture of curiosity and worry. "So now we're not blowing off the story? What about him? And what does it have to do with Tess's grandpa's urn?"

"Can we go outside?" Tess pleads. "Please? He can tell the story while I breathe some fresh air. Viktor probably has better taste than to attack us at IHOP. The smell from all this syrup is making me want to vom."

WEDNESDAY, 5:58 AM

ANNE

ETHAN CHECKS THE PARKING LOT AND DEEMS IT SAFE for now.

"I will totally not be your friend unless you swear to tell me the stuff you left out," Tess whispers in my ear as we exit IHOP. "You almost did it with him while stuck in his ex's bod! This is like the best story ever. I want every single detail."

"Trust me when I say it was not as fun as you think."

Outside, the sky's getting lighter, red streaks rising over Lake Michigan. There's a heaviness to the air. A storm is coming. Not now, but later. My chest tightens. I don't do well with storms anymore. I'd imagine it's the same for Ethan and Tess. Ben too. I scan the sky. Nothing but some wispy morning clouds, barely visible in the predawn light.

Tess and I perch on the hood of Ethan's car, Ben and Ethan facing us. I'm on alert but also so tired that I think I could curl up right here on top of the car and take a nap. I've got six missed calls from my mom. I haven't answered any of them. But eventually, I'll have to. And I'll go back home. I have no idea what will happen when I do.

Out of the corner of my eye, I watch Ben and Tess. He smiles at her, and she tucks a curl behind her ear. Tess and Ben.

Definitely didn't see that coming. Maybe on some level it's a relief. Enough of a relief that I'm good with them breaking the time-honored rule of "Don't date someone your best friend has gone out with."

Am I evolved enough to listen to any future love-life details? Maybe.

He rests a hand briefly on her thigh. Maybe not.

Tess flicks Ben's hand away and scoots closer to me. Whispers in my ear again. "Are you good with this? Because you know, if you're not, he'll just have to get over me."

I squeeze her hand. "We're good," I whisper back. "Golden. Really."

Ben folds his arms across himself, his gaze scanning right, left, above us. Like a bodyguard watching for danger. Ben with his military-cut blond hair, wearing faded jeans and a black Smiths' *The World Won't Listen* tee that hugs his muscles in ways I probably shouldn't notice since we're not together anymore. But mostly what I think as I look at it is that when I first started going out with him, Ben had cheery, happy taste in music. A few months with me, and he's joined the angst train. Tess will be a good cure for this. Tess and Ben. Maybe I really am good with that.

Ben catches me checking him out. The slightest of smiles quirks his lips, then he's all business. "So this Koschei. How did he keep from dying? And why do you suddenly think it's so important?"

"It's a tale my mother told us," Ethan says. "I'm going to tell it like she did. So you hear it exactly like I used to. When I'm done, I'll tell you what I'm thinking. And then you can judge."

"Fair enough," Ben says, and then Ethan begins.

"Once there was a powerful magician named Koschei. He was a great sorcerer. The clouds would move in the sky as he directed; the rains would fall where he desired. If he wanted wild mushrooms of a certain type, they would sprout in abundance where his gaze met the ground. If he desired a pretty young girl, he would take her and she would not resist. Just one glance and she was in his thrall. The snows would fall at his whim. The sun would bake the earth if he commanded it to. Grapes would cluster on vines for the fine wine that graced his dining table.

In summer he would ride his horse through the Caucasus Mountains, and his wild laughter would echo in the canyons. Koschei's legend was great. The villagers feared him. 'Beware the sorcerer,' people said. 'He is a tricky one, that Koschei. He can shift shapes and ride into the village in the guise of a wild black stallion or whirl through the air like a thunderstorm.'

If a mist hovered on the ground or a fog obscured a farmer's vision as he walked to his field before the sun was up, people warned that this might be Koschei, taking the shapes of nature. They were awed and afraid. Families would warn their daughters to beware. 'Koschei might steal you,' they would say. 'He loves beautiful women. Even your husbands cannot protect you if Koschei desires your company.'

But there was one thing that Koschei wanted that he could not have. Or rather, he could, but even his great powers could not promise it to him forever. Koschei wanted what many have desired but few have ever achieved. He wanted to live forever. And he had found a way, for one cannot die if one's life force is separated from one's body. If when Death comes searching, he finds only the outer shell and not the inner spirit.

Koschei had hidden his soul inside a needle in a duck's egg, hidden inside a hare, tucked away in a chest, buried under an oak tree that grows on an unknown island in the middle of an unknown ocean. He would remain unassailable and immortal until that egg was found. And if that egg was broken, his soul would return to his body and he could in turn be killed."

Ethan pauses.

"You Russians are seriously disturbed," Tess comments. "This was a fairy tale? About some lecherous dude that ended up inside an egg? How much therapy would I need if my mother read me crap like that? But whatever. That story is one of the ones Anne and I were researching before our whole whirlwind ride to Cossack land. In the version we found, someone smacks Koschei in the head with the egg, and Koschei dies. I guess I skimmed the rest of it so fast I missed the soul stuff. So he's not invincible, right? Is that the point? But seriously—what would a kid learn from this? 'Hey, Ivan, don't shove your soul in an egg 'cause eventually someone will smack you between the eyes?' And what does this have to do with—oh."

"Oh," Ben echoes.

"You see what I'm thinking?" Ethan nods like we're all on the same wavelength. Ben nods too.

It takes me a few extra seconds. Possibly because watching Ben and Ethan nod their heads like they're two old friends throws my universe askew. Ben hates Ethan. Ethan isn't much fonder of Ben. And now Ben is going out with Tess, which is weird but okay. My brain is already so full it's no wonder I'm the last one to catch on.

"Viktor is Koschei," Ethan says. "Or like Koschei. I don't think the distinction matters. My God, everything is finally making sense. When he walked out of Baba Yaga's hut and Lily shot him, he didn't die. And why didn't he die?"

"Because he'd hidden his soul." My heart thunders in my ears, and my chest feels tight again, like my lungs have forgotten how to work. "Because he found a way to get back what

I took away from him when we brought Anastasia out of the forest. He figured out another way to immortality."

I breathe through my nose, attempting calm. Instead, I almost hyperventilate. "Why is it," I squeeze the words out of my too-freaked-to-function lungs, "that every time you tell me some new fairy tale, it turns out to be real? You're serious, aren't you? My insane double-great-grandfather has actually found a way to hide his soul. Fabulous."

Ben massages the side of his neck. I watch his fingers dig, hear his neck crack as he turns it. "Assuming of course, that I haven't joined you guys in some group hallucination—which is still entirely possible as far as I'm concerned—where does someone hide a soul?"

Silence.

"Inside something?" Tess is a fan of the obvious. "I mean that's why my grandpa's ashes in the closet story made you go all *CSI* on us, right? But it would have to be a lot of things, right? Each one hidden inside the other. So you're saying that while Baba Yaga was holding Viktor prisoner, he found this whole pile of things that he stuffed inside each other and she like totally didn't notice? Because I'm thinking that's kind of strange. That witch is wicked observant. I'm not buying that she'd just miss something like that. I mean, the comparison makes sense, but what? While she's got her back turned, he rips his soul out of his body and shoves it in a piece of bread and feeds it to the cat or something?"

Something tickles the back of my brain. I see myself standing in the pounding rain as Anastasia chose not to be saved. As she begged me to send her back to die with her family like she was supposed to. In my memory, we stand in the street as she pulls the doll apart, showing me the smaller dolls tucked inside. *My mama told me to hold on to her. No matter what. That if I did not let her go, she would keep me safe. And she has. She has kept all my secrets. Even as I was hidden away like this*, she says.

I gasp, a tiny sound in the back of my throat.

"Ethan. That day I had to send Anastasia back. Think. It was the doll that helped me do it, remember? Her matryoshka doll. Like the Vasilisa the Brave story—her mother had given her the doll to keep her safe. Only Anastasia's was one of those Russian nesting dolls." I pantomime with my hands. "One doll inside the next doll inside the next. Like the Koschei story, see? Anastasia even compared it to herself when she showed it to me. She said it hid her secrets just like she was hidden away.

"And Lily—oh my God, Ethan—Lily mentioned it too. That first time she spoke to me at the pool the day you came back. Right after she told me that Anastasia might not be dead. Not that I believe that part of it, but she talked about the doll. That whole 'stories within stories, secrets within secrets' thing. All this time, I just tossed it off as Lily nuttiness. But what if it's not? What if she was really giving us a clue?"

"Clue?" Tess chimes in. "I think it's more than a clue. The doll was in Baba Yaga's hut with Anastasia, right? And Viktor was in the same hut. So if he was looking for a place to hide something— spare crumbs, a button, his soul—and there's this doll that has a ready-made hiding place, then why not? I mean the guy's wacked, right? He thinks he's Koschei the Deathless. So if somehow he actually has figured out how to do a Lord Voldemort, Russian fairy tale style, then why not put his soul in the doll?"

"Slavic folklore predates Harry Potter by centuries," Ben interjects. "Not that I'm an expert, obviously."

I gape at him. I knew Ben was smart. But I had no idea that he really knew stuff. Lots of stuff. The next time I use someone as a make-out buddy so I can feel normal, I need to talk to him once in a while too.

Ethan's brows furrow. "It makes sense as a metaphor," he says slowly, "but when Anastasia disappeared, when you sent her back, the doll went with her. So it would have been in the basement in Ekaterinburg with the Romanovs when they were murdered, this time with Anastasia present. Not exactly accessible."

"This is making my head hurt," Tess says. "Did he use the doll or didn't he? The doll can't be in two places at once. And neither can he."

"But what if he could?" Ethan rubs the back of his neck. "Think about our two time-travel events. You and Tess were there watching what happened to my father, but he didn't see you. The Cossacks didn't see you. You say that I did, but it's not how I remember the event. So something changed. Your presence, maybe. The magic and how it works? Something allowed two versions of that reality to exist. Not different by much, not enough to make a difference down the line, but not the same."

"Or us," I add. "In London. Until the whole body-meld thing happened, there were basically two of you—the past you and the present you—existing together. If—and it's still a big *if* at this point—Viktor really has hidden his soul to become immortal again, then it's possible he did figure out how to be like Koschei—by somehow placing it in Anastasia's matryoshka doll."

"So what you're saying is that this is hopeless." Tess dips her hand in her pocket, extracts a small elastic, and pulls her blond hair into a loose tail. The sun is up now, and I can see purple blotches of exhaustion under her eyes.

She goes on. "Think about all the possible places that doll was over time. And the Tsarina gave it to Anastasia, right? So it existed before then too. So let's just say that somehow, on some bizarre level, you guys are right. Viktor managed to find a way to be with a doll that technically doesn't exist anymore, rip out his soul, and stuff it in there, all without Baba Yaga knowing he's done this. Not that I'm buying it, but let's just say you're right. How do we find that right moment in time? That doll could be anywhere. So now we have to find it, destroy it, free his soul, and make him mortal again. Plus, did you ever think that it might not be just the doll? Maybe the doll is hidden inside something else. Did that ever occur to any of you?"

"Not to mention," Ben adds helpfully, "that even if by some miraculous turn of events, A: this is all true and B: you accomplish it, then what? It's not like this dude is stupid. Even if you destroy the doll and free his soul, all that means is that he's not invincible anymore. If this is a needle in a haystack, as you seem to think, then even if you succeed, Viktor could be anywhere by then."

"But he's not," I say. "Ben's right, Ethan. Viktor doesn't have to stay here. I know he's only been free for a few weeks. Who knows—maybe he's still planning what he wants to do. But he could go back to Russia, head to Europe, go anywhere he wants. Only here he is, stalking Tess and following us. Which makes me ask, 'Why?'"

The four of us ponder this as the sun continues to rise. The sky stays gray, the air humid. From over the lake, there's the vaguest rumble of thunder. My stomach clenches.

Why *has* Viktor hung around? Is it to stop me? Then why just stalk me? Why not confront me and get it over with? I'm not immortal. But if he is, then he's got nothing to lose. I could slice him through with a sword and he'd get up ticking. Or at least get up. There has to be a reason.

And then the other why, the part Ethan and I have still kept to ourselves. Why make Ethan powerful again? Why would Viktor loan out a piece of his magic? It makes no sense at all.

But at least this explains how Viktor was able to remove Lily's bullet from his chest. That's a step in the right direction.

"Well, I don't know about the rest of you," Tess says. She yawns hugely, and for one creepy second I think of Baba Yaga's jaw, stretching and unhinging to show those iron teeth. "But I'm wiped. We can stand here for the next million years coming up with possibilities, but honestly? Who the hell knows what Viktor did or thought while he was at Baba Yaga's. I say we all go to Ethan's and get some sleep. 'Cause unless things have changed since we got to IHOP, Anne's still kicked out of her house and no way am I going home alone. So I say daytime sleepover at Ethan's. Make s'mores. Take turns keeping guard. That kind of thing."

Ethan and Ben look lost in Tess ramble. But I'm not.

"You're a genius," I say, smacking a kiss on her forehead.

"Gross!" She swipes the spot with the back of her hand. "Don't get so excited. Ethan probably doesn't have marshmallows or graham crackers. We'll have to sit in his apartment, drink hot tea, and brood about the old days."

I snort a laugh. "No, you idiot. Don't you realize what you said?"

The only one except Viktor who knows what went on in Baba Yaga's hut is the witch herself.

I see the light go on in Ethan's head. "Oh no," he says. "It's too dangerous."

"Only way. Baba Yaga knows, Ethan. She may not be happy sharing, but she has to know. At least something. 'Cause let's face it—Viktor was mortal again when he offered himself up to her. And when he stepped out of her hut, he wasn't. Whatever he did, whenever that crucial moment was, it happened while he was her prisoner. And only one other besides him knows when that was."

As though the sky has heard me, thunder rumbles closer. To the east, a flash of lightning rips the early morning sky. Maybe she has heard me. Maybe I'm doing it on my own.

"I'm sick and tired of waiting, Ethan. Baba Yaga's right. I'm playing at this and playing at this while my friends are in danger and my family is totally falling apart. I'm the one who has to do something. I've always been the one—since this began. I mean, that's the point, right? So let me do it."

"Not alone. Not now."

"Then when? After something happens to Tess? After Lily comes back when I'm not around and convinces my mother to do something crazy? Or goes after my father? Or Ben? Or you? It's the same as it's been, Ethan. There's only one place to find the answers."

When the power begins to twist inside my belly, I let it. The forest doesn't scare me anymore. How can it? Since I made my bargain with Baba Yaga, it's part of me like it's part of her. I've resisted. I've ignored. I've pretended that this is going to go away. So what's happened? I've been dragged into the past on someone else's terms.

No more.

I lift my face to the sky. The storm rolls in because I bid it to. I've called her before, but out of desperation not strength. And it went badly because of it. I had to save Tess and Ben. I had to bring Ethan back from the dead.

Now my mother wants me to help her see her dead son. And Viktor wants us gone, hurt, dead—whatever he can accomplish. Lily, too, I realize as I raise my arms and feel the familiar heat of my magic crackle under my skin, fly to my fingertips. Lily, the pesky detail Viktor got wrong and is now paying for over and over. She didn't die like she was supposed to. She may be crazy and dangerous, but she doesn't deserve the fate she received. She lost her child—my mother—and then she lost herself forever.

Lily, who wasn't afraid of her magic but ended up punished because of it. A rusalka until her transformation can be avenged. Until Viktor's blood is shed.

It hadn't occurred to me. But now it does. He wants her dead too. How do you kill a Russian mermaid? I'm sure there's a story. There's always a story. That's the way my life goes now.

I summon the part of me that's Yaga's. Lightning etches the sky like a fingernail cutting a line. The sky splits open. I feel the magnetic pull of my power calling to its source.

"Anne, no!" Ethan's hands are on me, and then I feel Ben's. Powerful hands, gripping me. I shake them off. Ignore the dark surge of power pulsing from Ethan as I do.

Baba Yaga leans over the edge of the mortar. Her red

kerchief flutters in the wind. Her eyes glitter. Her hands clutch the edge of the huge black bowl separately from her body. "You have much to learn, girl. Are you finally willing to begin?"

I don't answer her. Just reach up my hand. Intuitively I know that this must be done on her terms. In her territory. One of her hands loosens its grip on the mortar and flings itself into the air, its enormous wrinkled fingers spread wide.

"No!" Tess screams. She grips me around the waist.

The disembodied hand hurtles earthward, impossibly fast. I push Tess off me. She hits the ground with a grunt. I have to do this alone. I'm convinced. Bringing anyone else with me will make her think I'm weak.

Somewhere, I hear Ethan shouting a spell. Feel his magic plow through the air toward the mortar. His thoughts are muddled, but the emotion comes through. Terror. Anger. Frustration.

Baba Yaga's hand grabs mine, rough skin rasping as it tightens around my hand, my arm. My feet scrape the pavement as I'm dragged forward. *Why not up? We need to go up to the mortar if that's how we're doing this.*

"Let go, Anne," Ethan yells. I hear his feet pounding the pavement behind me. Feel the swoosh in the air as he grabs for me but misses. Baba Yaga's hand tugs and I start to lift from the ground. But whatever Ethan is muttering—his own spell? Some part of Viktor's dark magic?—it's keeping Baba Yaga from pulling me to the mortar.

The witch leans over the impossibly large bowl, stirs the air with her giant pestle. The sleeve that waits for the hand holding me to return flaps empty in the wind. Thunder booms. Another streak of lightning cracks and sizzles.

My memory flashes to that horrible day on the beach. My

mother kneeling in the sand. Baba Yaga pulling me into the mortar. And what she said to me then about Ethan. *Here's what I did not expect, my girl. I did not expect you to love him.*

Why did she think that? I do love him. I've loved him since the beginning. It goes against everything rational in my brain, but I do. Only here's the problem: the fact that I love him and he loves me only makes things harder. How can I stop a crazy bad guy and a seriously disturbed rusalka when I'm worried about hurting the people I love? Maybe the real truth is that people like me don't really get a chance at love. It's just a cruel illusion. Loving Ethan makes me hesitate. And I can't do that right now.

"Stop it, Ethan," I shout to him. "I know. I know. This is nuts. I'm nuts. But let go. I've got to do this. Let me go, damn it."

My pulse kicks into overdrive. I could pull away. I should pull away. But something—some weird sense of honor or responsibility or love for the people I care about—propels me to continue. Is this what it's like when firefighters rush into a burning building? Are they as terrified as I am, even though they know that if they don't keep on going, all will be lost? How did I become this person? What power decided that I could handle it?

"Shit, Anne, don't." The words are Ben's. He's thrown himself into the mix. I risk a glance behind me. Ben and Ethan are running in tandem, both reaching for me. I don't see Tess. Where is Tess? The thought panics me and I try to block it out. *I have to do this. Tess will be fine.*

"It's time, daughter," Baba Yaga calls to me. "Time for you to use your gift. You know what to do. Just do it. And come to me." She laughs, a cruel sound that echoes in waves over the parking lot. One by one, the lights of the neon IHOP sign go dark, but not in order. HOP. HO. O. If I weren't clinging to a gross hand for my life, I'd find this funny.

For the first time, I don't think about the magic as it rises inside me. I just let it happen. Let it be part of me. Around me I weave a spell of protection. To keep Ethan from saving me. To keep Ben from saving me. I've been through that before. None of us needs a repeat.

The magic simmers low in my belly, fills me in a way I haven't allowed myself to feel. The elements are mine to control. This, I've learned, is the essence of Baba Yaga's magic. Of mine. I can stop waves—better now, I'd imagine. I can cause the wind to blow and fire to burn. I can make shriveled plants bloom on their vines. Some things I can't do. I brought Ethan back but only because there was a window of time. His lips were still warm. Air still lingered in his lungs. A few minutes more and the damage would have been permanent. There is still a natural order to things. Only so many rules that I can break. Always some consequence.

This is what I understand as my feet dangle almost comically above the IHOP parking lot, a huge wrinkled hand pulling me into the sky. And this: for the very first time, since I've used my magic, I think I kind of like it.

I close my eyes. Ignore the tugging sensation on my arm and the fear of flying with only this not-exactly-trustworthy witch's hand to keep me from falling.

Ethan's borrowed power is hugely strong. He just proved that in my backyard with Lily. If I hadn't been there to talk him down, who knows how far he would have gone.

But I'm strong too. Stronger maybe because the witch is

hovering above me and the connection between us feels like iron links. Maybe this witch thing isn't so bad.

I close my eyes and continue the spell I've started. Feel the air tighten behind me. Tighten and change form. An invisible wall is what I want. It's what I get. Ethan and Ben reach for me. I can feel the air bend as Ethan's magic attempts to ram through the barrier. I push back. Baba Yaga's hand slips a little and my feet scrape the ground again. So far we've avoided hitting parked cars, but now my hip collides with a Ford Explorer. Stinging pain shoots down my leg.

"*Atebis, babushka!*" Ethan shouts. He's so close that I think I can feel his breath on my arm.

Then smack. The wall of air solidifies. Ethan and Ben smash into it. The hand drags me forward, then slowly up. My heels, then the balls of my feet. Just the barest tips of my toes graze the cement.

Someone grabs my free hand just as I lift off again. Her nails dig into my palm as she tightens her grip. The one person I didn't think to block.

"Shit!" Tess hollers. "Don't you dare drop me."

Wednesday, 6:45 am

Ethan

D o something," Ben says. "Damn it, Ethan. We can't just let her take them."

I fumble for another spell. Do I have the power in me now to compel the witch to return? Even as I think it, the mortar disappears into the clouds. They're just gone.

"Let's go to the lake, then." Ben fishes keys from his pocket. "There's got to be a way to follow them. I'll drive. C'mon. That's how we ended up in that damn forest last time. At the lake. Maybe we can do it again. You're Magic Guy. You can figure it out, right?"

"Anne's the one who can access Baba Yaga's forest. Not me. It's never been me." Which, of course, is the problem.

"Viktor, then. You could find him, right? He controlled that witch, didn't he? Isn't that what you said? So he must know how to get to her forest. We need to go now. God knows what's going to happen there. Why the hell did Anne do that?"

I force myself to breathe. "Because she's Anne. Because she can. When Viktor used Anastasia the way he did, he created his own nemesis. Anne. It's what I never want to admit, but she and I both know that this can only end one way—with someone dead. Viktor. Anne. Me. You or Tess. Someone she loves.

Anne's gone because she doesn't want it to be one of us. And even if we could follow her, she's right. Our presence will only add more danger. Not just for us. But for her."

Ben's nostrils flare. The look in his eyes says that he hates me. "What then?"

We go after them anyway. We drive to the lake. We track down Viktor. I use whatever darkness keeps building in my veins and rip a hole in the sky and pull them back. This is what my brain is screaming.

But I tell Ben, "We wait. We stay together—safety in numbers. We swing by and check Anne's house. And Tess's. And yours—find out where your parents are. Make sure nothing weird is going on. Remember, Viktor's linked to Anne too. He may actually know what just happened here. I hope he doesn't. That would make things easier. But we can't be certain. So we need to be vigilant. Other than that, we wait. She'll make it back, Ben. They both will."

I say the words as though I know them to be the purest of truths.

Ben looks away. He knows bullshit when he hears it.

I set to work creating another spell. Cast my hands in the circle and work quickly to remove evidence of what just happened here. People's memories are fluid things, but a little magical push will help assure that. Like that horrible day when Anne and I found my friend Alex Olensky dying on the floor of his office. I used this spell then too. My hands shake a little as I say the words that need to be said. My dark borrowed power pushes the spell more intensely than I've felt before. A fear forms: Will Viktor's magic stop me? But I complete the spell without interruption. Some things inside me are still my own.

Ben watches in silence.

"They'll protect each other," I tell him. "Anne and Tess. We have to believe that."

We leave the rest unsaid. Is Ben in love with Anne? He won't pursue her. He's no fool. He's a strangely good match for Tess—both loyal to a fault. I have no interest in knowing his mind. I know only this: I've done many foolish things over the years, but there is one thing I did right. I fell in love with Anne the first time I saw her. I need to stay strong enough to deserve that love.

And then the thought: maybe I was never strong to begin with.

"All right." Ben studies the empty sky. The IHOP sign blinks back to life. "We wait."

"I would suggest a stronger plan of action."

Ben and I turn.

"And I would also suggest that we move quickly." It's my old friend Dimitri. He's leaning against a black Ford sedan, a wry look of amusement on his face, an unlit cigarette between his fingers. "That was quite the spectacle your girl and her witch just put on," he continues. "I see her time travel hasn't diminished her spirit. And don't look so shocked, Ethan. Did you really think I'd have let you walk out of that restaurant if you were the only one who'd regained some power?"

"Um," Ben says quietly. "Who the hell is that? And did he just say you have power again? When exactly were you and Anne going to mention this?"

I ignore Ben, keep my attention on Dimitri. His eyes are darker than they were when we met at the café. Not good.

"He's using us, you know?" Dimitri extracts a pack of

matches from his pocket and cups his hand as he lights the cigarette. He drops the match, still burning, to the cement. "I'm
assuming that if I've figured it out, so have you. You're many
things, Ethan, but you're not stupid."

I shrug. "I don't have time for this. If you want to tell me
something I don't know, then fine. I meant what I said to
you—I'm willing to work together until we stop him. I did not
say that I trusted you."

Dimitri walks closer, exhales smoke. Flicks ash into the still
heavy air.

"And I, Brother, did not say I trusted you. But I have done
what I promised. Although perhaps you are right. Your Anne
and her little friend are with the witch. I suppose this isn't the
time for small talk."

"And yet here we are," I say blandly. "Like two grandmothers
around a fire."

Above us, there's the faint echo of thunder. More than anything, I want to look up. But in this game we're playing, I refuse
to be the first to blink.

"You've left a trail of magic a mile wide, Ethan," Dimitri
says. "In the old days, you would never have been so careless. Then again, in the old days, we had our own power, not
Viktor's scraps. This is what I keep turning over and over. Why
would someone who wants the world at his fingertips gift the
two of us with part of his power? That seems odd, doesn't it?"

He pulls cigarettes from his pocket, offers. "I'm glad to see
you still have a few vices," he says, when I slip one from the
pack. "I make it a policy never to trust a man who has no vices."

I reach for matches. Ben extends his hand to Dimitri. "I'm
Ben. And you are?"

Dimitri cocks his head as if Ben has fallen from the sky. "Perhaps," he says, "it is time for a little demonstration."

He flicks his remaining half-cigarette to the ground. Flicks a finger. The ashes ignite. The flame travels a swift path toward Ben.

"Hey!" Ben dances back. The flames follow, lick at his feet.

"Enough." Cigarette still between my fingers, I spread my hands. Concentrate. The flames lower. Disappear. "Point taken."

Dimitri chuckles. Studies Ben. "This one must be Anne's, yes? I suppose we wouldn't want to damage him."

Inside me, power pushes against my will. The urge to let it free careens wildly. Images flash—none of them mine, yet rising full-grown: Ben, motionless on the ground. Dimitri, hands pressed to his slit belly, his intestines spilling out. The rusalka swirling in a whirlpool, her mouth open in a silent scream.

Something urges me to let it rage. Instead, I push the power back below the surface. And decide to resort to the truth.

"Viktor's hidden his soul." Has Dimitri understood this as well? "Like Koschei—the story we all heard as children. The Deathless wonder. Unkillable until his soul is set free to return to him. It's why Anne's gone to Baba Yaga's. She thinks the answers are in the hut somehow. Some clue to explain how he did it or where it's hidden."

Dimitri arches a brow. "And so it comes back to that every time, eh? Our eternal lives in the hands of a girl. I'm sure the irony is not lost on you. But my question still stands. Why give us part of what makes him strong? Here is what I think, Ethan. Because he has to. Because whatever it is he's done, however he's managed to divest himself of that which once again makes him human, he needs us still."

"But for what?"

"I don't know," Dimitri says. "But I have a feeling we'd better find out before he decides to use us. And I know exactly how we can do that."

"Oh?"

"Ask him face-to-face."

In Baba Yaga's Forest, Wednesday

ANNE

My stomach pitches as Baba Yaga's detached hand hoists us through darkening clouds to the mortar, then above it.

"Don't drop me!" Tess screeches.

"Hang on! Holy crap, Tess. You're slipping. Hold my damn hand."

We're right above the middle of the mortar, but the hand drags us higher. Baba Yaga tips her red scarf-covered head back and smiles, her iron teeth glinting in the lightning.

We fall. Not descend, just plummet. The hand is still holding me and I'm still gripping Tess—still screaming—but we fall fast. We slam facedown into the mortar—Tess first, then me. I smack down so hard that my breath seizes in my chest and I see tiny black dots.

I groan and roll over and suck in painful, rasping breaths as my lungs refill with air. Baba Yaga drapes her arm with the flapping sleeve over the side of the mortar, and the hand shoots back up and reattaches.

The storm disappears, but not the clouds.

Tess. She's saying something, but my ears are still ringing and my head throbs with each jackrabbit beat of my heart. We link fingers and stand. I touch my pulsing forehead. My fingers graze a bump the size of a small egg from where my head hit the mortar.

Baba Yaga swivels to face us. Her mouth is huge, her chin solid and muscular, the bones jutting against her ancient skin in the spots where I've seen her jaw drop and unhinge. Both hands now back in her sleeves, she reaches for us and smooths a sandpapery palm across each of our foreheads. In unison, we recoil, but there's no place to go. The mortar is sticky under my feet. I try not to think about what it's sticky with.

"What say you, Daughter Anne?" Baba Yaga glowers at me with her black eyes. Tess squeezes my hand—hard.

"I'm not your daughter, Yaga. Never was. Never will be. But I am asking for your help again. And willing to return to your forest."

Baba Yaga smiles, and the wrinkles etched into her leathery brown skin deepen into canyons. I watch my reflection in her iron teeth—my hair all tangled, my eyes huge and darker than they're supposed to be, my mouth fixed in a straight line. I look old—well, older.

The air around us shimmers. I blink. We're in the forest as though we've always been there. The hut breathes in and out in front of us. The chicken legs claw at the ground. The skulls on the fence glow, lighting up their empty eye sockets. I hear a hissing and then a meow and Baba Yaga's *koshka*, which I know now is Russian for *cat*, slithers out of a shadowy corner and flicks its pink tongue at us.

"I don't want to be here," Tess says under her breath. It is a little late for her to come to this particular conclusion.

Baba Yaga smiles again. "I can arrange for you to be gone."

We move the party inside the hut, the huge wooden door closing behind us with a thud that makes my pulse jump.

The room is as it was the last time I saw it, as it always is in my dreams: wooden floor, narrow bed, table, chairs, and a deep fireplace in the corner. Floating in the center of the fire, a bleached white skull grins at us. Flames lick the centers of what used to be eyes.

I shiver, gooseflesh prickling my skin. Tess rubs her hands over her arms. The room feels icy even though a fire roars in the fireplace only a few steps away.

Baba Yaga flicks one enormous, leather-skinned wrist. The sleeve of her brown dress ripples as her hand detaches and scuttles across the wooden floor. Tess blinks. Suddenly, I can't breathe, can't swallow. The hand is wrapped around my throat, the fingers squeezing like giant snakes.

"If I killed you right here—just because I can—would it still be worth it for you to have come? Imagine, girl. You dead. Your Tess keeping me company. Is this what you want? Think, Anne. So much that you should be doing. So much that you have promised me. You are not the girl you were. You will not be her again. Desire does not make things so. Look at me and know this."

I don't want to look at her. I absolutely do not. The hand turns my head, and then the pressure is so great that I can't even close my eyes. My vision starts to go spotty again—more little black dots flickering everywhere. I tell myself not to pass out. I need to keep Tess safe. I need to—

She squeezes my neck tighter. I remember that horrible moment on the El train last fall when Viktor tried to kill me. It felt like this, didn't it? Somewhere I think I hear Tess screaming.

"You have questions, girl. I know this. What did I see? What did I know? Perhaps you think me the fool. Your Viktor managed to get the best of me, you think. Here I am, his captor, the mighty Baba Yaga, and yet he escapes. With your help, of course, but not the same as when he entered my forest. Perhaps I will answer you, daughter. Perhaps I will eat your friend. Grind her bones between my teeth while you watch.

"Time will tell, as it always does in my hut. But first this: you know only what I am now and what I was before. Let me show you the in between, girl. The thing I am. The thing the Victor and his Brotherhood and even your silly Ethan diluted when they compelled me to protect Anastasia. Look. Listen. Learn. You will see me. You will be me."

I try to look away, but it's hopeless. I sink into her gaze, deeper and deeper. Then it's like when I used to dream I was Anastasia. The piece that's me and the piece that's the witch soften and meld until I can't tell what's me and what's her. The story that unfolds is familiar. Then it creeps into places she has not let me see. Like my journeys to the past, I think before my thoughts are only hers. Returning again and again as long-hidden secrets rise. The dark parts that lie in all of us. The ones we never share.

I sit in this same hut, staring into my fire. It warms me, but not enough. Never, ever enough. I used to love the sun on my face, I think. I used to run in the woods and pick bright yellow and pink flowers to make wreaths and necklaces. But one day it wasn't enough. Maybe it never was. This is what I think now as I rock in my chair and my koshka winds himself around my ankles. As the fire crackles and burns, and the skull that was once the head of an enemy hovers in the flames.

Beauty betrayed me. Or perhaps I betrayed myself. In my mind, I see the man that I loved, the one I gave myself to, completely and joyfully. He is tall and his brown hair is thick when I stroke it. His cheekbones are sharp and his face thin, his green eyes thoughtful. He has long fingers that set sparks in my skin when he touches me. I remember the feel of his lips as they press against my cheek, my neck, my mouth. Did I love him? I no longer know what this word means. What does it mean to love someone—to be loved in return?

I only know the anger that burned in me when I saw his hands stroking another woman's face. Had he ever really seen me? Loved me? His child was just barely planted in me at that moment. Not even a full month, but I knew. I pressed my hands against my still flat belly. When I told him, he shrugged. "That is your business, Yaga," he said.

This is how things were then, in the old days. The child was my concern, not his.

I wept for a very long time. But nothing changed. Tears do not have power. Only actions do. I had always known I was different. Even then, when we lived close to nature, I was closer. The elements had always felt a part of me—my herbs grew more lushly, deer ate from my outstretched hand. My journey to the Old Ones did not take me long.

"Be certain," they told me. "We do not give this gift often. Its price is steep."

Inside me, I felt his child flutter. I was certain. I would give up my beauty for the power they offered. I would do it with a willing heart. I would teach this child my ways, not his.

The pain was enormous. It ripped through me, over me, inside me. All change comes with pain, but I had never known something like this. In the end I lay alone in the forest. I crawled to the stream and stared at my reflection. A monster stared back. Eyes black as pitch. Nose long and hooked under as though it wanted to meet my lips. I pulled them back into a smile. My teeth glinted in the water. I reached up to run my finger over them. They were iron, now, dark gray. Inhuman. My skin, once the smooth color of almonds, was now dark and wrinkled. Age spots, huge as saucers, covered my body.

I looked down at my hands. They were huge, each knotted knuckle the size of a walnut. When the first hand slipped from my wrist and dropped into the stream, then flicked its fingers and scuttled back onto the ground at my feet, I felt myself sway on the verge of unconsciousness.

The hunger came next—huge as the new body that housed the woman who used to be me. I stumbled to my feet. My new hand marched on fingertips up my leg and angled itself back to my wrist. The reattachment burned, but I was too ravenous to feel it.

I came to the apple tree first, studded in small blooms that would not be fruit for weeks. I slammed into it, wrapped my arms around the trunk. Apples. Apples. Full, lush, red. I ripped them off the branches, bit into their flesh, the juice running down my face, sweet and sticky. I ate until the tree was empty. And still I craved more.

It was then that I remembered the child inside me. The image of the tiny baby mixed in my mind with the red, red of the apples. Perhaps if it was a girl, I would call her Rose. The apples were a sign. Her tiny cheeks would be red and plump. I pressed my hands to my stomach, those ugly, hideous monster hands that were now mine, the ones which had just climbed the apple tree to pluck the highest branches for the fruit I'd devoured, seeds and core and all.

Was it my new self that told me? Or would I have known even as I used to be? The child was gone. Not miscarried, not born. Not ripped away. Just simply absent. It was then that I began to understand the price of what I had asked. To be more than human was to be less than human. I had stepped into a different forest. There would be no going back. I do not know how long I wept.

The hunger returned, sharper than before. I stumbled through the *forest, wound my way in the direction of my home. But I could not cross the stream. I could wade almost to the opposite shore, close enough that I could almost touch it. But not quite. I stood in the water, the bottom of my dress soaked and heavy. The sun beat down on my head. Somehow the heat made the hunger worse.*

In my pocket was an old red scarf. I wrapped it around my head, tied it under my chin with clumsy fingers, pulled it forward to hide my face in its shadows. It was then that I saw him—a boy of about six or seven, walking along the opposite shore.

"Babushka!" he called to me, and I knew how I looked to him—a grandmother, an old woman. The hunger grew even more.

"Babushka," he said again. "Are you stuck? Do you need help?"

I nodded, keeping my face half hidden in my red scarf. My empty belly growled. He waded to me. Held out his firmly fleshed little hand. My own hands were stuffed into the pockets of my dress. I waited until he came closer, too close to escape. I remember that he smelled sweet and young and juicy as the apples.

I devoured him whole. My mouth opened, my jaw dropped impossibly wide. I reached for him with those hideous hands and stuffed him inside me. He had offered help but I had not wanted any. He had been kind. I ate him anyway. His bones crunched between my teeth. My heart beat wildly with each bite. The part of me that remembered what it was to be human tried to resist. The power I had welcomed did not hesitate.

Afterward I cried again. It was the last time I would ever weep. Back in the forest, I built my hut. Manipulated wood and stones to form a structure. Once I had raised chickens for meat and eggs. Now I placed my hut atop two enormous enchanted chicken legs. Function and amusement. My home would move from place to place. I would outwit my enemies, especially those who would see this strange hut and think it less for its appearance. I would know better. I would know all.

The heads of my enemies began to line my fence. Each skull placed neatly on a pike as though I was planting sunflowers. The legends had begun by them, most of them true. The Russians called me Baba Yaga. Auntie Yaga. The name was a dark humor. I was not benevolent Auntie, stirring soup and boiling potatoes. I was Baba Yaga—the most powerful witch that ever lived. The Death Crone. The Bone Mother.

This is what I remember as I sit before my fire. This is what I know as I rock in my chair. This is—

The connection between me and the witch breaks. Well, mostly. I'm half in and half out of her head. Rocking in the hut, thinking her thoughts—and standing in the hut awake, with her hands squeezing the last bit of breath out of my lungs.

I can barely see, and I definitely can't breathe, but I understand anyway. What I am now. What I'm capable of. I'm not her, not yet and maybe not ever, but I've got a piece of her.

I let that piece—dark and angry—rise inside me. Rip her hands from my neck. She makes a surprised cry as one hand stays attached to her wrist and the other flies across the room. It lands on the wooden floor, turning in confused circles before scuttling back to her arm. She's watching it when I rake my nails down her cheek. Blood oozes dark and red.

The hut ripples with energy. Mine. Hers. The flames in the fireplace grow so bright and hot that sweat beads on my forehead, drips down my back. We stand facing each other, me and Baba Yaga. The cut on her face heals almost instantly. She laughs. Her breath is hot and horrible.

Next to me, a small whimper. Only then do I realize Tess is still standing at my side.

"Anne?" Her voice a tiny question. I shove her behind me.

"I get it," I tell Baba Yaga. I'm shaking with anger and fear and a whole bunch of other emotions that I don't have time to name. I hate her.

"I get it. You can stop choking me and all the rest of it. I get it. You've given me something awful. But I asked for it, didn't I? Just like you did. So now what? Wait for me to get hungry?"

The witch smiles slowly. "So now you ask. And then you move on. Stop Viktor as you promised. Free your silly grandmother from her rusalka spell."

"Whatever. You've just made it clear that it's more than that. I'll do what you want but it won't matter. Like you and the Old Ones. You didn't control that bargain, did you?" In my head I see her eating that little boy whole. Correction: I see her doing it through her eyes, like it was me. And let me say this is so disgusting that I will possibly never eat again. I can still taste little boy bones in the back of my throat.

She exhales more foul breath in my face. Tess peeps her head around my side, and I elbow her back.

"Ask," Baba Yaga says. "The questions that you did not have before. I cannot tell unless you ask."

"Oh, for God's sake." Tess is shaking, but she steps forward again. "She's changing the rules as she goes along." I elbow her again and hope that I don't get pissed off enough that I end up biting off her arm or something.

I swallow. Find my voice. "How did he compel you?" I ask softly. Then again, louder: "How did Viktor do it? You must know. You give me this whole vision of you, and yet here you are—just as stuck as I am. So how? That's my first question."

Her eyes study mine. She traces one wide finger over my eyebrows. My eyes close, and briefly, she strokes the lids. I try not to shudder. Tell my thundering heart that I shouldn't be afraid.

The pressure of her finger lifts, and I open my eyes. Tess is still tucked against me not saying a word. Is she too scared? Or has the witch done something to her voice? I don't dare take my gaze away long enough to check.

"How do people get what they want? Force. Flattery. The illusion that they are either powerful or indispensable. Kindness, sometimes. And do not look so shocked, Daughter Anne. Even I still know what it is to be kind. To be thankful."

Oh, right. Who would she need to thank? And even worse, now that I've seen into her head, why would she ever feel thankful again? Because she's alive? Because she's powerful?

I do my best to sound calm. Nonchalant. I've fought back, after all. Give me magic and don't be surprised when I use it. "So. Which one was it? Or don't you know?"

Tess digs her nails into my arm.

"Sometimes, daughter, we get what we want only because someone else believes she will profit."

I let this sink in. Baba Yaga holds my gaze again, so deeply and so fiercely that for a second or two, I think that she's going to burrow her memories into my head again. Make me be her. But she just smiles and waits.

The words tumble out. Suddenly it's like I must say them; I must know. "What did you think you could gain from him? You were already manipulating him, weren't you? Taking out your vengeance on his mother, Marina, or something like that? She came crawling to you to ask you to give her illegitimate son the power he deserved and you told her okay, knowing all the time that down the road, some of that power is going to seep through to his descendants, including me. All of whom are going to be girls because somehow you knew how to make that happen. You already set him up so that his own need for power would defeat him—which, let me add, hasn't exactly worked like you planned since he's still out there roaming around making my life a living hell. So what could you possibly want from him?"

Her silence wraps around me, filling the hut with unspoken answers and questions yet to be asked—mine and hers. The memories she forced me to share with her tunnel deeper, sink into my skin, my pores, my everything.

She had eternity spinning out in front of her. What could Viktor give her? What had she wanted?

The answer comes not from Baba Yaga, but from my own heart, beating furiously in my chest. The painful images return, just as she's shared them. Without thinking, I press my hands to my belly like I'd felt her do in my head. That horrible moment when she understood the price of her power. The daughter she would never have. The one she dreamed of naming Rose.

"How could you?" I ask her. I don't want to cry in front of her, but this is what happens. Hot, angry tears well in my eyes.

"Forever is a long time," she says.

"*You* chose forever," I tell her. "You. Not her. Not Anastasia. How could you do that to her? You're not totally evil, you know. You have choices. Okay, a lot of them are gross, but even so. Screw with Viktor—that's one thing. Hurt a girl who never asked anything from you? Why? My God. All this time I'm thinking only Viktor could be cruel enough to use someone whose only sin was loving him like a brother. But no. Now it's you too. And you know what? I think what you did is even worse."

"Anne." Tess tugs on my arm. I can see in her eyes that she understands. "Anne. Anastasia was going to die, remember?"

"So?" My throat is so tight that I have to force the word out. "Shit happens. Haven't we all seen that lately? People die. History is full of bodies. It sucks, but it happens."

I turn back to Baba Yaga. Her face is enigmatic, her eyes giving away nothing while mine are full of tears. "Coming here—it was worse than death. And why? So you could relive the whole Vasilisa story like in the fairy tales? Pretend you had a daughter? Pretend you were a mother and not just a witch who let some jerk use her so he could live forever? I hate you right now. I hate you more than I've hated anything. More than I hate Viktor, and that's saying something.

"And you know what else I hate? That I'm stuck with you forever too. In a different way from Anastasia, but it amounts to the same thing, doesn't it? You're right about one thing, though. No one does anything just to do it. I gave myself to you so I could save Ethan. You know, the guy you think I'm too afraid to love. Maybe that's the lesson here. Sacrifice is a load of crap. Everyone wants something. And I guess we all get what we deserve."

She watches me impassively, her eyes still giving nothing away. Do I have what it takes to ask my other question? Will she answer?

"Anne," Tess whispers. "No. Is that what you think? You're wrong. It doesn't matter what she did. What you promised her. You're not her. You never will be. Don't let her get in your head."

"Your friend is a nuisance." So swiftly that I don't even see her hand move, Baba Yaga slices one long nail down Tess's face. Blood speckles in a line down Tess's cheek. One dot, then two, then more than I can count. The skin splits apart in slow motion, the cut far deeper than it looks at first. Tess opens her mouth—a perfect O of shock. Then she presses her lips together, a tight seam. The skin around her lips whitens. She is refusing to scream.

"You cut me. I cut her. My rules, girl. I have allowed you here to ask your questions. But one thing will never change. Nothing is without cost. My own story confirms this. It is the way of nature. You take and you must give. I know you understand this. I am like the world that gives me my power. It is not cruelty, just the way things work. You cannot spill my blood without blood spilling in return. Yours. Hers. Someone's. I allowed Viktor to use me so I could use Anastasia. I have paid for that weakness many times over. But never more than what it was worth. That is how my forest works."

I reach to press my hand to Tess's wound to heal her.

Baba Yaga's arm is faster. Her hand tightens around my wrist, a vise of pain.

"No. She has bled on your behalf before. Clearly she is willing. Let her bleed until we are done. You are a powerful girl, Anne. Use that power on your emotions. It is a lesson you will need. Look where your anger got you, unchecked. You let your fury at Lily, at that worthless rusalka, guide your actions. You opened the door to the hut. Not fully, but enough. Viktor went free. I know what you will ask me next. It is the only possible question. But know this, no matter what my answer, true or a lie, he could not have used anything he managed to gain unless you let him free. You are complicit, girl. Just as I am. Oh, you think yourself more. Your friend whispers this in your ear. But only you know the truth of what lies inside."

What lies inside me right now as the strange odors of the hut filter into my lungs—spices and tea and earth and death—is this: I've been walking around so absolutely certain that I am not a person capable of taking a life. Right this second, I think that's a lie.

I force myself to push the thought aside. I have other business now.

"Viktor's been gone for weeks now," I say. "You've had time to think—at least when you weren't shipping me off to get some lesson from the past. So tell me. How did he do it? I'm assuming you know what we do. He hid his soul. We're thinking in Anastasia's matryoshka doll. So how? When? And where the hell do you think that doll is?"

Baba Yaga's laughter echoes against the walls of the hut. The cat—*koshka*—skids toward her from whatever corner it's been hiding in. She bends, lowers herself impossibly in a movement that is at once bulky and graceful, and strokes its head. It closes those yellow gleaming eyes and purrs with pleasure.

"Souls are tricky things, daughter. They are not easily taken and not easily divested. Of course, you must understand—it has been centuries since I relinquished my own to the Old Ones. Theologians convince humans that the soul goes one place or another. But like everything I have taught you, things are not that simple. It is the oldest of tricks—far older than I or even those who gave me my power. Remove the essence and the body waits for its return. Mortality hangs in the balance until that which gives humans their humanity is once again in place."

"I get all that." My gaze shifts to Tess's bleeding face. But I form my words calmly, like I've got all the time in the world. "But how did he manage to do it, do you think?"

She shrugs one giant shoulder. Her joints crack—a powerful snapping sound, like the warning boom that signals the beginning of an avalanche.

"How is not important. What's done is done. The question is where. Maybe the doll. Maybe something else. This will be for you to discover."

I gape at her. "No. You need to tell me. You have to tell me. I have no idea what you're going to want from me in the future. Isn't that enough? If I destroy him, won't that make you happy anyway?"

"Will it please you?"

"Stop with the damn questions. Just tell me."

"A story, then."

"Let me heal Tess."

"After."

We growl at each other—really, that's how it sounds. But she gets her way. We seat ourselves at her table. She places a mug of tea at each of our places—hers, mine, Tess. Tess holds a hand to her cheek. Blood seeps between her fingers. Drips into her cup of tea.

Baba Yaga takes a long slurp of tea. She swallows, the liquid flowing audibly down her throat like water swirling in a drain.

"As you say, daughter, forever is a long time. The things I once was, once dreamed of being—they were gone. Eventually, certain desires eased. I was lonely, yes, but time—even here—has a way of filling the gaps. Years do not pass as years but as days, moments, seconds. I found ways to control my hunger. I picked my victims thoughtfully. The greed of the thing I'd become settled into a routine.

"Still there were moments when I found myself thinking of

the girl I once was. Almost as though I dreamed of a stranger, I remembered her smooth skin, her bright eyes, her shiny dark hair that glinted hints of gold in the sunlight. That girl had desires, appetites. And sometimes in the remembering, I understood that there were ways to satisfy them. I could force matters, certainly. Or use my power to glamour my appearance. Show myself only when my needs were filled and I had no more need to hide my true nature. A certain pleasure is to be had from the fear on a man's face when he understands that his lover is not who he believed she was.

"And then I came upon Koschei. Monsters we were. Both exchanging our human frailties for the promise of power, of life everlasting. We fell upon each other like two starved animals.

"For a while.

"Eventually, I saw him for what he was. Do not think me hypocritical or blind to my own truths. I knew what I was, just as I know now. But Koschei was different. He had always been an evil thing—just in human form. Taking what he wanted, who he wanted. Like the man whose betrayal had loosed my own desire for power. The one who never knew and would not have cared about the child I lost when I turned. Here is where we parted ways: Koschei always believed that he deserved to be the Deathless. And there is a recklessness that comes with such arrogance. For when one is absolutely certain that he will never suffer defeat, he sets his own downfall in motion.

"You have read the tales about me. Not a single one mentions my demise. Always, I return. I may be tricked. I may be evaded. But no one mentions a plan for my destruction."

Baba Yaga leans across the table. Her enormous face looms next to mine, our foreheads touching. Her breath makes me want to puke. Bile rises in my throat, burning my tongue as it spills upward into my mouth and burns again when I swallow it back.

"I will not give you the answers you desire. But understand this. Viktor believes himself to be Koschei resurrected. In all ways, this is how he presented himself to me when he was my captive. For a time, I thought him quite delightfully mad. For a while, I hated him. Either way, I was willing to use him and he was willing to be used.

"You already know the folklore. Koschei hid his soul inside a needle, hidden in an egg, stuffed into a duck, placed in a hare, then locked in a box as iron as my teeth, and buried under a tree on an island. That is how the story goes. You, of anyone, should know that stories are only that. Your travels to the past—have they not shown you that memories are malleable? That truth has many guises?

"Viktor thinks himself to be Koschei, but know this, girl, he is not Koschei. Not exactly. He is a man who has found another way to cheat death. And death can only be cheated for so long. The natural order, girl. Remember. You must follow truth. The doll is only part of it. Koschei's story is not truth—it is only a reflection of it. To know how to find Viktor's soul is to understand what he most desires. As I have asked you. As you have answered."

Baba Yaga pauses for another gulp of tea. She drains the cup, slams it on the table. The sound echoes through the wood. The walls of the hut shudder in and out like they're breathing. Below my feet on the wooden floor, a skittering vibration. The chicken legs must be running. Taking us who knows where.

Really, I want to strangle her. If I could, I would. Questions.

Riddles. Circles and circles and what? Tess still bleeding and me still sitting here listening to a crazy witch babbling.

"Here is the rest of it—all I will say. I used Viktor and he used me. I learned what he wanted, but he also saw my failings." She points to the fireplace. The skull glows; the flames leap wildly inside it, around it. I see my own face, Ethan's, Anastasia's. She walks with her sisters. Her brother. Then the flames darken, the visions dissolve into smoke.

"I missed her," Baba Yaga says. Her gaze is locked on the skull in the fireplace. "I mourned for her. I had not thought it possible and it was happening. Her memories that I had pulled from her to keep her mind in shadows, I went to them once she was gone. The past, Anne. You are a smart girl. You have already understood that the answers lie there. You must pick the rest of your journeys carefully. Only you can do this."

I slam my fists on the table. "But you've sent me. First me and Tess, then Ethan and me."

"Perhaps. Perhaps not. Maybe you have sent yourself."

In a sudden quick motion, she wraps her fingers around my wrist. Lifts my hand and slaps it against Tess's still bleeding cheek.

"Hey!" Tess yelps.

I feel the magic flood from my body into Tess's wound. When I lift my hand, her skin is smooth and unharmed. I take Tess's hands in mine. Her face is pale and sweaty, and her blond hair is plastered in thin strands to her head.

"You're okay," I murmur. "I'm sorry it took so long. God, Tess, I'm so sorry."

"I'm fine," she whispers. "Really."

I push my chair back. Stand.

The memories of Anastasia fill me. She is so much a part of this place, a part of what's happening to us, what keeps happening over and over as though it needs to repeat itself until I get it right. I've failed her. I saved her and then sent her back to die. Viktor used her. Baba Yaga used her. Just as they've used Lily. Used me.

I see her sitting on the bed in the corner. Holding her doll. Sweeping this floor. Bringing sweet tea to the witch. Staring into the fire that still burns just inches from where I am now. Why was she here in the first place? Because she thought she could save her family.

In my head, I see her as I once dreamed—talking to Viktor. *I promise you*, he says to her. *I give you my word.*

Where would someone hide his soul? It's not quite the right question, is it? Where would Viktor hide his soul? What memory of Anastasia's would he slip into?

One with which he was already familiar.

One that allowed him access to her, to the Alexander Palace, to the Tsar—the father who kept him hidden like Viktor was about to do with his soul. That's what a man like Viktor would think. Not enough to just hide it. But to hide it in a place that represented everything he wanted but never got.

A place like the room he was coming out of when Ethan and I got zapped to the palace and I decided that my date to the Cubs game was more important.

Really? Is it possible that I'm just that stupid?

Um, maybe.

"Yaga!" I shout. I grab Tess's hand. "Are you telling the truth? I can go where I want? Come back as I choose?"

"Always," she says, her dark, skull-filled eyes still focused deep within the fireplace. "Do you not understand, daughter, how much of myself I have given to you? Are you so afraid of your own power that you would deny having mine?"

"Why wouldn't I? Viktor's done the same to Ethan, you know? Stuffed him full of something dark. Why should I trust you?"

Baba Yaga turns then, her face huge and lined and hideous. "If this has happened as you say, then you have even less time than I thought. He is not me, child. Believe or not. That is your choice. You think I have taken choice away from you. I have not. Go. Do this thing that needs doing. But hurry. The darkness stirs everywhere, in everything. It cannot be contained much longer."

She stretches her hands to the fire. I grip Tess's hand tighter.

"You ready?" I ask her.

"Oh no," Tess says. "You've got to be kidding me."

"Close your eyes," I tell her. "And hang on."

My own eyes are open when the hut contracts and folds. When Tess and I move forward into time and space.

And when we land on our asses in the snow—in front of the Alexander Palace.

Wednesday, 9:25 am

Ethan

F<small>ACE-TO-FACE</small>?" I <small>ECHO</small> D<small>IMITRI'S</small> <small>WORDS</small>. "A<small>ND</small> <small>EXACTLY</small> how do you plan on achieving that?" *Just yesterday you seemed shocked that Viktor was alive. Perhaps not so shocked after all.*

"There are ways, Ethan."

"A tracking spell?" We'd used them over the years—with varying degrees of success—as we searched for the girl who could save Anastasia. Now, of course, I know that only I was really trying.

"Something like that. It's the modern age now. Magic takes its own fascinating forms." He reaches into his pocket. Pulls out an iPhone.

"There's an app for this?" Ben peers at the phone.

Dimitri chuckles. "It's magic, boy, not the movies. My guess is that he hasn't strayed far from us. I don't know if he can't, or if he won't. Don't you feel it, Ethan? You should, Brother. It's how I found you here, you know. What can track one can track the other. Whatever magic he's given us, it's sensing its source. You two can stand here in this parking lot and wait for the little woman and her friend. Or you can come with me and push this thing into motion."

"But they'll be back soon." Ben's voice is steady but his tone urgent. "You end up where you start, right? So what—they come back and we're just gone? No way. You want to leave? Fine. I'll swing by Anne's and Tess's. Check on their parents. Then I'll come back here and wait. When I've got them, we'll find you."

"Not safe, Ben," I tell him.

"For who? Me? You? Don't you get it? We're already screwed. All of us. Just by this whole situation. Go ahead, tell me I'm wrong. Tell me this is all going to work out. It's a lie, man. You think you love her. But you let her go without you. And then you stand here and give me this bull about how going would be more dangerous. Dangerous for who?"

Ben turns to Dimitri. "So what the hell is the phone for?"

Dimitri grins. "This."

He taps a number. Presses the phone to his ear. "Brother," he says. "It is I. Dimitri." He pauses, listening. Then: "Of course. You had prepared me last fall, yes? That when you returned, I would know it. Feel it. You are well, then? I am glad to hear it. I have waited for you, Brother. It is a relief to know that you are alive and well." Dimitri listens again, nods. "The usual place, I assume?"

He listens some more, then ends the call. Gestures to me and Ben.

"One of you or both of you. I have no particular preference. He'll meet us downtown by the Art Institute. During the past few years, he's gained a fondness for that park—the one with the curved steel sculpture. A public space with lots of people so as not to call attention to ourselves. And don't look so shocked, Ethan. I still want him dead. I'm just a pragmatist. Did you think our meeting meant that Viktor and I had broken ties? Even you couldn't possibly be so naïve. Contingency plans, Ethan. Did you honestly believe I wouldn't have one?"

Ben's eyes widen. "Just like that? You called Viktor. What kind of idiots do you think we are?"

The kind that have no choice but to go with him, I think. *And he knows it.*

"He still trusts you, then?" I ask Dimitri.

Dimitri shrugs. "I took a chance. He did not sound surprised. Other than that, I have no idea. After I met with you, I started to check his old haunts. He has an apartment here, you know. But it was empty. Still, I felt his presence. So I took a calculated gamble. If indeed he believes himself to be invincible, it may explain why he'd take the chance of showing himself. Of talking to me. Why not? We can't harm him."

"I'll go," I say. "Just me."

Ben nods—a quick jerk of the chin.

"Keep them safe," I tell him. "Bring her back to me. I have to do this, Ben." But it is not what I want to do. And if I am certain of nothing else, I know it will go badly. How could it not?

I scan the sky. Nothing. They're in Baba Yaga's forest still; I'm sure of it. The link between me and Anne weakened, and I knew she'd crossed the boundary. It takes every ounce of control that I have to go with Dimitri rather than wait for Anne to return. But we need to take the fight where it belongs.

I move to go. Then find myself hesitating. There is no time, but I do not trust him and I will never trust him. And so I ask, "Why? Why help me?" If that's what he is doing.

The expression on his face is strange and undecipherable. The combativeness leaves his voice. "Yesterday I told you that I believed in happy endings. Maybe once."

"What changed?"

"Viktor took the only thing I ever cared about. The only person I ever truly loved."

I wait for him to finish, suddenly knowing what he is going to say.

"Anastasia," Dimitri says. "You want to understand why I'm willing to join forces with you? This is why. She didn't only trust Viktor. She trusted me. I told her someone would come for her. When it was all over and the Romanovs were saved. That Viktor or I or you would come. Only after did I under-stand what we'd done. By then it was too late. And the worst part? I never told her. Just accepted what he promised me. That if I helped him do this thing, then he'd bring us together. She was his sister, after all. And she cared for him. What cause would I have not to believe him? Later, he told me. Later there would be time."

He laughs, a bitter sound. "Funny, eh? Time was what we ended up with. All the time in the world, but no one to share it with."

Has he told us the truth? Maybe. At least this part of it.

"Go," Ben says. "Go. I can't fight Viktor. But you can. Go. I'll be here. And Anne and Tess? Not even that wicked witch can stop those two. Trust me. When they get back, I'll keep them safe until we can meet up."

"I'm counting on it," I tell him.

In Alexander Palace
outside St. Petersburg,
Definitely Not Present Day

Anne

WE ARE SERIOUSLY GOING TO DIE, AREN'T WE?" TESS brushes snow off her butt. I do the same. We're both wearing jeans and T-shirts and flip-flops. In the snow. It is entirely possible that we will freeze to death before we manage to do anything of value.

"Would you stop saying that?"

"Only when you stop dragging me into life-and-death situations. It was bad enough to smack my face in the dirt when we thought the Cossacks were chasing us. But that was like a walk in the park compared to letting that crazy witch slice open my face." She runs a finger over her cheek. "Do you have any idea how much I wanted to scream? But I wasn't going to give her the satisfaction."

I kiss Tess on the cheek. "You're the best. And I'm sorry."

"Talk is cheap." Tess rubs her hands over her arms. Stomps snow off her feet. "So where to? Inside, I hope. I can't feel my toes. Leave it to us to get here in the winter."

"Actually"—I point to some flowers poking their tops out of the light covering of snow—"it looks more like spring."

"Whatever. What are you now, a meteorologist? I'm assuming you've got a plan. So why don't you share it? And maybe poof up some boots for us while you're at it."

I study the enormous palace sitting a few hundred yards away, its white columns shining in the sun. Not exactly where I'd aimed for—which was inside. But it will have to do.

"You were right, Tess. At least I think you were."

She smiles, then her forehead wrinkles. "Right about what?"

"Ethan and I should have stayed. Whatever it was that Baba Yaga wanted to show me—I need to see it. I need to finish the visit. Anastasia was talking to Viktor. I need to hear what they said. I need to know why he was inside the palace. It may not be the whole answer. But I think it's important."

Of course, I could know already, if I hadn't gotten all pissy and stopped Baba Yaga from sending me here. But I was on a date. We were kissing! We had peanuts! Ethan's tongue was in my mouth! Who thinks straight at a time like that?

Tess rubs her arms. Her goose bumps have goose bumps. "Beyond my general brilliance and all, could you make this a little less vague? What exactly are you thinking besides, 'Hey, time travel—there's some fun we need to have again'?"

"What I think is that Baba Yaga missed Anastasia. And maybe she compensated by bringing up memories of her in the fire. You know—in that creepy skull. So there's Viktor, right? Trapped in the hut watching Baba Yaga do this day after day. Who knows how long it felt like to him there. Maybe like centuries. And at some point, he figures it out. How to do what we've done—go back and forth in time. Stick his soul in Anastasia's doll one trip. And hide it somewhere during another. That's why he's trying to stop us now, I think. Because there's a chance that we might figure it out too."

"So somehow he butted into one of Anastasia's memories

228

while Baba Yaga was looking at them in her fire? Took the doll and hid it here in the past? This is what you're telling me?"

"Yeah. Too crazy?"

"Is that even possible anymore? This isn't because of the Ben thing, is it? Because you know, I took psychology. You could just be acting passive-aggressive or something and making me suffer."

I roll my eyes. Even my eyeballs are cold. The expression on Tess's face shifts from joking to serious.

"Omigod, Tess. No. Is that what you—no." The idea of Ben and Tess had slipped from my mind in Baba Yaga's hut, but now it's back full steam ahead.

"'Cause it's weird, right? I know we haven't had time to talk about it. But I want to talk about it. Okay, maybe not right now because I'm freaking out that someone is going to suddenly notice two strange American girls and run us through with a sword or throw us in a dungeon. Did the Romanovs even have dungeons? Whatever. He's nice, Anne. And God, he's smart. You know I like smart—not that you could tell with Neal. Which probably should have been my clue that that whole relationship was doomed. But Ben is—"

I rest my hand on her arm. "I know. He really is. And it really is okay. I told you that at IHOP. It's more than okay, actually. I think it's great."

"Honest? Because I've been worried that this makes me look totally lame. Like all I can do is take your leftovers or something. Plus, there's the whole blonde thing. People stereotype, you know. Barbie and Ken or whatever. Not that I'm a Barbie. I'm way too flat-chested and—"

"Tess. You could never be lame. Trust me."

She wrinkles her nose. "Well, okay, yeah. It's just that—I was totally not expecting to feel like this. And I only gave myself permission to feel like this when you told me that it was over. I mean, he drove back for me in the middle of the night. I'm standing in my bedroom so scared that I think I'm gonna pee my pants, and then I hear his car on the driveway. And I run down and open the door and realize that I've never wanted to see anyone so much in my entire life. You should have seen his face when I leaped on him and kissed him. I was all 'Thank God almighty, you're here and at least I don't have to die alone in the suburbs.' And then I looked at him. And he looked at me."

She blushes. "If it wasn't a cliché, I'd have jumped his bones right there in my foyer. Only that would have been slutty. Right?"

"Um, yes." I change the subject. "And did I tell you that when Baba Yaga first became a witch she chowed down on a little boy? Like swallowed him whole, bones and all. I saw it in her head. Correction—I lived it in her head. If you ever hear me say that I wish I knew what someone was thinking, just slap me, okay?"

"Ewww."

"You don't really have to hurt me."

"Not that. The other thing."

We schlep through the snow as I explain the rest of my plan to Tess. Find the room that Viktor was coming out of when Anastasia saw him. Go inside. See what we find. As long I don't body switch with anyone, we'll be in good shape. Unless, of course, this is the wrong year. Or Viktor didn't actu-ally tell Anastasia anything relevant because he was already an evil, conniving bastard who could anticipate a need for future secrecy. Or any one of a trillion depressing possibilities.

We could seriously be here forever.

I picture Ben and Ethan still standing in the IHOP parking lot waiting for us to—I don't know—fall from the sky or something. Maybe they'll end up eating more pancakes.

We make it to the stone pathway by the palace. Various groups of people stroll by us—guards, an older woman who looks like she could be a nanny or governess or whatever they would have had, and two guys in long black coats, both wearing gloves. My heart jumps every time one of them comes close. One of the coat guys actually brushes against Tess's arm. He stops and she lets out a soft gasp. But he just says something in Russian to the other guy and then walks on. No one seems to sense our presence.

Everyone looks slightly cold and more than slightly anxious. The political tide had already begun to turn, I know. I guess everyone was aware. Except the Tsar.

"So." Tess stops and turns to me. "If we're looking for the matryoshka doll—at least maybe—where do you think Viktor would have put it?"

"That's what we have to figure out."

"I shouldn't have asked, should I?"

A tall dark-haired guy with a mustache, wearing what looks like a guard uniform, steps out of the palace. We slip inside before the door closes.

It's gorgeous. And ornate. And really, really huge. Crystal chandeliers. A fireplace. Groupings of tables and chairs.

"This is crazy," Tess whispers. "We're going to see them, aren't we? Anastasia and her family."

"It would be easier if we didn't, but, maybe. Yes." And if we're lucky, they won't see us. At least that's my plan.

Tess sucks in a breath through her nose, exhales through her mouth. "Okay, boss. Where to? And let's do this fast, okay? Your parents are still in the middle of their freak-out, remember? I really don't want to get back and see your dad going medieval on Ethan because neither of them knows where you are."

Yet another level of fun in my world.

We begin to wander. Argue about what we'd seen in the various website pictures. We find ourselves in what turn out to be the servants' quarters. Then some kind of sitting room. Another room with a wall covered with religious icons—picture after picture of gold-haloed saints, each one looking more unhappy and tortured than the next. After that, we get turned around and end up back where we began.

Servants bustle here and there, carrying this, cleaning that. Everyone's blabbing in Russian, which doesn't exactly help. Possibly I should have asked Baba Yaga to conjure up a decent Alexander Palace blueprint before we left the hut. I do a mental run-through of Spells I Think I May Know. I can light candles, heal wounds, make the wind blow and plants grow. I can read Ethan's thoughts. I may or may not have been able to put a protection spell around my house. And I've burned a few rusalki and, in one unfortunate incident, Ben's face. But not even Baba Yaga seems to have a spell for how to find the bad guy's soul while time traveling to the past.

"What about that way?" Tess points to our left. "I don't think we've…" Her mouth sags. Her face goes white.

A tall wild-bearded man in black walks toward us, deep in conversation with a regal-looking woman, hair pinned in some kind of updo, wearing a long, cream-colored high-collared dress. She's gesturing with her hands and he's nodding. He says something and she clasps her hands together, almost as though in prayer.

"Is that—" Tess whispers.

I hold up a hand for her to be quiet. Not that they can hear us. Or see us. Just that I need to make sure that—

He stops dead in his tracks. Twists his head left. Right. Tilts his chin up, his gaze skimming the high ceiling. When he looks down again, I see his eyes. Dark. Gleaming. Evil.

I hold my breath. Stand absolutely still.

Father Grigory—aka Rasputin—circles his gaze round and round and stops. He stares directly at me. My heart skips a beat. Then another. The breath I'd been holding freezes in my chest.

Tsarina Alexandra—the woman cannot be anyone else—turns to him and says something.

He ignores her like she's not there. I see her face flush, but she waits for him to do something. Defers to him and I want to scream at her to tell him to get out. To call for the guards or her husband or someone to get rid of him. He's going to destroy her family and she has no idea.

Rasputin walks toward us. Tess makes a strangled sound in the back of her throat. I stand very, very still. He stops just inches from me, smelling rank, his beard greasy. His close-set eyes darken to black.

Everything in the room seems to hold its breath.

And then he bursts into Russian and laughs.

"Holy shit," Tess whispers when he finally, finally walks away.

He knows, I think. He knows there's something. But even he can't figure it out. Point for our team.

Neither Tess nor I move another muscle until Rasputin and Alexandra both walk out the door toward the park.

"How could she trust that guy? Just looking at him makes me want to hurl." Tess's eyes are wide as I motion toward the direction from which the Tsarina and her creepy priest have just come. The family must have rooms there; maybe one of them is the right one. If not, we'll have to try upstairs.

"She was desperate," I whisper. Rasputin didn't see us, but I have no idea if maybe he could manage to hear us. Whispering is good. "Anastasia's brother was so sick. Father Grigory promised her answers. I think that's really all there is to it."

Tess makes an ick face. "So she trusts the king of the creepers and Anastasia trusts Viktor. I feel like I need to do an intervention or something. Don't you? I mean it's sort of your family and all. Well, more than sort of. Don't you wish you could go back in time and—oh. See? This is how grossed out I am right now. We are back in time. Never mind."

I nudge her toward the wing we haven't explored. How many hours have passed since we've been gone? How long has it been since I've actually slept? A day? Two? I'm oddly alert—the magic maybe? Maybe just adrenaline. Was it only yesterday that Ethan and I were sitting at Wrigley Field?

Ethan.

Tess touches my arm. Only then do I realize I've said his name aloud.

"Hey." She gives my shoulders a quick squeeze. "You know you're really brave, right? Bravest person I've ever met. Okay, maybe not the smartest sometimes." She grins, but her eyes are serious. "It'll be okay, Anne. Even if it's not. Do you understand what I mean? This whole crazy thing—it's going to end soon, one way or the other. And it may not be the way we think. Or the way you want it to. But don't ever believe that the outcome is about you. That whole destiny bullshit? You know what I think? I think we make our destiny. And I think you're amazing. If you weren't, I wouldn't be your friend."

So there we stand, me and Tess, crying our eyes out in the middle of the Alexander Palace. She's right, of course. Tess, it turns out, is almost always right, which is something that most people don't understand about her. She is a highly underestimated human being, and that is exactly why she is my best friend.

"But what if I can't—"

Tess presses her hand to my mouth. "Don't. Not helping. Besides, what's the worst that could happen if you don't find crazy Viktor's hidden soul?"

I stare at her.

"Okay. Maybe that wasn't the best question."

"You think?"

We laugh so hard that we forget to whisper. So hard that we don't hear the voices down the hall right away. We're laughing and walking, and then Tess grabs my arm again, really hard.

"Ow."

She presses a finger to her lips. I follow her gaze. My heart sticks in my throat, beats there furiously like a trapped bird trying to free itself.

Anastasia Romanov—about ten years old—stands at the doorway a few feet from us. It is in some ways like watching myself. I've been her, dreamed of her, watched her life in one way or another over and over. Saved her and sent her back to die.

Her eyes are blue like her father's. It's a softer blue than Ethan's but just as familiar. Her hair falls down her back in gentle waves, her bangs curving slightly on her forehead. Her nose is long and straight. She's wearing a dark skirt and a white blouse tucked in, and a tiny strand of pearls adorns her neck.

"Why so sad, brother?" she says softly, and at first I think it must be Alexei that she's talking to. That would make sense. Her mom was just down here with horrible Father Grigory. Alexei must have been sick again. She's trying to cheer him up.

Tess and I edge closer. If I wasn't invisible, I could talk to Anastasia again like I did that horrible day in front of the Jewel Box when everything went both right and wrong. This is what I'm thinking as her brother walks out of the room.

In that moment it's like lots of things we wish for, search for, hope for. Sometimes getting what you want is as painful as wanting it.

"I am of the Brotherhood now," Viktor says as he steps from the room to Anastasia's left. He looks just like he did when Ethan and I made our brief guest appearance yesterday. Younger. Thin. Dark eyes. Long, angular face. I hate every inch of him.

Next to me, I feel Tess stiffen. My little flapping-bird heart beats its wings some more in my throat. I try to swallow, but my mouth has dried up.

"Like Father Grigory?" Anastasia says. She makes a face that looks a lot like Tess's ick face. If I wasn't frozen with fear, this might make me smile. "He was just here, you know. Talking to Mama."

Viktor arches his dark brows. "Was he now? I thought as much. But I came today to speak to your father. To show him what I have become. Not like Father Grigory, sister. Do not fear. I would never be like that man." His lips curve in his own look of disgust. I guess that's the one thing he and I finally agree on.

"Papa will be happy." Anastasia smiles shyly at him. For like the zillionth time, I want to run up and shake her. Tell her no, no, no. Don't smile at him. Don't trust him. No. Don't.

"Perhaps he will, sister. But somehow I doubt it. Your father does not approve of me." He pauses, seems to consider whether or not he should go on. Then adds, "If he did, then perhaps my portrait would also grace that lovely new addition to his desk in the study."

Anastasia frowns. "I will tell Papa, then. He will listen to me. I am sure of it."

Viktor's eyes glitter. He gives a short laugh.

Tess grips my arm.

"So," he says to Anastasia, "you are Anastasia the Brave now?"

She nods. "Like the story Mama tells. Like Vasilisa. I will go into the forest of my father's study and tell him that you are very nice. And if there are any witches in there like Baba Yaga, I will beat them over the head until they are gone."

I listen to her tell him this, and suddenly I know how someone's heart can break. Mine feels crushed right now. Smashed into the tiniest of bits possible.

Viktor leans and brushes a kiss to Anastasia's head. Stoops so they are eye to eye. "Be careful, little girl. I have met Baba Yaga. She is not particularly nice. You would not want to be eaten. Although I do thank you for your kind wishes on my behalf."

Like Rasputin, when he walks by Tess and me, he stops. Just inches from my face, he stands and sort of sniffs the air.

"Yaga," he says so softly that even though he's just like an inch from me, I can barely make out the word. "Is that you? I thought you did not leave your forest. Perhaps I have more to learn. Or perhaps you just can't stay away from me." He chuckles. "A witch, yes. But still a woman. So predictable. Do you hear me, Yaga? Perhaps my sister would appreciate a visit."

Wonderful. He sniffs the air around me and smells witch. Fabulous.

When he's gone, Anastasia steps into the room. We follow her.

"Do you smell me?" I whisper to Tess. "Do I smell like a witch?"

"You smell kind of sweaty."

"I smell?"

"You asked."

I look around. More chandeliers. A bunch of paintings. A fireplace and a pool table. And a huge desk cluttered with papers and pictures and various clocks and knickknacks.

I came to speak to your father, Viktor had said.

We are in Tsar Nicholas's study. But it's just me and Tess and Anastasia. No Tsar. Maybe there's another exit. Maybe he never was in here in the first place. That would make sense, wouldn't it? To be seen with his illegitimate son right in his own house? Out there in the park, maybe, like I'd seen in one of my dreams. But not here. Not on his own home turf.

"Now what?" Anastasia still doesn't see us, but still Tess whispers her question.

The answer happens quickly, almost too quickly, like maybe I'm dreaming. Only I'm not.

Anastasia walks to the desk. Moves past the clutter of stuff and bends to look at something displayed on a little stand at the far end.

"Oh," I say. A tiny sound that makes Tess shift her gaze to me.

It's not just a random something that Anastasia's studying. It's something I know. The last thing she thought about before I sent her back to die.

In my head, I go there again. See myself standing on Second Street, the Jewel Box destroyed, rain streaming in buckets. Baba Yaga's tears pouring from the sky. Anastasia and I had held her matryoshka doll between us and I'd placed my other hand over my heart. I was supposed to be sending her back. I *would* send her back a few seconds later. But right then, our minds linked together, Anastasia and I weren't thinking about death. We were thinking about this room and this Fabergé egg that sits on her father's desk.

The egg with all their pictures on it. Anastasia's and her brother and sisters'.

Perhaps my portrait would also grace that lovely new addition to his desk in the study.

Every part of me starts to tingle. Magic. Fear. Memories.

Sometimes you just know.

"It's the egg," I whisper. "All those pictures. Oh my God. It's the one thing Viktor wanted and never got—to be an official part of the Romanovs. This is the moment. This is the memory. I can feel it."

My impulse is to grab it. But would Anastasia see? Would she realize she wasn't alone? That could ruin everything.

So we wait. One minute. Two. Three. Five excruciating minutes click by on the clock on the Tsar's desk. Then six. Seven minutes she stands there studying the damn egg.

In the hall, a female voice calls out. "Anastasia. Anastasia. You are supposed to be at your lessons. I saw you come down here, Anastasia. Answer me."

Anastasia hesitates. Sighs. I hear my own heart beating.

When the door closes behind her, Tess huffs out a huge breath.

Pulse flying, I step to the desk. Will I be able to touch it? I half expect that my hand will just slide right through.

But my hand tightens around the egg just fine.

If I were in a museum, I'd admire how beautiful it is. So white and shiny, the decorations exquisite. The little picture panels each exactly perfect in shape and size. Each one with a picture. And seven of those pictures of the family. Nicholas. Alexandra. Alexei, the heir to the throne. Anastasia and her sisters—OTMA, they called themselves—Olga, Tatiana, Maria, and Anastasia.

I turn it every which way as I look at it. And then I turn it upside down.

An eighth picture panel.

Viktor. The panel underneath is an image of Viktor.

"Holy shit." Tess touches a finger to the picture.

"Don't," I snap, a whip of panic hitting me. "What if it disappears or something?"

She snatches her hand away like the egg is on fire.

"This is it." I'm half crying, half laughing, mostly feeling so giddy that I think I'm going to float up to the ceiling.

"Does it open? It has to open, right?"

"Here. On top. Shit, Tess. He did it. He changed this one thing in history. This has to be it."

I'm having trouble getting my brain around it. This Fabergé egg is in someone's art collection in the present. In the present, it has just seven portraits. But in the past, it's been altered to have eight. How can that even be? But it is. I'm looking at it.

"It's perfect," Tess says. "It's what he always wanted, isn't it? For his dad the Tsar to acknowledge him. So he can't get that in real life. But he can fake it here. He had to wait until he was Baba Yaga's prisoner, but he got what he wanted. He found his way into Anastasia's memories. He changed the thing that pissed him most."

And if we're lucky, it's where he hid what we're looking for.

"How big was that doll of hers anyway? Bigger than this egg, right?"

"The whole doll, maybe. But not the ones inside. Dolls within dolls. Stories within stories. The littlest doll. That's all he'd need."

"So are you gonna open it?" Tess looks at me. I look at the egg.

I find the tiny hidden clasp. Ease it open with my finger.

We peer inside.

A wooden doll just slightly larger than my little fingernail stares up at us.

I lean back in case it leaps up or says something. But it just lies there with its painted eyes and thin painted smile.

"That's it?" Tess tilts her head. What did she expect? "So, is Viktor's soul really in there? Like how? Taped inside with magic Gorilla Glue or something?"

"Um, yeah?" Our command of the existential is a little rocky. We've leaped into the past with no planning whatsoever, other than a limited working knowledge of the Koschei fairy tale. It's like feeling qualified to do brain surgery because I've watched *Grey's Anatomy*.

The door to the study creaks, then opens enough for a brown little spaniel to trot into the room.

The dog yips.

I jump. Smack heads with Tess.

The egg slips from my hand, but I manage to catch it. The doll, however, flies out and nosedives to the floor, bounces when it hits. Bounce. Bounce.

Spaniel chases it.

Noooooo, I think in slow motion. *Holy shit. No.*

For a second I think I'm going to black out. I see stars. My skin feels like ice.

Spaniel noses the doll. Its pink, spitty tongue licks it.

Get it, my brain commands. But I feel like everything is moving in slow motion. Vomit rises in my throat. A wave of dizziness spins my head.

"Anne!" Tess's cry is sharp, but when she repeats my name, her voice fades.

My brain tries to process what's happening.

Viktor's soul is in the doll in the egg. That's what we think. Not that I want to hurt this wonderful historical egg, which I haven't because I just caught it and I'm clutching it in both hands, but so? I didn't hide *my* soul in it. The doll smacking the floor should be a good thing, right? Okay, the dog possibly eating it isn't good, but isn't that how all those Koschei the Deathless stories go? Break the egg or toss the egg, and his soul gets knocked around and then goes back where it belongs so he can die like he's supposed to? Maybe we've done it. Maybe this will all be over.

Then why do I feel like I'm about to pass out? Or vomit? Or worse?

Tess falls to the floor. Her head hits the carpet with a muffled thud.

My knees buckle. My head feels strange and floaty. My vision blurs.

"Here, doggy," I say weakly. "Give me the doll. C'mon, dog. Open your mouth and spit it out."

My jumbled brain attempts to work. Egg—jostled. Doll—falls. Doll—bounces on carpet. Tess—lying on floor looking really bad. Me—fading fast. Somebody's spaniel swallowing the doll with Viktor's soul attached like it's a magical Milk Bone. All of the above not working well for Tess and me. Well, one question is answered. What would happen if we tried to destroy the doll right here rather than bringing it back to our time?

Someone's damn dog would try to eat it and kill us in the process, that's what.

"The doll!" I hit the floor on my knees. "We need to get the doll away from the dog."

We both start to crawl. Spaniel thinks we're playing. He runs in happy circles, the doll still in his mouth.

How do I know it's in his mouth and not crushed between his doggy teeth? Because I'm still here thinking these absurd thoughts.

"Dog!" I say. "Oh, please, doggy. This cannot be happening."

Behind me, I hear the door creak again. Does it open? I can't turn my head.

"The doll," I say, more weakly this time. "We have to get the doll."

"Jimmy!" a girl's voice says. Then she says something else in Russian. *Jimmy? Wait. I remember this. Jimmy is the dog. Bad Jimmy. Give me the damn doll back, Jimbo.*

"Jimmy!" the voice says again. The spaniel stops racing in circles. Sits. *Good Jimmy.*

Through blurred vision, I see the dog drop the saliva-covered matryoshka doll into someone's hand. The hand places it gently on the Tsar's desk. Then reaches down for me.

My head clears.

Anastasia Romanov, still holding my hand, stares at me like she sort of knows me. Says something in Russian. Then looks curiously at the egg, the doll, the dog, and me.

WEDNESDAY, 9:48 AM

ETHAN

So what now?" We come to a stop at the huge sculpture in one of the tourist-jammed plazas of Millennium Park. "Just stand here and wait?"

Dimitri scowls.

I check my phone—just like I've been doing every minute or so. Nothing. It's almost ten in the morning. Anne and Tess have been gone for over three hours. Three hours real-world time. Who knows how long—or how short—a time frame has passed in Baba Yaga's forest. If that's even where they still are. For so long, Anne and I have drifted in and out of each other's thoughts. Now there is nothing. The absence of that connection frightens me. Where is she?

A quick phone call from Ben. "Anything?" he asks.

"Not yet," I say.

The unsaid commentary is much longer.

Ben is right. I never should have let Anne go without me.

Ben is wrong. My presence would have changed nothing. Would have made it harder for her. A rule of combat: never risk something you are not willing to lose.

A problem: Anne is not willing to lose me. But in going she has asked me to accept the possibility of losing her.

Thus the one thing on which Ben and I agree: to lose her is unthinkable.

"Americans and their art," Dimitri comments dismissively. He's looking at the sculpture—the one everyone calls the "Bean"—made of smooth curved panels of stainless steel more than thirty feet high with an arch beneath it, tall enough for people to walk under.

"Sculptor's British," I tell him. As though it matters. The mirrorlike surface reflects the crowd. I can see the two of us at the left corner. Even close up we'd be warped by the curved shape. *Like the truth of us*, I think. The steel's reflection altering what we are, just as we ourselves are not what we seem. Dimitri and I are from another age, another place.

"The Brits aren't much better." His nostrils flare in disdain. "God, Ethan, don't you miss it sometimes? Russia? The old days. We were men, then. Now—look at us. Still waiting for that bastard to show his face and your little girl to wrestle information from a witch we once thought was beneath our concern."

"No." The one-word answer suffices. I have no interest in listening to him wax poetic about Mother Russia. I have never known him well, and now is not the time to start. He came from a more privileged background than I did—that much I had gathered long ago. As for me, I had thought there was nothing left to lose when Viktor took me in. Offered me the Brotherhood's protection.

Now, I wonder. Was my family's death not just random destruction? Was that Cossack who killed my father actually connected to Viktor? Did he make me an orphan so that I would be of use?

I scan the plaza. No Viktor. Just Dimitri and me and a crowd of strangers.

And this: "What did he promise you?" I ask him. "Before he promised you Anastasia. When you had a choice. What made you join the Brotherhood?"

He stares at me oddly, as though this is the first time he's considered this particular question. I don't expect him to answer. But he does.

"I'd been sleeping with one of our maids—Sonia was her name. We lived in Minsk, a nice house. Nice for then, at least. When she told me she was pregnant, I said I would marry her. My father disagreed. He fired her on the spot. Sent her packing in the middle of the night. It was weeks before I tracked her to an aunt's little house in some country village."

Something hard and cold flickers in Dimitri's eyes. "Sonia's father had his own opinion on the subject of her having my child. There were ways—even back then. The women, they knew how to take care of unfortunate circumstances. Sonia wouldn't speak to me. I told my father to go to hell. He disowned me, told me to get out. A few weeks later, someone introduced me to Viktor."

His gaze rests on the curved steel sculpture. "I should have fought for Sonia. But I didn't. I don't even know why. Stupidity. Fear. Arrogance. But Anastasia—she didn't see that. She saw only a shallow fool who was kind to her. Who was a friend of her 'secret brother.' The truth? She had no idea how I felt about her. But I saw in her everything I had lost with Sonia. And when Viktor promised that he would help make the match, I believed that too."

"You were young."

He shakes his head. His dark eyes focus somewhere that only he can see. "What fitting punishment our lives have been, eh, Brother? To keep repeating one age over and over, and still we never get it right."

"We're moving forward now," I remind him. "Things are not the same."

"People don't change, Ethan. All these years, and this is what I believe. What is that saying? 'A tiger can't change his stripes.' I think that is it. If I had it to do over again, any of it, would I behave differently? Would I choose more wisely? You tell me. We are what we are, my friend. No more. No less."

"What are you prepared to do?" The question slips out without me being consciously aware that I was about to ask it.

He hesitates for a long moment. Long enough that I grow uneasy.

"Kill him if I can. If death isn't possible, then destruction, suffering. Whatever I can manage. We have part of his power now. Who knows what will happen?" He tilts his head, then flicks a finger toward my throat. Against my will, my breath seizes in my lungs.

"I know you remember this trick, Ethan. He's used it on you, after all. So I ask myself: even if a man could live forever, what life would he have if he couldn't breathe? He might not die. But my power would still squeeze at his neck. It is an interesting conundrum, wouldn't you say?"

The finger flicks again. Air rushes back where it belongs.

And I realize that I'm standing here with a madman.

He moves his hand again, but this time I'm quicker. The magic I've been repressing, holding deep inside me, rises swiftly, hungrily.

"I wouldn't do that if I were you," I say. His feet lift from the ground because I tell them to. He shoots across the plaza toward the sculpture, knocking a few tourists off their feet as he goes. The back of his head smacks against the left side of the curved steel. He slumps to the cement.

Part of me registers shock at what I've done. Part of me finds it amusing.

"Ah, Ethan," says a voice behind me. "Showing your true colors at last. Perhaps our friend Dimitri was wrong. People can change. Look at you—finally enjoying yourself."

Viktor, thin but no longer skeletal, claps his hands in slow applause. His dark hair is streaked with white. Deep lines etch the skin around his eyes. A small scar runs from the corner of his mouth to his chin. Dimitri struggles to his feet, a crowd—as yet unaware that I'm responsible for what just happened—gathering around him.

"I'd thought to share with both of you," he says. "A man needs options, you see. But I see now that I need to make some alterations in that plan. Don't worry, Ethan. This won't hurt. Not much anyway."

Dimitri has shaken off the crowd. I see when he recognizes the man who's joined me. He walks faster, then seems to change his mind. Stops.

Inside me, the magic anticipates. *Block him. Hurt him. Do damage. Survive at all costs.* This is what my brain interprets from the power.

No, I tell myself. *This was a mistake.*

Viktor clears his throat. Angles his gaze to our old friend who stands reflected in foot after foot of dark, curved steel.

Dimitri raises his arms.

I double over in searing pain. Fall to my knees on the concrete. My body feels like it's on fire. What has he done? I was going to stop him, wasn't I? But the pain burns and my mind blurs. Through the haze of red, I manage a glimpse at Dimitri. He is standing in the middle of the plaza, a perplexed look on his face.

Every movement an agony, I hold out my hand. My brain struggles for a spell to stop him. And then my gaze falls on the swirling dark tendrils of power flickering at my fingertips.

What the hell is this?

Viktor pulls me to my feet. "You know," he says. "There are so few surprises for us, Ethan. We have seen so much, after all. But who knew that after all this time, Dimitri would share his sad, pathetic tale with you. Who knew that he would prove such a liability. But you—this is a much better plan. I can feel the difference already, can't you?"

He claps me on the back. "Enjoy, Ethan. Enjoy. This will all be over soon, I'd imagine. We will all go our separate ways— some more permanent than others. But until then, live a little. Let loose. See how much fun it really is."

He smiles, then walks in front of me toward Dimitri, moving purposefully but with the casual stride of a man who is in no particular hurry. One step away. Two. Three. Understanding washes over me.

"Don't worry, Ethan," Viktor calls over his shoulder. "Even that is only a small taste of what I've managed to get back."

Asking why is pointless right now. The why will come later. Now I only know one thing. He has transferred more power to me. It writhes inside me, darkening my own thoughts, smudging the lines between what is me and what is not.

No. I control what I do or don't do. I will not give in. I need to wait for Anne. We need to find Viktor's soul. We need to stop him. I have to protect her from Baba Yaga. Anne, who's given her life for mine. That is who I am. Not this. Not…

Viktor closes the distance between himself and Dimitri.

A smile tugs, unbidden, at my lips.

The power surges from me. Smashes into the ground. The concrete plaza cracks, spiderwebs of lines running everywhere, ground buckling and bending. The enormous steel sculpture groans as the earth beneath it vibrates.

"No!" I yell it aloud.

The power screams back. And keeps on going.

Still at Alexander Palace
and Not Happy about It

Anne

S HE SEES ME. ANASTASIA SEES ME. HOLY CRAP, SHE SEES me. Like little Ethan saw me. I really do need an instruction manual for all of this.

"Um, hi," I say. "Hello."

"I speak English," she says. "You are English?"

"American." I gesture to Tess, still sprawled on the Tsar's carpet in a rather unladylike position. "Both of us."

Anastasia's forehead wrinkles. "I am sorry about Jimmy. He is not an obedient dog." Then, "Do I know you? I think I know you. What are you doing in my papa's study? Did Viktor bring you with him?"

Tess snorts. I flash her a look of warning.

"Sort of," I say slowly. "But we need to get going now." *And take the dog-spit matryoshka doll with us, which is going to be problematic since it's sitting on your father's desk and Tess and I don't belong here and any second now you're going to sic your spaniel on us. Or the dog is going to swallow the doll, and Tess and I will be lying dead on your carpet.*

"That's mine." I point to the doll. "The dog startled me and I dropped it. Thanks for getting it back. He's quite the scamp, huh?"

Anastasia looks from me to the doll to the dog to Tess.

Then back at me. Or rather, at my hands. More specifically, at the Fabergé egg I'm still holding on to for dear life. The one that Viktor has altered by adding his picture. Will it stay that way? Or if we get his soul back where it belongs, will everything else revert to normal too? Unless Tess and I don't make it out of here because Jimmy is a bad little spaniel.

"You cannot touch that," she says, holding out her hand. "Those are very special."

I hand her the egg. "Sorry. And yeah, Viktor brought us. I guess we got turned around or something."

I can tell she doesn't believe me. She shouldn't believe me. I wouldn't believe me. Hell, the dog doesn't believe me.

Any second now, here's what's going to happen: she's going to call for help. Scream to a guard or her father or a servant or someone. Will they see us too? That's anyone's guess. If they do, we're in even bigger trouble. And if they don't, then guess what? I'm hurting Anastasia even more than she's already destined to be hurt. This is the last thing I want for her—to be the girl who gets in trouble for messing around with her father's things and spinning some crazy story about two girls and a little doll. A piece of the same doll her mother hasn't even given her yet.

Slowly, gently, so I won't spook her, I rest my hand on Anastasia's. Look into her eyes. Hold her gaze and let my magic do the rest. Manipulate a person I care about. A person who deserves the truth but is never going to get it, not even from me.

She hands me the soggy matryoshka doll. Careful not to jostle it, I slip it into my pocket. For a second, I feel a ripple, but I will it to stay still. Use Baba Yaga's magic to weave a protection around it so it can stay whole and solid until I need it to be otherwise. Would have been nice if I'd have thought of this before. I'm learning. Slowly. Painfully.

You won't remember us, I tell Anastasia in my mind. You will think that you have come in here to find your dog. That you found him and he bumped your dad's desk and you had to put the egg back on its stand.

I motion to Tess. She stands. I'm going to take us out of here and get back to Ethan and Ben and our world. Fix this whole mess and then go home and deal with that mess too.

I don't consciously plan what I do next. Or if I do, I don't admit it to myself.

"Anastasia," I say. "You won't remember me the next time you see me. But I want you to remember this. Viktor is going to promise you all sorts of stuff. Don't believe him. Terrible things may be happening. But you're going to have to stay strong. Your mom is going to give you a bigger doll, just like the one you just saw. She's going to tell you to hold on to it, and she's right. Do what she says. But not Viktor. You can't trust him. I know you think you can, but you can't."

"Anne." Tess's eyes are wide. "You can't do that, can you? I mean, isn't that going to…"

She's right. I know she's right. Everything we've been doing—even everything good that's come from this, like Ethan and me—I might have just ruined it. In my head, I do my best to take it back. Is it too late? I guess we'll know soon enough.

"We've got to go now," I say. "You won't remember that we've been here. At least I hope you won't."

I pat my pocket. Make sure the doll is still inside.

Jimmy the spaniel gives a cheery woof.

I take Tess's hand.

And find myself turning again to Anastasia.

"I'm Anne," I say. "Anne Michaelson." Will she remember? When she sees me again when I come for her in the forest, will some tiny molecule of her recognize me? How nice it would be to know that in her grief and terror, she remembered a girl named Anne who told her to be careful.

I close my eyes. The world folds and contracts. My stomach pitches.

Just like that, the Alexander Palace disappears.

In its place stand the IHOP parking lot and Ben.

Just Ben.

"Thank God," he says. "Are you guys okay?"

Tess leaps on Ben like a crazed spider monkey. "You are so not going to believe what happened."

"Wish that were true," Ben says. "You can tell me in the car. We need to go. This guy named Dimitri showed up right after you guys left. Ethan's gone with him to confront Viktor. At least that's what they said. Who knows what's really going on."

"Dimitri? Gone where? Ethan left? Before we got back?" Why? Why? He should be here.

"Downtown to Millennium Park."

"It's a public place," Tess says. "That should be safe, huh?"

"No. Shit. Where's your car?" My head is still spinning from the time travel. Does Ben even drive a car?

Ben points, and the three of us sprint across the parking lot. To his Saturn two-seat convertible.

We head downtown, Ben driving, Tess in my lap.

ETHAN

CHAOS. THE ENTIRE PARK IS IN TOTAL CHAOS.

The plaza buckles and cracks. People fall, scream. They stream toward Michigan Avenue. They back away as the huge sculpture groans and shakes. The steel plates reflect the scene like some horrible Bosch painting.

"Get away from there!" someone shouts. The Bean's arch shudders as people run under it, escaping to the plaza beyond.

"More!" shouts the power that's not mine. No. No. Everything inside me continues to burn, smolder. I have to stop this. Whatever Viktor's purpose, whatever he's about to do or reveal, I can deal with that later.

Spells streak through my head. Dark. Wrong. Unfamiliar.

"*Ya dolzhen*," I begin. *I must.* Must what? I struggle to pull the words from the heaving mass of magic that's been forced into me.

Viktor strides into the maelstrom. The crowd swallows him.

"He's getting away!" Dimitri is somehow next to me now, gesturing, shouting.

Everything in my world reduces to one desire: control the magic. If I don't, nothing else will matter. It will all be gone.

In my head, a voice. Anne.

"Ethan. We're coming."

"He gave it all to you, didn't he?" Dimitri grabs me by the shoulders. "He took it from me and gave it to you. I have nothing left."

I can feel the lie pulse from him. Viktor's power is gone. Yes. But not Dimitri's own. Like me, it wouldn't be much. But maybe it's enough. So here's the question: can I convince a man who's no longer sane—probably hasn't been for years—to help me?

Across the plaza, a hundred tons of steel rise into the air.

"The Bean!" someone yells. "It's floating."

"Work with me," I tell Dimitri urgently. "Please."

The sculpture undulates, shifting over the crowd like silver mercury. A panel falls. Someone screams.

"I need to tether myself to something," I tell him. "And it's going to have to be you. Now, Dimitri! Before anyone else gets hurt."

I sense this is not a priority for him.

The sculpture dips right, then left.

My nose begins to bleed.

I let my magic twist Dimitri's arm. Literally, that is.

He squawks in pain. I twist it tighter.

"*Ya dolzhen*," I say again. The rest of the spell follows—slowly, agonizingly reining the magic in.

It settles below my skin, an unwilling truce.

Concentrating, clearer now, with Dimitri rubbing his arm and now my very unwilling accomplice, I force the heavy steel sculpture back to earth. It hits with a thud, but stays more or less in one piece. Emphasis on the less rather than the more. The arch is considerably lower now.

I let out the breath I didn't know I was holding. And realize that our little display has gathered quite a crowd. Mostly they're staring at the ruined mound of stainless steel. But some of them are watching us…putting two and two together.

"Go," I tell Dimitri. "Now." We walk across the plaza, now pockmarked with cracks and holes, increase our pace to a jog, then sprint toward where Viktor disappeared. On the streets bordering the park, sirens have begun a persistent wail. Two squad cars bump over the curb and squeal to a stop somewhere behind us.

We run faster. Work our way into the crowd, which is as yet unaware that we're the cause of what's happened. In front of me, a man in plaid shorts and walking shoes stumbles. I grab him before he falls. Keep moving. It's impossible to see or hear beyond the sea of bodies. Safer to stay with the group at this point.

Viktor is probably long gone.

The crowd winds around the regrounded sculpture. People try to squeeze into the restaurant that's on the far end. But the place is already packed. A cop shouts something through his bullhorn.

Under my skin, the magic growls in frustration. How long can I keep it at bay?

We keep moving. Stumble down. Under my feet, water.

We're wading in the reflecting pool.

The noise begins as a low hum, then rises to shouts and gasps.

Dimitri points. "Look!"

Tourists come to Millennium Park for many reasons. Music, gardens, the sculpture I have now half destroyed. But they also come for this:

Two fifty-foot towers of glass, one on each end of the shallow pool which is now soaking its way up my pants legs. Each tower projecting images of faces. And from the mouth of each face that fades in and then out of the glass tower, water streams into the pool. It is designed to mimic the mythological gargoyles of older architecture—life-giving water flowing from their mouths. Like magic.

"Jesus," says the guy next to me, the earbuds of his iPod hanging at his neck. "That is one unfortunate-looking old lady. Who wants to look at a picture of that?"

I lift my gaze to the top of the tower. Stare into Baba Yaga's eyes, skulls gleaming. Water spouts from her huge mouth, glints off her hideous iron teeth.

The sky darkens. Thunder peals, and above the fountain, lightning sears the sky.

"Mommy," says a boy about five or six, clinging to his mother's hand. "Is that a witch?"

In the glass tower, Baba Yaga smiles. The water gushes faster. Then she purses her lips and blows.

"Give me my magic back," Dimitri says. "You can do it."

WEDNESDAY, 11:53 AM

ANNE

WE DRIVE ACROSS THE BRIDGE OVER THE RIVER, AND THE traffic on Michigan Avenue slows to a dead halt.

Five minutes later, we've moved exactly half a car length.

"Sit still," I tell Tess. She slides half off my lap, but there's no place to go.

"Screw it," Ben says. "C'mon."

He slams the Saturn into a no-parking parking space off Wacker. We climb out. My legs are sweaty. Tess is more solid than she looks.

"Can you three read?" A very large, very cranky policeman poses this question.

Well, yes, officer. But obviously we can't read, panic, fight the bad guy, and notice that Ben has parked—illegally—behind your squad car. Guess who was also stuck in traffic?

Tess grabs the keys out of Ben's hands. "My boyfriend isn't the brightest," she informs the cop. "I told you that wasn't a legal space, honey."

The cop lowers his sunglasses and eyeballs Tess a little more closely.

Everything inside me turns to a jittery mess. We need to get to the park. Now. Before now, actually, but I'm not up for any more time travel.

"What's the big hurry, folks?" the cop asks. He peers into the backseat of the Saturn. Clearly we're headed into search-the-car-for-drugs territory.

"Well." Tess smiles sweetly. "We were going to meet my brother downtown for lunch. Only I had to help Anne here with something first. An important something. And I really never drive down here. My dad says taking the train is always the better option. But the something took so long that I had to ask my boyfriend, Ben, for a ride.

"Say hi, Ben. He's so sweet. Sometimes I call him Benbo, but he doesn't like that, do you, Benbo? Anyway, we're really sorry. I'll move the car, and they'll go ahead and tell my brother that I'll be there as soon as I can, okay?"

Turns out it's not okay. And that he plans on doing a search of the car.

"You try," Tess hisses in my ear. "Magic, girl, remember?"

"He's a policeman."

"You just told the future to Anastasia. You're choosing a funny time to draw a moral line in the sand."

The cop's walkie-talkie blares. He answers. Listens. Looks down Michigan Avenue.

I begin to get a really bad feeling. This is saying a lot since I'm in full panic mode and I've got a magic doll in my pocket with someone's soul attached to it. I hope.

The cop's face turns serious.

"You three need to turn around and go back the way you came," he says. "Some kind of riot at Millennium Park. Just get the hell out of here. Now."

Tess starts to cry. Hysterical cartoon crying. Damsel in distress crying. Huge tears pour from her eyes and stream down her cheeks. She sounds like she's hyperventilating. Ben looks at her like he's staring at an alien.

"My brother's down there," she wails. "That's where we're meeting him. At that restaurant right by the Bean. He's waiting tables there until he gets into medical school. He needs to take his MCAT again." She clutches at the cop's arm. "You have to take us with you. If something happens to Zach, I don't know what I'd do. Our parents are in Belgium on business."

I gape at her.

There's a slight pause in the action while the cop contemplates. His radio is screeching, and the traffic keeps building, and some guy gets out of his Ford Focus waving his BlackBerry and yelling that the world is ending and we'd all better repent.

Officer Shanahan—this is the name on his badge—makes up his mind. Or maybe he just decides that he can't leave Tess here squalling like a crazy person. "Get in," he huffs at us, opening the rear door. "All of you. We'll find your brother."

We squeeze into the backseat—me in the middle, Tess on my right, Ben on my left.

"Was any of that the truth?" Ben whispers in my ear.

"Her brother's name," I whisper back.

Officer Shanahan cranks up the siren, makes a U-turn into traffic, and heads us up Wacker.

Tess's tears dry up. She is seriously the best fake crier I've ever seen.

"Gonna have to detour around the river," Officer Shanahan says.

"Did you put a whammy on him?" Tess's mouth is wet from all the crying when she breathes this in my other ear.

I shake my head. I would have. But he decided all on his own.

"Do you think it's terrorists?" Ben's brow furrows.

"Probably not," I whisper, although obviously I'm not totally certain about this. "But I bet Ethan and Dimitri have found Viktor."

The whispering is getting annoying, so for the millionth time since we headed downtown, I try Ethan's phone. For the millionth time, he doesn't answer.

For the first time, I notice a missed-call message from my dad's phone.

I so can't deal with that right now.

Later, I tell myself. If there is a later.

I lose track of how many different turns and back alleys we take. Twice, we drive down the sidewalk, siren screaming, horn honking. About two blocks out, we bounce so hard that the matryoshka doll flops against my hip. I press my hand over it as we sway back and forth. At one point I think Tess throws up in her mouth.

"Stay in the car!" Officer Shanahan directs us. "Your brother's Zach, right?"

"Zach Edwards," Tess says. Why she gives him her real last name is a mystery to me. But that's Tess.

"I'll find him," the cop says. "But you three need to hunker down and not move. Understand?"

Of course we understand. We just don't plan on listening.

Actually, we shouldn't have worried.

Because one look at the glass walls of the fountain in the reflecting pool is all it takes.

Officer Shanahan's mouth hangs open.

Even then I don't think he'd have unlocked the door to let us out. But Baba Yaga leans out of the glass, and her huge jaw drops and unhinges.

"Jesus Christ," says Officer Shanahan. "What is that? Some kind of hologram?"

"Let us out." Tess bangs on the window. "You want it on your head when Baba Yaga eats your squad car with us inside like the cream in a Twinkie?"

"Baba who? You know what that thing is?"

"Don't worry," Tess says. "Anne's a superhero. It'll be okay. Really."

Overhead, thunder booms so close it feels like it's in the squad car with us. Raindrops start to pelt the car. I lean over Ben to the window and crane my neck. It's pouring rain—complete with lightning and thunder—but only on Millennium Park. I can actually see the lines of demarcation in the sky.

"What the hell?" says Officer Shanahan.

"You have to let us out," I holler. "Please."

And when he doesn't act fast enough, I take matters into my own hands, just as one of Baba Yaga's hands detaches from her wrist and scampers down the glass tower to splash in the reflecting pool.

Officer Shanahan leaps from the front seat at the same moment I use my magic to pop the locks. We scramble out of the police car behind him and into the pounding rain.

Ben's face drains of color—not that there'd been much left from the crazy police car ride.

"Shit." Tess grabs his hand.

"We have to move," I say. "Now."

"Is that a hand?" Officer Shanahan's brow furrows as he tries to make sense of what he's seeing.

"Her hands unscrew," Tess says. "It's really gross. But you get used to it."

My own panic tightens. Spreads through my belly, legs, arms. Can a person actually break into a million pieces? Because that's what it feels like I'm about to do.

The wind has picked up and not because of me. A garbage can flies into the air and smashes into some guy's head. He crumbles to the ground and people trample over him, fleeing the witch in the glass tower that they've obviously decided is real and not a hologram.

Officer Shanahan doesn't offer any further direction, just muscles his way through the wind and rain toward the fallen man.

Baba Yaga leans farther from the tower. Rain is falling into that enormous, extended mouth. Somewhere deep in my veins, the magic she's given me begins to simmer. The sides of my own jaw begin to ache. My wrists tingle. And deeper still, something else. Something very dark and wrong that I can't quite name.

"Daughter," she says. She doesn't say my name. She doesn't have to. "I know you are here. Are you ready to show the world what's inside you?"

The memory she'd forced into me comes streaming back. That mixture of horror and hunger as she'd swallowed that little boy the day she turned into Baba Yaga and left her human self behind.

Is that what's going to happen to me? Is that my future?

I press my hand against my pocket. The doll is still there.

If I do this and make Viktor mortal once again, what happens next? Does Viktor have to die to free Lily? Will I end up with Baba Yaga, two crazy witches dancing around the forest? I feel like it's the last minutes of the Super Bowl and I still don't understand the rules of the game.

And none of it can ever undo the tragedy that's Anastasia. She probably thinks she dreamed the whole thing with me and Tess and the doll and the dog. The stuff I told her—it will fade away just like things do. She'll believe Viktor and she'll let Baba Yaga take her because she'll think she's saving her family. By the time she realizes that it's all a lie, it will be too late. But Ethan will find me and I'll do what I have to do and eventually she'll end up dying.

"This is crazy," I scream to Tess and Ben. "It's just an endless loop of crazy over and over. Every time we solve one part, something else just takes its place. I can't do this anymore," I tell them. Suddenly that's all I feel. "I just can't. It won't make any difference. What's changed? Except"—I gesture to the rain and the people running and falling and the hand splashing and the witch in the tower—"that now I get to add Millennium Park to the list of things I've destroyed."

Tess grabs my hands and pulls me eyeball to eyeball with her in the rain.

"It'll be okay," she says. "We haven't come this far for it not to be okay."

It is the absolutely worst thing she could possibly say right now.

"No." I rip my hands from hers and step back. Then back again. "How can you know me and then say that? Sometimes things aren't okay. Things don't work out. People die. People suffer. Don't you get it, Tess? Weren't you just with me at the Alexander Palace? This isn't some Disney fairy tale where everyone lives happily ever after. Or even where everyone lives. So just shut up."

I have never told my best friend in the world to shut up. Not like that. Not like I meant it.

I see the hurt on her face. And the pissy look on Ben's.

And I don't care.

I could lie and say that it's just Baba Yaga's fault. Her power is making me angry and angsty. Soon I'll be dressing in all black and listening to emo music and writing sad poetry about how I want to beat my head against a brick wall. Or trying not to eat people. Tess would believe this.

But it's all me. I'm scared and exhausted, and I have my insane ancestor's soul in my pocket. How could things possibly be okay?

The only thing I'm sure of is that I need to see this thing through because if I don't, it will keep following me. More bad stuff will happen and it will never be over.

Only one person really understands this. Only one person that I need to find. The person I keep running from.

I don't look back at Tess and Ben when I push into the crowd and race toward the glass-wall fountain. I just go.

Magic and fear surge through me in equal doses. Is this how Baba Yaga felt that day she changed? Is this how Lily felt as she opened her mouth to the water and found herself changing into a rusalka rather than dying?

When I see him standing in the reflecting pool, I feel a sharp pang of relief. I run faster. Almost there now. Did he hear my thoughts when I told him I was on my way?

"Ethan!" I shout. "Ethan." It was a mistake to go to Baba Yaga's without him. I thought I was protecting him. I wasn't. I was just protecting myself. Baba Yaga was right. I couldn't stand the thought of losing him. So much easier if he has to lose me.

No. Not easier. Just selfish and afraid. If you don't commit to love someone, no matter how oddly they've fallen into your life, then what are you? Really, what would I be? I would be her—that huge witch reflected in the glass-tower fountain. Powerful but alone. So lonely that she allowed herself to be used just so she could pretend Anastasia was her daughter.

But it's so hard. So much easier to run. To hide. I think of what I told Tess in Baba Yaga's hut. *People die. History is full of bodies.* But we go on anyway, don't we? I can accept Baba Yaga's power, but maybe I don't have to be her. And I don't have to be Lily either. Or even my mom. I don't want to be so crushed by loss that I lose myself to it. But it's a chance I have to take. A chance I want to take. Maybe my heart is more resilient than I think.

"Ethan!" I call to him again. I could lose him right this second. He could lose me. So I have to chance it. I have to try.

Ethan turns. *Yay,* I think. *Oh yay.* His shirt is ripped at the bottom and his hair matted, but he's in one piece. He's Ethan. I made it back to him. I wade through the water…

Ethan's eyes are all wrong again. Dark. Angry.

Also, unless my memory got shaken loose in the wild ride in the police car, that's Dimitri with him. Dimitri—the man who not too long ago was willing to kill me because Viktor told him to.

"Give it back," Dimitri growls at him. "You can reverse it, Ethan. You don't want it anyway. Give it to me."

"I can't," Ethan says. "Wouldn't if I could."

Can't what? Give him what?

"He'll just use you, you know. And you're too much of a coward to kill him if you get the chance. Concentrate, Ethan. Get rid of what you don't want. I'll do the rest."

I hear Ethan's voice inside my head. *Run. Go.*

Is he kidding? I've just gotten here. I've had a romantic epiphany. If I can get this soul out of my pocket, maybe there can be more peanuts! More kissing! Other stuff!

"Anne." Baba Yaga's voice fills the air. Or maybe just my head. Her hand has climbed back up to her. Now it's only her face looming in the glass fountain, her jaw still open impossibly wide. She locks on to me with those hideous skull eyes I know so well. My panic mixes oddly with the familiar feel of her.

"You think you know me," she says. "You think you understand. Girl, you know nothing. But you are about to find out."

Blip. She's gone. The glass tower fills with the image of some normal-looking woman. A general sigh of relief rises from the crowd. Possibly they hadn't been as much terrified as grossed out.

Dimitri is still focused only on Ethan. "We can work together," he says. "Find a way to give me back that power."

"No." Ethan's pale. Sort of shaky looking. Dark flickers of power dance at his fingertips.

When Dimitri hits him in the jaw, Ethan staggers. Dimitri punches him again.

"Don't," Ethan says. "You really don't want to do this."

Dimitri's fist plows into Ethan's belly. "Go on," Dimitri says. "Stop me."

I start to move toward them. Everything is going crazy and Dimitri wants to fight him? It makes no sense.

Run, says Ethan's voice in my head. *I need you to run.*

Dimitri grabs him by the shoulder. Ethan's hands glow darkly as he shoves Dimitri off him.

The air around them sizzles. *What the hell is going on?*

Dimitri laughs. Lunges at Ethan again.

"It should be mine," he says. "All of it. You know what he's taken from me. Give this back."

"I can't," Ethan says. "I wouldn't if I could." He holds up a hand. Sends Dimitri skimming across the water.

A tall guy in khakis and a dress shirt helps Dimitri to his feet. "Should I call the cops?" he asks. Dimitri shoves him aside.

A woman with two kids on either side of her hollers for them stop it.

"I'll handle it," I tell her.

"Are those contacts?" the boy on her left asks me. "Those skulls in your eyes are really scary. Like that witch lady in the tower."

The three of them run before I can respond.

"Anne," Ethan says. "You need to get out of here. Now." His body begins to vibrate. A low hum fills the air. "Shit." He doubles over. "Go, Anne. Please."

Dimitri comes running, a grim look on his face as he plows through the shallow water.

In that moment, I recognize the darkness that I've been feeling. I don't understand how it's happened, but the dark power inside Ethan is enormous now. The power that Viktor has somehow forced on him just like Baba Yaga has placed her own magic in me.

"No!" Screaming the word, I start to run. Not away but toward him. *Please don't let me have been too late. Please. Please.* "Ethan! No!"

He tries to stand, then doubles over again. The magic streams from his hands.

VIKTOR

I FEEL IT BEGIN. I SMILE. ETHAN, ETHAN. I TOLD YOU IT would be fun. Of course, you are a tough one. Lucky you have Dimitri with you. No one can force an issue quite like Dimitri. Except, of course, for me.

The boy, Ben, lies on the ground, unconscious. Better to let him live. I am not like the witch. Not a monster. Just Koschei come to life. He was a hindrance, this Ben Logan. Now he is not. But to kill him—I am not cruel, just a pragmatist.

"Let me go." Tess Edwards struggles against me. Her eyes show the terror that her voice does not betray. A strong girl. A loyal girl. Worthy of Anne's friendship.

But friendships are liabilities. Like love, they make us weak.

"She's going to come after you, you know," Tess says.

"Not yet," I tell her. "But soon. I'm counting on it, actually."

When she struggles again, I point to Ben Logan. "If you'd like him to stay alive, I suggest you do as I say."

ETHAN

THE MAGIC POURS FROM ME. I WILL IT NOT TO, BUT STILL it moves, even as Anne approaches, running.

"What's happening?" Anne grabs me, and her momentum has us stumbling, falling into the water.

No. She shouldn't be here. She can't be here. Where the hell is Dimitri? How much glass is in two fifty-foot towers? How much death?

Seconds. Mere seconds. This is all I have. No time to counter the spell that is not mine but has come from my hands nonetheless.

Protect. It's all I can do.

We hit the water.

Slow. Protect. Minimize.

One second. Two. Three.

The spell hits its target. First one, then the other fifty-foot glass tower explodes.

Wednesday, 12:43 pm

Anne

We're falling too fast to right ourselves. We smash together to the shallow pool, skid along the bottom as glass begins to rain from the sky.

Ethan pulls me under him. Covers my body with his own.

"*Ya dolzhen*," I hear him say. *I must…*The rest of his words are blotted out by rain and falling glass.

Must what? Stop what's already happened?

I do what I can to slow it down. Visualize rounded ends, not jagged. Small nuggets, not huge shards. At one point, I think I even push some of it back into the air. But the rain and wind work against us. Glass flies everywhere, swirls in the wind like millions of tiny daggers.

Nearby, someone screams. Harsh. Loud. Then the sound is gone, sucked into the huge noise of falling glass and rushing water.

A wall. I work to build that invisible wall. But there are so many people, so many bodies to protect. My own body heaves with the effort. Power bursts from me—more than I've ever used. More than I've ever felt. *Protect. Protect. Protect.*

Magic streams from every inch of me as I lie with Ethan in the shallow water. It burns my hands, my arms, my insides. Does my life flash in front of me? Not really. I think stupid thoughts. Will Buster the cat miss me? And not so stupid. My parents. Tess. Ben. When they find our bodies—Ethan's and mine—under a mountain of glass, will someone be able to identify us?

And the biggest thought. Don't let me die. Not here. Not now. Not yet. Not when I finally figured out how I feel about him. About us.

Ethan presses his body against me. The world continues to explode.

Eventually, it's over. One fountain tower completely destroyed. The other missing only a few blocks of glass. What I felt as we hit the ground—that I'd collided with Ethan in time to divert part of it. A small miracle. The rain eases to a drizzle.

We stagger to our feet. I'm shaking hard, and my nose is bleeding freely. I lick my lip and taste blood. Sirens are wailing and people are screaming. The back of my head feels like it's been hit with a sledgehammer.

Ethan's shocky, pale. There's glass in his hair and blood—his or someone else's. He coughs. When he wipes his mouth, there's blood on the back of his hand.

"Viktor," he rasps. "He'd given magic to Dimitri too. Dimitri's gone mad, Anne. He'd come back to try to kill Viktor. But Viktor knew. He took the magic from him. Put it in me. I still don't know why. But Dimitri wanted the power. He thought I could…I couldn't—it…"

He looks away and stiffens. I track his gaze.

We wade a few feet through water and glass to the body lying face up in the shallow water, a huge piece of glass protruding from his chest.

Dimitri.

Crouching down, Ethan feels for a pulse. I stare at the piece of glass. It must have sliced right through his heart.

What happens next is a blur. We try to revive him. Briefly, we discuss removing the piece of glass. I press my hand to his chest. Feel magic rise again in my fingers, flow into his body. This comes easily to me now, I realize. Even in panic. Even in terror. My body seems to know what to do.

But here is what I also know. Nature has its price. Death— at least in the real world—is still death. Some things cannot be undone.

Ethan stares at Dimitri's body.

"He wanted someone to die," he says. It sounds as cold as I feel. "I guess he got his wish."

It's my turn to throw up. After, I wipe my mouth with the back of my hand. My head throbs. I see a man limping— his leg is cut. A woman helps a guy who looks about four- teen to stand. Here and there, more of the same. Cuts. Bruises. A girl walks by, crying but ambulatory, a deep cut on her forearm.

I brush my hand over it. Close the wound. Not completely enough to freak her out, but enough for me not to worry.

We're lucky. Most people had cleared out once a witch appeared in the fountain. Dimitri's is the only body.

He won't lie here for long. On Michigan Avenue, a stream of cop cars, ambulances, fire trucks. Two helicopters, then three swing into view.

We leave. Fast.

"There was a cop with us," I say, remembering. We're sprinting now, getting out of sight. We can cut through the garden that runs by the Art Institute, I tell Ethan. Get back out to the street that way. "He gave us a ride here because we got stuck in traffic right after we crossed the river."

"We?"

"Tess and Ben. They're here somewhere. Ben drove. We need to find them."

Ethan looks at me blankly. "You shouldn't even be near me," he says. His tone is as blank as his expression.

Guilt. His. Mine. No shortage, that's for sure.

We wind our way through a garden that was probably full of people until a few minutes ago. The huge lawn ahead of us makes me nervous—so big and out in the open. No choice but to chance it. I scan the sky—no Baba Yaga

"I'm sorry I left like that at IHOP." I reach for his hand. He pulls away. "I thought I was protecting you. Maybe I was. But I only made things worse, didn't I? I mean if I was there, would you have gone with Dimitri to meet Viktor? I don't think you—oh!"

I pat my hip. Feel relief when my fingers meet the doll's hard shape. "Wait," I say. "God, Ethan, it's been so crazy, I haven't even told you—showed you. Whatever." Gently, I pull the matryoshka doll from my pocket. "Look."

"Where did you get that?"

I talk quickly as we move through the garden and cross the huge lawn that leads to the street. I tell him everything. What Baba Yaga showed me about her past. Her loneliness. What she said about using Anastasia. How she, too, thought that Viktor believed himself to be like Koschei. And how she was certain that he had accessed Anastasia's past memories while Baba Yaga watched them in the fire.

"So we went to the Romanovs," I say. And then I tell him

the rest of it. He cradles the doll in his hand. I tell him about Anastasia. And Rasputin and the Tsarina. Even about annoying Jimmy the spaniel.

We're walking west on Randolph Street back toward Michigan by the time I finish.

"I always hated that damn dog," Ethan says, and I roll my eyes.

He studies the tiny doll as we reach Michigan Avenue, now a sea of people and emergency vehicles. We need to get out of here. It isn't going to take long for someone to recognize one of us. Or connect us to the dead man lying by the smashed fountain.

"Do you think it's really in there?" I ask as he hands the doll back to me—possibly so he's not holding on to it if he goes dark again. He's still pale as a ghost and keeping his distance.

"Only one way to find out."

"Now? I mean, like, just what? Slam it to the ground? Crush it? What? Everything went wonky when it bounced on the carpet in 1911. So I brought it back with us. Tess thinks that…"

Tess. I stop walking.

I'd shoved my phone back in my pocket so I didn't have to answer the message from my father. It's vibrated on and off, but I've ignored it.

I pull out my phone. Check my missed calls.

Dad.

Dad.

Dad.

Dad.

Tess.

Then nothing. The last message from Tess is a text.

Vktr, she's typed. Nothing more.

Shit. My pulse quickens.

"Something's really wrong," I say, showing Ethan the text. "Why would she text that unless he had her. Or almost had her. Or…"

I press Tess's number. Her phone goes immediately to voice mail.

I do the same with Ben's number. Same result. *Why did I leave them? Why did I run?*

"He knew you'd come to me," Ethan says. "This whole thing—it was some kind of distraction."

Is he right? Are we that predictable? Okay, we are. But that doesn't explain it all. There are lots of ways to distract someone. Why juice him up with power and make him more dangerous? Only to kill Dimitri? A million easier ways to do that. There's something we're not seeing. But there's no time. Where the hell are Ben and Tess?

"Hey!" a voice behind me booms. "Tess's friend? Anne, right?"

Officer Shanahan, his uniform torn, his face weary. Relief washes over me. Officer Shanahan. Tess must be okay.

Except what he says is, "The guy who was with you? Tess's boyfriend? I just put him in an ambulance. He must have been hit by something in that freak storm that blew up. I thought he was dead. But he was just unconscious. They've taken him to Rush."

My brain doesn't shift gears fast enough. "They what?" *Ben? Hospital?* "Did Tess go with him?"

"He'll be okay. One of the paramedics is my wife's brother Nick. He knows what he's doing." Then, "Tess?" The cop stares at me. "I thought she was with you."

No. No. No.

In my hand, my phone vibrates. Dad again.

"Hi," I snap. "I'm okay, Dad. I just can't talk right now. I—"

"Have you talked to your mother?" Dad's voice is panicked. In my head, I see him all wild-haired like when Lily made her guest appearance and he was standing in our backyard.

"Mom? Why?" The words come out strained. My throat dries up. How long has it been since I've had something to drink?

"You're okay, though?" my father says, and I realize how much I love him. "Sweetie. Anne. You're safe, right?"

This is highly questionable, but I tell him yes.

"Your mother's disappeared," Dad says then. "I'd gotten her to bed after you—well, after. I thought she'd finally fallen asleep. I must have dozed off. When I woke up, she was gone."

"Gone? Like gone somewhere? Or just gone? Did she leave a note? Did you call her cell?" I try not to shriek but fail.

"Just gone," he says. "She left her phone on the kitchen table. She was telling me all these things, Anne. I don't know what to believe anymore. That woman in the yard. Ethan. You. It's like I got out of bed and fell into some alternate…Your mother kept insisting that the thing in the backyard was her birth mother. That she wanted to be with her. That this Lily was the only one who could understand. That she knew what it was like to have no more hope. That Lily was the only one who could help. 'She told me where it happened,' your mother kept saying. 'She showed me.'"

My father's voice breaks. "Anne. Who is this Ethan, really? What's been going on in my house? Where is your mother?"

"She went to find Lily," I say, and as the words come out

of my mouth, every molecule in my body tells me that they're true. But where?

"I even drove to the cemetery." My father's crying on the phone now. "I thought if she was upset like this she'd go to David's grave. She's done that before, you know. Some of those times when she's disappeared. She'll walk. Or go to the movies. Or sometimes she just sits at the cemetery."

I thought he hadn't noticed. He had. He just hadn't done anything about it.

A mixture of fear, anger, and frustration swirls inside me.

"I'll find her," I promise and end the call.

"It was my dad," I say. "My mom's missing."

Officer Shanahan furrows his brow. That muscle in Ethan's jaw pulses.

Where could she be? And why now? I have to find Tess. Ben is in the hospital. Ethan's hanging on by a thread. Viktor's soul is still in the matryoshka doll that's back in my other pocket. My life is imploding and now, unless I'm really mistaken, my mom's gone to search for Lily.

Lily. *She showed me where it happened.* This is what Mom told Dad.

The one thing Lily would want my mom to see, to understand. In the end, the only place she'd go. The place that held her trapped, the place where she was when she became a rusalka. The one she had to haunt.

"She's gone to find Lily," I tell Ethan. "We need to go to the river. Now."

"What about Tess?"

The answer comes quickly even though I don't want it to be true. "If Viktor has her, he'll follow us," I say. "Or he'll make sure we know. If he took her, he took her for a reason. Plus, he's not going far from you, is he?"

"Something's happened with Tess?" This question is Officer Shanahan's. "Maybe," I say. *Yes.*

Do I unconsciously use magic on my new friend the police officer when he offers to drive us in his squad car? Or do I just look that desperate? Surely he's blocking out the information that I seem to be connected to the still-ongoing chaos around us. Maybe he just likes Tess. She has that effect on people.

All I know is that Officer Shanahan, sirens blaring, drives us back to the bridge at Wacker. He gets another call on his radio as we leap out.

"By the boats." Ethan points below us. "It happened by the boats."

Once again, we run.

WEDNESDAY, 2:02 PM

ETHAN

I WASN'T THERE WHEN IT HAPPENED. BUT I'VE REPLAYED IT in my head a thousand times. The night I saw Lily—human Lily. The night she didn't die but instead became a rusalka, an evil thing. Viktor had already identified her as the one who might be able to save Anastasia. I had no idea. He told me the trail had gone cold. Why would I have doubted him? By then I had believed him for almost fifty years.

The truth? I was tired of this little game we were playing. Fifty years in, that's how I saw it. Later, I regained my vigilance. I found Anne. I became the man I wanted to become. But then—it seemed to me there were better things to do.

It was another woman I saw first—the one I later learned was Nadia, Lily's friend. Nadia who would take the identity of Amelia Benson and continue to protect Lily's baby. Baby Laura, Anne's mother. Fate is a funny thing. Another minute and I would have seen them both together. All our destinies, I think, would have vastly changed. But I didn't. I stopped and lit Nadia's cigarette as she fumbled for a match.

I thought it strange that Viktor kept walking; usually he was a man of good manners, especially in public. We had both kept some of the old ways—a courtliness that came with having lived in different times. But that night, he didn't stop. Years later, I would understand why, but not then. All I knew was that I'd given a small favor to a woman I'd never seen before and never planned on seeing again.

I was almost to my hotel when I saw the other woman. There was something so sad about her gray eyes; this is why I was able to recognize them a few weeks ago. Why I was able to connect these events that had happened so many years apart. To understand even more painfully what I had already come to know—that I had been betrayed by many people, but most of all by Viktor, a man I had trusted with my life. The woman with the gray eyes had bumped into me as I passed by a small bookshop, stared at my face, then run.

It should have bothered me more. I should have followed her. But I didn't. Of the many things I regret in my very long life, this is one. Now I understand that I had a chance to save her. I, Ethan, who knew that magic existed, that there is a world beyond what most people see. That seventeen-year-old grand duchesses can be swept away by the hands of a witch, and women can meet hideous fates in the water.

This is the trick about destiny. If we are not watching, it can pass us by. We can miss the signs and the opportunities and the moments. Only if you live as long as I have, can you truly understand the tragedy of this.

That night I saw Lily—daughter of Natasha, granddaughter of Irina, great-granddaughter of Marina, Tsar Nicholas's lover, and Viktor's mother—she leaped into the Chicago River rather than be traced back to the infant daughter she'd hoped to save by giving up for adoption. Viktor had already killed her husband, Misha, in his attempt to do away with her.

Would he have pursued this had he known then that Lily was his own blood, that the girl who could rescue Anastasia was not just connected to the Brotherhood but to him? I do not know. I only know that Lily also ran because she saw me. And I was too much of a *zalupa* then to question why.

When she was drowning, when it was too late to turn back, when she opened her mouth to the water and let it rush into her lungs, they came for her. Rusalki, we call them in Russia. Mermaids. Lethal. Seductive. Malevolent. Cursed. Each unable to find rest or peace or a true death until the blood of the person who killed her—or betrayed her or caused her death—is shed. This is the way the folk tale goes. This is the destiny that found Lily.

Here is what I believe as Anne and I race along the river, desperate to finally bring this thing to an end: Lily's fate is not just on Viktor's head. It is also on mine. Everything that has come from that moment until now, I take responsibility for it all.

"Over there!" I shout now as I see Anne's mother leaning toward the water. "Hurry."

WEDNESDAY, 2:03 PM

ANNE

HERE'S THE STUFF MOST CHICAGOANS KNOW ABOUT THE Chicago River. You can go on a Wendella boat ride. On St. Patrick's Day, they dye the river green. Yellow water taxis zip back and forth, taking people all the way from Michigan Avenue down to Chinatown and some other stops in between. In the winter, parts of the river sometimes freeze if it gets really cold. Some of the bridges that go over the river have to open and lift up when sailboats are passing.

Here's what almost no one knows: in 1961, a woman named Lily tried to drown herself in the river and instead was turned into a rusalka. In part, she did it because she was afraid. In part, she did it to save her daughter, Laura, who happens to be my mom. Lily has not been able to rest since. She can't die, and she can't go free until the person responsible for what happened to her has his blood shed.

It's a creepy story and a creepy curse, and if Lily wasn't my birth grandmother, and the guy who tried to kill her wasn't my ancestor Viktor, who makes me connected to the Russian Romanovs, I probably wouldn't know it. But I do. And my mom hasn't been the same since she lost her son, my brother, David, to cancer. Anyone standing by the river right now needs to understand this. Otherwise I'm just a girl running to save her crazy family from even more unhappiness. It is not looking like I'm going to succeed.

"Mom!" I call to her. "Mom."

My mother sways on the edge of the sidewalk, the river below her. She's wearing a gauzy flowered sundress—cream-colored with tiny little sunflowers—and gladiator sandals. Her hair is hanging loose, blowing behind her in the wind. One of those yellow water taxis chugs not far out in the water.

When she hears my voice, Mom looks up. Her gaze meets mine, and she smiles, but then she turns her attention back at the river.

"Laura," Ethan says. "Look at me. Look at Anne."

We're almost to her now. As if with one mind, he and I slow to a brisk walk. Don't want to frighten her. Don't want her to move.

I hear their crooning sound before I see them. Like in the Jewel Box when they tried to lure Ben. At least a dozen rusalki bob in the river below us. One of them blows a kiss to the driver of the water taxi. And in the center of the pack is Lily, with her tattered lilac dress, her wild gray eyes, her dark hair snaking this way and that in the water and wind.

"I can be with him if I go to her," Mom says. She looks up again. Her eyes—brown like mine—are blank looking. Like with Ben, I think. The rusalki are luring her. Lily is luring her.

"No," Ethan says. "You won't be with David. It's a lie. That's what they do. They lie. She's lying, Laura."

Mom tilts her head. "She wouldn't do that. Mothers don't lie to daughters."

Of course they do, I want to scream. Especially if they're evil Russian mermaids. And even if they're not. We lie for all sorts of reasons. Sometimes just because the truth is too awful. It doesn't make it right. It just makes us human.

"Mom," I say as calmly as I can, given the circumstances, "Lily isn't ever going to tell you the truth. She can't. It's part of her curse. I know it sucks, and I know you're sad, and I know you want things to be different. But jumping into the river isn't going to do anything but make it worse. Is that what you want for me and Daddy? To be sad enough that we want to die?"

Mom hesitates, then teeters closer to the edge. My heart catches in my throat. *This isn't her*, I think. *She's not herself.* No matter what, my mom wouldn't do this to me.

Slowly, I edge closer, ready to grab her. Ethan maneuvers himself to the other side.

"Laura," Lily calls up from the water. "It's not so bad once you let go. You'll be with me then. We'll see my grandson. I promise. The pain will stop."

"Liar." I spit the word between gritted teeth. "You horrible liar. I hate you. Oh God, how I hate you." I would kill her right now if I could. With magic. With my bare hands. But she's not human. Which I guess is the point.

I take another step, almost to her. My body is shaking—with fear, with exhaustion, and with the power that's building inside me, readying itself to do whatever I ask.

Protection spell. Yes. I need to do that. But I can't even…it comes anyway, flowing easily. My mind builds a cocoon of safety around my mother, like tucking an invisible comforter around her as she lies in bed.

Then terror grips me once again. The spell protects her from Lily. But it does nothing to stop my mother's free will. No magic will stop her from jumping. Only me and Ethan.

On the other side of Mom, I see Ethan shiver. Black tendrils of power flow around him like before. He shudders. Closes his eyes, and the threads of magic fade.

"You okay?" I can see that he's not.

"For now."

In the water, Lily laughs.

Behind me, so does someone else.

Viktor. He holds Tess next to him, his arm draped casually over her shoulders like they're the best of friends. There's a purple bruise under her eye. But she's alive. *Tess. Oh, Tess.*

"Anne," she says, and Viktor's hand moves to her throat. She winces. "You need to—" Tess rasps. Viktor's grip tightens.

"I had no idea," Viktor says, "that we were having a party. I thought Ethan, here, would be quite tapped out from his little escapade. Ah, Brother Ethan, I do believe I have underestimated your stamina. How fortunate."

My mother looks from Lily to me to Viktor and Tess to Ethan. Her pretty sundress whips around her thin legs in the wind. The rest of us look like we've been through twelve tornadoes, but my mom—poised on the edge of no return—looks like she's stepped out of a fashion magazine. If I wasn't panicked to the point of nausea, I might find this funny.

"Laura," Lily calls from the water. "David is waiting for you. You need to come now."

It is at that moment, as everything prepares to explode again in one way or the other, that Tess does something very Tess-like. She stomps with all her might on Viktor's foot. Then she knees him in the groin. It isn't magic. But it gets her point across.

"Do it!" she screams at me when he loses his grip on her throat.

Does she not see that my mother is about to leap into a scrum of rusalki?

Ethan lunges for my mother.

I pull the matryoshka doll out of my pocket.

I guess what happens after that is just my mother being a mom. Okay, a very depressed, hypnotized-by-her-evil-mermaid-mother mom, but a mom.

A mom who sees that her daughter's best friend since pre-school is being hurt by some guy she doesn't really know. I assume she sort of recognizes him, but it isn't enough.

My mother ducks from Ethan's reach and tackles Viktor like she's trying out for the NFL. He loses his hold on Tess and she scrambles free.

"Mom!" I scream, and keep on screaming as Viktor and my mother twist and turn, like they're dancing at the edge of the water. And then in a blink my mother falls, flailing, into the river. Into the circle of rusalki. Did he push her? Did she jump? Did my protection spell fail?

Ethan never even hesitates. He dives after her.

After that, I don't think. I just do what I have to do.

My hand uncurls. In my palm sits the tiny, fragile wooden doll that somehow one day in another time and place will end up being Anastasia's. I place it on the sidewalk. Raise my foot and smash it to pieces.

Like that day last fall when we returned from the forest and Ethan and Viktor got their mortality back, the world fills with light. Viktor's eyes widen in shock. *Didn't think I was going to do that now, did you? Yeah, me—just a stupid girl.*

If I make it through this and anyone ever asks me what I think about the human soul, here's what I'll say: people choose how they act—good, bad, homicidal maniac on a power trip. But the soul—it's all light and energy. I can't explain it beyond that. I just know that the light finds Viktor. It pours into every inch of him. Makes him stumble and sink to his knees accepting that energy. Life force? Soul? I'm not the person to ask. I just know what I see. The light pours out of the broken matryoshka doll and into Viktor. Who, let me add, does not look pleased.

"Gotcha!" Tess says. She's doing a happy dance over by a tree.

But I don't have time to celebrate. My mother is still in the water.

Wednesday, 2:41 pm

Ethan

My hands slice through the water just as everything inside me begins to pull and twist and burn. For a second, I think I've hit my head because even as my body goes underwater, the world seems full of light.

Only as I surface and get my bearings do I understand. Anne has done it. Viktor's soul really was in Anastasia's matryoshka doll. Now it's back inside him and he's vulnerable. We can stop him. He can die.

Laura flounders in the river a few feet from me, Lily treading water at her side. The rusalki have made a circle around them. If we're lucky—if this has really worked—Viktor is no longer invincible. But his magic still writhes inside me, stronger than anything I've ever felt. Viktor's power has used me. Now I use it.

Magic streams from my fingers through the water. The mermaids shriek and howl as the air around them grows warmer, then warmer still. I kick toward them, flick a hand. Heat. Smoke. Flame.

I dive beneath them as they scream. As their hair burns but they find themselves unable to sink into the cooling water. Inside the circle, I grab Laura. She struggles. Lily has her mind still.

"Look below the surface," she tells Anne's mother. "You'll see your boy. Your son. You can't leave him. You can't leave me."

She reaches out her skeletal arms, covered in dark lines of seaweed. The light that's everywhere, the light that means that Anne has succeeded—we've succeeded—illuminates everything—Lily, me, Laura, and the singed, screaming rusalka circle.

Lily lifts her gaze to the sidewalk above us. To Viktor, bent over, arms resting on his thigh, one knee on the ground. Lily gasps, stays very still in the water as Viktor stands.

I start to swim, pulling Anne's mother with me. Toward the closest safety I can find—the yellow water taxi chugging swiftly toward us. Someone pulls her up. They reach for me next. But something drags me back and under. Begins to claw at my face. Not Lily. But another rusalka. The rusalka who used to be Nadia. Nadia—Lily's friend. Nadia, whose cigarette I lit all those years ago.

Sharp talons of nails rake my forehead, dig into my eye. Blood spurts, blurs my vision. Pain. Hot, searing. *My eye.*

The magic rises again. I send her under, as deep as she can go. If I could kill her, I would. Maybe I do.

Only one eye is functioning as I swim back toward Anne. My only thought is to reach her. I keep swimming, my own blood slick on my face.

WEDNESDAY, 3:02 PM

ANNE

RELIEF SPILLS THROUGH ME. MOM'S SAFE, AT LEAST FOR now. The rest of it—we'll deal with it later. But in this moment in time, she's on the water taxi.

Ethan's swimming back to me. Another check in the plus column. Then I see his face—covered in blood. A red trail streams behind him in the water.

"Anne!" Tess's voice knifes through the air. A warning.

I pivot. Viktor ages as he strides toward me, the youth he'd regained peeling off him like pieces of skin after a bad sunburn. But he doesn't slow. He doesn't do us all a favor and just drop dead.

So here's the problem. Well, beyond all the other problems. Like Ethan, I've been holding back. That gnawing hunger—all those pancakes!—that aches in my jaw. I know what I've taken from her, but I've resisted it. Kept it under. Hidden.

Maybe I always would have. Maybe I'd have just lived the rest of my life in a sort of Dr. Jekyll–Mr. Hyde kind of way. Kept the witch buried except for surface stuff like making my mom's tomato plants grow. I think I could have done it. I really do. I'm a rising senior at Kennedy High School. Not a witch in a freaky chicken-leg hut in some forest.

But threaten everyone I love and then come after me even though you're now gnarly looking and old? I let the witch rise.

I'm not Baba Yaga. I haven't traded beauty for power. I haven't let the Old Ones turn me into something just so I don't have to bend to other people's will. I'm not standing somewhere in Russia, my hands pressed to my stomach knowing that my lover's baby has been obliterated because I'm no longer human. I'm not going to eat all the apples from a tree and then gobble an innocent little boy.

I took what she offered only to help save the people I love. Because Ethan was dying and Ben was hurt and Tess was in danger. Because my family had been turned upside down by fate and destiny and crazy mermaids and death. Because I'd sent a girl who deserved better back to die like she was supposed to. I tell myself that it isn't the same. And I really do believe this.

Viktor hesitates as he hears me groan. Maybe he thinks I'm sick or afraid. I double over, but I still know where he is. The hunger feels all-consuming when I let it. A raw ache in my belly, my blood, my teeth.

My jaw loosens. Unhinges. Drops. I think I even get a little taller. Maybe I'm just imagining that.

He's almost on me when I stand up, open my witch's mouth, and lean forward to take a bite.

Viktor's eyes widen. He makes a noise that sounds like "eep."

Somewhere, I hear Tess shout, "Holy shit."

I'm very, very hungry. My jaw widens even more. Viktor begins to backpedal. I stalk after him.

He smells sharp and dark, and his blood will taste rich in my mouth. This simultaneously pleases me and disgusts me.

But it doesn't make me stop. The anger about so many things rises with the witch's power. I have magic. I am a very powerful woman. But I cannot make my mother better. I cannot make her stop wanting something—someone—she can never have. I can only destroy this man whose selfish desire to live forever has destroyed so many lives.

This is what it comes down to—we get the time we get, and we try to make the best of it before it's cut short by circumstance or illness or chance. For Viktor this was not enough. He took Anastasia and he took Baba Yaga and he took Ethan, and because of all that, he took me. He killed Professor Olensky. Lily is cursed. My mother inherited her sadness. It will never be enough.

And so the witch in me will eat him. I will chew his flesh and his bones and his desire, and when I am done, I will spit the pieces on the ground. I will put his head on a spike, and I will place it on Baba Yaga's fence. When I visit her again— which this man has made my fate—I will look into his empty eyes and know that I put him there.

This is what crawls through my veins as I reach for him. Part of me screams that the thoughts aren't mine. But I'm tired. So tired of all of it. I decide not to listen.

A hand pulls me back. A very strong hand. Actually, just a hand.

"No," Baba Yaga says. She hasn't mortared in. She's just there. *When did she arrive? Is this real? Am I real?* I strain against the hand. I want to destroy him. I have to.

"No," she says again. She doesn't elaborate. Doesn't give me some witch-to-witch lecture. "This is not Russia, daughter. You are not me. You made him mortal again. That is enough."

Then she smiles with those iron teeth. Her skull eyes light up kind of cheerfully. "But that doesn't mean I can't do it. You let him free, after all. I am no longer compelled to protect a Romanov. Especially one so unworthy of their legacy. And mine."

She uses the hand that isn't holding me to lift Viktor in the air. Studies him like he's a bug under a microscope. And begins to bend him backward. I think she plans on breaking him in two.

He screams.

And in the water, still coming back to me, so does Ethan.

I turn. Ethan is treading water now, struggling. He jerks. Goes under. Swims to the surface. His face is covered in blood. But something else is hurting him now. He screams again. Lifts above the river and bends backward. Like something wants to break him in two.

This time when Viktor screams, he also laughs. Blood is oozing from his mouth, so it comes out as sort of a gurgle.

"Go ahead, Yaga," he says. "Kill me. But you'll kill her hero, Ethan too, you know. I still have some tricks, Yaga. Do you think I wouldn't have a plan? My soul in the doll. And a part of my magic hidden elsewhere. Enough to do the job. I live. Ethan lives. I die. He dies. Such a perfect safeguard, yes? Your darling Anne wouldn't kill her lover, now would she? How will she feel when you do it? But maybe that's what you want. Your precious Anne all to yourself. Not quite your Anastasia. But good enough, eh?"

Baba Yaga licks her lips. Opens her own enormous mouth.

My head swirls with all that's happening. I'm still dizzy with hunger. But I need to stop her. She's going to kill Viktor.

Ethan will die. Then she touches me on the forehead, and my jaw becomes just my jaw again. The power inside me shrinks back. Hides.

"No!" Tess yells. She rushes toward Baba Yaga. "No. You can't."

In the water, Ethan screams again.

And then I see Lily.

Wednesday, 3:18 pm

Ethan

LILY PULLS ME UNDER WATER. THE PAIN IS UNBEARABLE. The vision in my left eye is gone. And now I'm being torn in two by something I can't quite identify. Vaguely, I hear Viktor scream. Where is he? Is my pain connected to his? I don't understand. I just know I'm dying. Here in the Chicago River with Anne on the sidewalk above me. I'm dying and I can't seem to make it stop.

Anne, I call in my head. *Anne. Can you hear me? I love you, Anne. I've always loved you. I will always love you. Know this. Remember this.*

"Be still," Lily says. Can I really hear her underwater? Am I dead? "I hold you accountable," she croons in my ear. "Just as Viktor. But there is value in love. You saved my daughter, even from me. You did not stop. Your heart—it is far purer than mine ever was. You have suffered as I have. You will suffer more. But know this, Ethan. Had I not become what I am, destiny would not have brought you to Anne. Love, Ethan—it finds a way. There is value in it. You were willing to die. Be willing to live and love instead."

Her hands rip into my back. Nails dig. I feel my skin tear. Skeletal arms hold me under. My body bows and bends—a different force. But under the water, in the quiet, it is just Lily and

I. She scrapes deep into my back, nails sharp as talons raking the skin near my shoulder.

"Do not be afraid," she murmurs. "I will release you from him. I will set you free. Already his life force is waning. I can feel it, Ethan. I can die now. But you—you must live. Live, Ethan. Love my granddaughter. Do right by her."

She claws my back again. *So much blood in the water. Is it all mine?* My body writhes, twists. The magic that is Viktor's magic howls inside me. *Can magic feel pain?* He's dying. Viktor is dying. And so am I.

"There," Lily says. Her voice is gentle. "It is done. I have removed the thing that binds you to him. Did you not know, Ethan? Did you not understand? No matter. It is gone. You are free. And so, it seems, am I. Love her, Ethan. Live."

She floats in front of me now, her hair snaking around her, those gray eyes locked on mine. In that instant, there is light again. Sparkling like crystal in the murky river. Lily smiles. Then shimmers into the light.

Somehow I swim to the surface.

ANNE

Two things happen at once. Ethan rises to the surface of the water, still gloriously alive. And Baba Yaga cracks Viktor's back and tosses him into the river. First one rusalka, then another and another and another surround him in the water. Closer and closer they swim, circling so fast they make a whirlpool. They disappear into its vortex, dragging Viktor with them.

Is he alive when he sinks? Blood has been shed. I don't know if this means he has to die. I don't choose to ask.

Baba Yaga sends both hands to the edge of the river. They lift Ethan up and out. Lay him on the grass. He's bleeding—so much blood on his face. His clothes are ripped and torn. Tess and I kneel next to him. She pushes his wet hair off his forehead.

"Your mother," he gasps. His head tilts oddly as he looks at me.

"Safe," I tell him. "Viktor's gone, Ethan. Baba Yaga broke his back. The rusalki took it from there." I'll tell him the rest of it later. No time for stories now.

"Lily did something to my shoulder," he says. His voice is so faint that I can barely hear him. We need doctors. A hospital. An ambulance.

He struggles to sit, but manages only to roll slightly to one side. I suck in a breath when I see it. The back of his shirt is ripped almost completely off. His skin is a bloody mess. It takes me a few seconds to see what's gone.

"Your tattoo," I tell him. "She dug it off your back. The lion tattoo. Ethan—it's gone."

In his head, I hear the rest of it. What Lily told him about the tattoo and how it kept him linked to Viktor.

Baba Yaga moves to stand over us. Her hands skitter back to her and tug the hem of her skirt as they begin their climb back to her empty, flapping sleeves. In the distance I hear sirens. Out in the river, my mom is still on the water taxi.

"I have given us protection, daughter," Baba Yaga says. "Do what you need to. The real world can be held at bay for only so long. People's memories are short, though. I will not have to do much to make them forget what they've seen."

I rip the bottom of my T-shirt and use it to wipe Ethan's face.

"His eye," Tess whispers in my ear. "Anne. His eye."

Ethan's right eye is blue and whole. But his left eye has been jabbed. Something has gone straight through it.

Gently, I press the piece of shirt to Ethan's eye.

"Rusalka," he whispers. I don't ask him to tell me more.

Rage rises inside me. Rage and grief and a million other emotions too dangerous to identify. But not the hunger. Somehow, for now, that's gone.

I have no idea how much power I have left—maybe none. Maybe all of it. But everything inside me pushes into my hand as I press it to Ethan's damaged eye. *Heal*, I tell the wound. *Please. Heal.* In my head, I imagine the eye knitting itself together. Becoming whole. Healed. The pain gone.

My hand feels warm against Ethan's face. Something is working. *Oh, please, let it work.*

When I peel my hand away, his eye looks like his eye again. Happiness floods through my veins. Softly, I press a kiss to his lips. "It's going to be okay," I say.

"Did you do something?" Ethan asks. "I can't see from that side."

How can that be? I healed his eye. Healed it. But when I look, I see the truth. One eye—his left eye, still blue as a summer sky—is blind.

"Nature commands a price, daughter," Baba Yaga says. Her voice is calm, matter of fact. "You have brought him back to you a third time. Always there are consequences. I believe in time he will find it a small price to pay."

I stare at her, then back at Ethan, then at the river now calm, not a rusalka in sight.

"Your debt to me is paid, girl. You have given me my chance for vengeance. You are released from your bargain—but only if you want to be. I have lived a very long time. I can wait a bit longer for your response."

In that instant, she stops being there. She doesn't rise up to her mortar. I don't see the sky rip as I have before. She is just here and then she's not here.

"Is it over?" Tess asks.

"Yes," I tell her. "I think so."

A Month Later

Anne

It has taken a lot to un-implode our lives. We're still working on it, actually. My mother's in therapy, and she'll probably be going for a very long time. Maybe forever. Some of that is my fault. Most of it really isn't. People are what they are, and they feel what they feel. Sometimes a hole is so deep that you can't get out of it. And the magic stuff just made it all more complicated.

A week after that horrible day downtown, my parents announced that they were separating for a while. It was Mom's request, not Dad's. But she was insistent that she needed time to figure things out and eventually he gave in.

My father has rented a small apartment in Evanston, not far from where Ethan lives. This wasn't on purpose, by the way. It's just there was a newer building with studio apartments available. At least that's what my dad says—my dad who seems to have accepted that I'm with Ethan now, whether he wants me to be or not. As I've yet to find him peeping in Ethan's windows when I'm over there, I guess I have to believe him. He has a view of the lake, although lately I'd rather not look at the water.

Dad goes with Mom to some of her therapy sessions, and

they're seeing a marriage counselor too. They both say that they want to make our family work again. I hope that they can. I sleep at my dad's on the weekends, and we all have dinner together on Sunday nights when he drives me back home.

It's all very calm and civilized. At least on the surface.

Underneath, of course, is a different story. But like in the fairy tales, no one goes into Baba Yaga's forest and comes out the same. No one really lives happily ever after. But at least now we're all moving forward.

Doctors have confirmed that Ethan has no sight in his left eye. No one can understand how it looks so healthy otherwise. So far he has chosen not to explain it to them. Like everything else, it could all be a lot worse. I was able to use my magic to close the wound on his back. The skin is smooth now and unblemished. No sign of that lion tattoo that I always found so sexy.

As for Ethan himself, my heart beats faster when he walks into the room. He is the only one I'll ever want. The only one I've ever wanted. His hair is still a little bit too long, and his eyes—both of them—are still a stunning blue. His skin smells earthy and spicy and clean, like soap. When he kisses me, my body tingles in a way that is its own kind of magic. We don't seem to be able to read each other's thoughts any more—at least not the way we did. We're both okay with that.

Most days, we're together. School starts for me in another few days, so this is going to change. But for the past month, it's been Ethan and me. We talk and eat and listen to music, and lately in the afternoons we've started walking to a little park not far from where he lives.

We lie on a blanket under the trees and he kisses me and

I kiss him back, and sometimes he even reads me poetry like we're in a romantic movie. I think about how lucky we are to have found each other. I ponder what Lily told him—the story he murmured to me that night after Baba Yaga's hands pulled him from the river and brought him back to me. He was dopey from painkillers and lying on our guest bed. I'd pulled the rocking chair next to the bed and was curled up there with my pillow and a blanket. My mother was sedated and sleeping, and my father had finally drifted off.

He hadn't argued about Ethan staying the night. He was just happy Mom was alive.

I climbed into the bed and slipped under the covers with Ethan. We pressed against each other and he told me what Lily had done. What she'd said. That if he'd stopped her from jumping that night so many years ago, things might have been different. He might not have followed the path that ended here with me. I might never have been the one to save Anastasia. Everything else might have been different too. It had taken seeing her in the river again for him to truly understand.

We whispered together in the darkness until he fell asleep with me tucked in the crook of his arm. In the morning, we woke peacefully, the sun shining in the window, my head still resting on the pillow next to him.

"I'm so sorry," I whispered to him that next morning. My fingers caressed that beautiful unseeing eye.

His answer had been to kiss me and pull me close. I felt his heart beat fast against mine. And for the first time since we'd met, I understood what love really was.

In other matters of love or at least lust, Ben and Tess are still together too. Ben didn't remember much of what had happened. But he'd been conscious by the time he reached the hospital. Tess had gone over there as soon as things were finally over. Her brother, Zach, stayed with her until Ben's parents arrived. She'd called me about a dozen times so I could help her craft a plausible story for everyone. So far it seems to have worked.

"Thank you," Ethan told Tess the other day when the four of us went out for pizza. We sat at a little table at Lou Malnati's, stuffing our faces with deep-dish cheese pizza and onion rings—the official food of people who have endured magical trauma.

Tess narrowed her eyes at him. Crunched a piece of Lou's famous butter crust between her teeth. A string of cheese was stuck to her lip. Ben leaned over and ate it off her lip, then kissed her.

"Eww" was my personal comment. If someone is going to eat pizza off me, we're going to do it in private.

"Why are you thanking me?" Tess picked up the spatula and helped herself to another slice.

"Because you never give up. Because Anne and I wouldn't be here without you."

"That?" Tess dredged an onion ring in ranch dressing and shoved most of it in her mouth. "Guess you owe me, huh?"

As for me and Baba Yaga, well, I still don't know how that story is going to end. She'd told me that I owed her nothing, but it's not like there's been an official de-powering. Mostly it feels like a "don't ask, don't tell" sort of thing. I won't bother the magic, and so far it hasn't bothered me. All I know is that it feels wrong to give it up completely. And until it doesn't, I guess I'll just live with things as they are. I'm not the same girl who went into Baba Yaga's forest. I'm done pretending I am.

I think this is why last Sunday I used the magic again. Like saving Anastasia regardless of how it eventually turned out, sometimes there are things that we just have to do. I don't know why I did it exactly, except that my dad had grilled steaks and suddenly there the three of us were, remembering how much David had loved my dad's famous rib-eye marinade. These are the moments that happen when you've lost someone— one second you're chomping on steak and salad, and the next you're having this flashback to the way things used to be. We don't lose people all at once, I guess. They disappear in stages.

Later, after Dad had gone back to the apartment, Mom fell asleep on the couch watching TV. I watched her lying there in shorts and a T-shirt, still too thin, too fragile. And I thought about all those nights she'd spent sitting in David's hospital room. About the look on her face out there in our yard that night when Lily came to her.

I didn't think about the rest of it. Just pressed my hand to her forehead, and as gently as I could, I took us both back. April 5. David's twelfth birthday. I was just ten, still in middle school. We'd come downstairs for breakfast, and my mom had put twelve candles in David's waffles—six in one and six in the other. This was our tradition as far back as I could remember— birthday breakfast candles.

My dad was late and rushing, and I had done something

really geeky to my bangs with the curling iron and Mom's hair spray. But we all gathered around the table while David made a wish and blew out his candles. My mom kissed David on both cheeks and my dad patted him on the back. Later we'd all go out to dinner. On the weekend, David would take his friends paintballing.

None of us had any idea what was coming. I guess you never do. This is what I showed my mom. Let her put those candles in the waffles one more time. Let her hug my brother and bury her nose in his hair and have no fear that this might be the last time. One small moment. One ordinary day.

Why had I possibly refused when she had asked? Many reasons, I suppose. But as Ethan reminds me, it does us little good to look backward.

In her sleep, my mother smiled.

The Swedish Film Festival,
One Month and Three Days Later

Anne

"Vats of coffee," Tess says. "Do you think they serve it in a bucket? I mean seriously, I need a caffeine IV. Who watches crap like that? Unhappy blond people yapping in Swedish. Plus, the subtitles. I can't watch and read at the same time. Was anyone else getting dizzy?"

Because of a certain set of events a little over a month ago, the Art Institute has postponed its Swedish Film Festival until today.

The Swedish Film Festival, let me add, should be renamed the Narcolepsy Film Festival. Tess is right. Ten minutes into the first movie, the subtitles had lulled me into a semiconscious state. Somehow we'd managed to sit there—me and Tess sandwiched between Ben on Tess's left and Ethan on my right—for two films in a row: the first about some guy who lives on a farm in rural Sweden and falls in love with his next-door neighbor's wife. They spend most of the movie casting longing looks at each other until finally she ends up moving to Stockholm to run a pastry shop and he throws himself into his thresher and dies.

The second one seemed happier—something about a street musician and his dog. Honestly? By then I was focused on Ethan's lips and how his hand was resting on my knee.

We leave the museum and head out to Michigan Avenue. It's the first time I've been back since what we all have decided to call "the incident." So far we're all in one piece. The Swedes can jump into their threshers. Ethan and I and Tess and Ben are going for coffee. Maybe pastries too. Those pastries looked good in the movie.

"Do you know any place that makes cream puffs?" I ask the group. We're at the stoplight, waiting to cross. There's a place that makes great lattes a couple blocks away.

The light turns and we start to walk, and that's when we see her. A girl about ten years old, walking with her mother. She's slim and pretty, and she's got eyes as blue as cornflowers and light brown hair. Her nose is straight and so is her posture, and I notice that she looks an awful lot like her mother. She says something to her mom that makes them both laugh.

In her hand is a little wooden doll with a painted face.

"Anne," Tess says. "Do you see that?"

"Yup," I say. "I do. Ethan, do *you* see that?"

He turns so he can look with his good eye. "Oh," he says. "Hmm."

"Not again," Ben humphs.

"Is it possible?" Tess asks.

Is what possible? I think. Did Anastasia really take my warning when we visited the past and somehow escape the massacre and live happily ever after, and these people are her descendants? My fingers give a suspicious little tingle.

"Nah," Ethan and I say in unison. We hurry across the street. On the other side, I tilt my face and encourage him to kiss me. Ethan kisses very, very well.

The girl and her mother go somewhere I don't see.

I hook my arms around Ethan's neck. His strong arms lift me, twirl me in a circle. A happy dance.

"I think Anne just told destiny to suck it," Tess tells Ben.

"You've got that right," I say against Ethan's lips.

And then I kiss him again.

ACKNOWLEDGMENTS

As usual, this cannot be done alone.

Jen Rofe, my wise and wonderful cowgirl—chai lattes for life.

The Sourcebooks team: intrepid editor Leah Hultenschmidt, Kelly Barrales-Saylor, Kristin Zelazko, Kay Mitchell, and Derry Wilkens—a million zillion cupcakes. And even more thank-yous.

Critique partners Dede, Kim, Bob, Suz—red boas all around.

My tribe of fellow writers and artists: agent sisters, 2k9ers, Houston YA crew, Austin gang, and more—my life is fuller, my writing stronger, my heart happy.

My readers for everything else. It is always about you and telling you a story. Without that, there is nothing.

Rick, Jake, Kellie—for cheering me on always and always and always.

ABOUT THE AUTHOR

Joy Preble grew up in Chicago where—possibly because she was raised by an accountant and a bookkeeper—she dreamed of being a backup singer, but instead earned an English degree from Northwestern. Eventually, she began to write books so she could get paid for making up stuff. She now lives in Texas with her family, including a basset-boxer named Lyla who never met a shoe she didn't want to eat. Visit Joy at joypreble.com.